you

A NOVEL

should

SMILE

more

ANASTASIA RYAN

sourcebooks
casablanca

Published by Sourcebooks Casablanca, an imprint of Sourcebooks
P.O. Box 4410, Naperville, Illinois 60567-4410
(630) 961-3900
sourcebooks.com

Cataloging-in-Publication Data is on file with the Library of Congress.

Printed and bound in Canada.
MBP 10 9 8 7 6 5 4 3 2 1

For my mom.
It's an honor to follow in your footsteps.

Chapter 1

"We don't like your face." Xavier Adams stared unblinkingly at me from across the conference table.

What? Surely he hadn't said what I thought he'd said. "You called me in here because you don't like my face?"

"It's been brought to our attention, and we've started taking notice," Xavier replied. "Both your face and your expressions aren't acceptable in the workplace and especially not at Directis." Xavier leaned back in his chair and made aggressive eye contact.

I reached up and touched my cheek. It wasn't a *bad* face. I was pretty attached to it. "I don't understand," I managed.

I looked him over. He wasn't exactly someone to be offering advice about appearances. I knew he was tapping his bare feet against the floor from the slapping sound they made against the hardwood. And the fact that he never wore shoes. His graying hair was swept back from his forehead as if he wanted people to think he was outdoorsy in a rugged yet high-end sort of way. He owned the company, which I suppose gave him a lot of latitude. He'd only noticed me in passing before, offering unsolicited advice about herbal teas in the break room or mansplaining why women aren't as good at high-endurance sports as men. I honestly hadn't thought he knew my name until he called me into the conference room. To complain about my face. A man who never wore shoes.

On my first day, he'd whizzed past my desk barefoot, his dress pants rolled up to the ankles. "That guy forgot his shoes," I had whispered to the person sitting next to me.

"That's Xavier Adams. He's the boss. Bare feet connect him to nature and ground his circle of energy," she'd whispered back. "He has a pallet of grass under his desk that he rubs his feet in while he's working. It keeps him centered."

"Hm. I think shoes are always a good idea at work," I'd mumbled back.

I couldn't remember her name. She was gone less than two weeks later.

Across from me at the conference table, Xavier was flanked on either side by a member of the HR department, Gary, who was portly and unassuming, and Xavier's second-in-command, Bobbert. Management called him *Bob*, and his employees called him *Robert*, so I'd taken to referring to him as *Bobbert* in my head. He was an overgrown frat boy in a suit. He always had a smarmy smile and winked at everyone. Once, I'd thought he was flirting with me, but then he'd turned and winked at Gary in just the same way.

"We've called you in here," Xavier explained, adjusting his Christophe Claret watch, "because we're going to terminate you."

"Like Liam Neeson style?" My heart stopped for a second.

"Your services here are no longer needed," he clarified.

I let out a breath. In that split second, I'd taken mental stock of the room. Xavier was about five four, and I was pretty sure I could take him. I had at least a couple of inches on him, and one good stomp on his naked toes would probably stop him cold. Gary seemed unlikely to participate. Bobbert gave me pause, though. He looked slippery.

"I'm being fired?" I glanced over at Gary, who was staring at the ceiling and chewing on his lip. He didn't look at me. Bobbert was now doubled over, sweating profusely. He looked like he was about to vomit.

I focused again on Xavier's face, trying to tamp down my panic. I was a good employee. I'd worked for Directis—"Telemarketing with a Personal Touch!"—for almost two years. Not that you had to be great to be a telemarketer, but I was. I hadn't done anything wrong. "For my expressions?" I asked. "Over the phone?"

"Your face makes it clear you don't think very highly of the management here. Quite frankly, it gives the impression that you have a dark soul. You can gather your things, and Gary will walk you out."

He was right about the first part. I *did* think everyone in management was useless. Xavier's pretentiousness was really annoying. A few days after my coworker had told me about his pallet of grass, I'd dropped off a document in Xavier's office. He hadn't been there, so I'd taken my chance and gotten down on my hands and knees to see under his desk. The "grass" had looked kind of shiny and short. Who watered it? Where was its light source? So many questions. My heart beating fast, I'd leaned over and touched a blade. It had felt like plastic. *There's no way this dude has a square of Astroturf under his desk*, I'd thought. For weeks after, when I was falling asleep, I couldn't help thinking about Xavier and his feet and his Astroturf. Did being a CEO automatically make you weird? Could fake grass connect you to anything?

I didn't like Bobbert either. His hands were always wet, and he laughed loudly at his own jokes. But I hadn't said that out loud, had I? At least not to anyone except my closest friends, when no one else was around. Had my resting bitch face awakened? And even so, shouldn't they just give me a warning?

But the other part? WTF? "I have a dark soul?" I asked. "I foster kittens for the Humane Society."

"Dark soul. Walk her out, Gary." He slid a piece of paper toward me with my name, Vanessa Blair, handwritten across on top. A box labeled INSUBORDINATION was checked. I almost laughed out loud, despite the panic flooding through me. The number of people throughout my life who had probably wanted to call me out for insubordination…and I'd made it to twenty-eight before it had actually happened. Because of my face.

"How in the world do you know what kind of soul I have? And how is this relevant to my job performance?"

"As I just explained, your face." He looked at me as if I were a small child for asking.

An ill-timed snort escaped me. This was beyond ridiculous, and yet they all looked perfectly serious. I opened my mouth to request the real reason they were firing me, but Xavier shook his head and said, "Go!"

Gary, the HR guy, who had been silent the whole time, got up and opened the door. He still wouldn't look at me. Bobbert shrank farther down in his seat. I followed Gary out of the conference room, my legs shaky, making eye contact with my coworker Jane as I walked past. "Fired," I mouthed to her as I went to pack up my mountain of coffee mugs and fancy pens in an empty box that had appeared on my desk during my absence.

"*What*?" she mouthed back. "No way. What for?"

I shrugged, still reeling from the unreality of it all. I said, "I don't like his feet, and he doesn't like my face."

"Are you all high?" Jane asked, wide-eyed.

Gary walked me toward the door as I heard Xavier say behind me, "Jane, please come in the conference room to meet with me, Bob, and Gary."

Shit. Jane too? What was wrong with *her* face?

Gary escorted me all the way to my car. A slight rain had begun to fall. Balancing my belongings on my hip, I fumbled in my handbag for my keys but couldn't find them. I dug through all the sample lipsticks and old receipts, searching as hard as I could. Gary turned around to go back inside. I set my stuff on the curb in a heap and slumped beside it, letting the rain ruin my makeup as I looked up at the clouds and waited for Jane. The September air was colder than it had been earlier, and the concrete curb felt like a block of ice through my dress pants. I shivered. I was pretty sure I'd left my jacket inside somewhere. I wasn't going back in for it, even if now I wouldn't have the money for a new one. I had five mouths to feed at home. All of them kittens.

It took Jane less than five minutes to show up with her box. "Those dudes are *all* high," she proclaimed, flipping Gary off as he hurried back inside. She dumped her stuff in the trunk of her car and turned to me, fuming. "I hate them all."

"What just happened?" I asked numbly.

"Beats me." She closed the trunk and turned to face me. "I have to take off before I punch them."

"Something rotten is going on in there—"

"It's probably just Xavier's feet. I'll text you later."

After I found my keys, I drove around aimlessly for a while, not knowing where to go, before finally heading home. I kept waiting for the tears to come, but my eyes stayed dry. I felt like I was falling, like the ground itself had been pulled out from under me. No one says, *I want to be a telemarketer when I grow up*, but a job is a job, and it kept me in my apartment with a car and food and soap. Without it, I could end up on the street, just me and the kittens, who would inevitably wander away. The only thing keeping them with me were four walls and no thumbs. I would be totally alone. Maybe I'd end up living under the bridge down the street, slowly going insane, admonishing myself for even having a face.

When I stepped inside my apartment, I kept the lights off and stumbled down the hall into the living room. At least it was warm in there. For now. I lay down in the middle of the floor and stared at the ceiling, trying to figure out why I wasn't crying yet. Because I hated working there? I had, but it was more than that. It was the injustice of it all and the sneaking suspicion that my firing didn't make any sense, not with my production numbers. I'd be hard to replace. So would Jane. Whatever the reason, I was now on a path to paranoid homelessness, to ending up as barefoot as my new archenemy. The apartment was small, only one bedroom, but it was mine, and it had a washer and dryer in the unit. That wasn't common, and I'd paid extra for it when I'd signed the lease. Everything felt like it was slipping away.

The kittens tiptoed over one by one and had begun to purr when one started to settle its fluffy calico rump on my face. I sat up, gagging on the fur and the indignity, when there was a pounding on the door.

"I've been meaning to talk to you about your face," a familiar voice yelled as I made my way to the door. Jane was standing on the other side, her eyeliner winged out and her blond hair in a messy bun. She shifted against the doorframe, and I saw Trisha, another one of our coworkers, behind her. Jane was tall, and her frame had hidden Trisha completely. I hadn't expected her, too. I wasn't as close with her since we had never hung out outside of work before. She gave me a little wave as I moved aside to let them in.

Jane headed down the hall to the living room and squinted. "Why's it so dark in here?" She turned on the light and settled onto the couch, propping her knee-high boots on the armrest. A kitten bolted, and I cringed a little. That couch was one of the only furnishings in my apartment I'd bought for myself: it had been either that or take my mother's floral sectional sofa. I'd chosen a modern, sleek couch that didn't attract cat hair. I guessed, at this point, it didn't matter if Jane's dirty shoes were all over the armrest since it wasn't like she could do more damage than the mud under the bridge. I was taking the damn thing with me when I got evicted.

"I'm practicing living without electricity," I said.

Trisha settled onto the corner of the loveseat, diagonally from the couch, trying not to dislodge two kittens playing on the cushion. The loveseat was a hand-me-down from my dad's corner of the basement and was now showing signs of kitten claws. I decided I'd leave it here when I became a squatter under the bridge.

"What excuse did they give you?" I asked.

"Smirking and laughing will not be tolerated in an office setting," Jane answered, using air quotes. "Not Trisha, though. She had to kiss Xavier's feet to keep her job."

I gasped. "You kissed his naked feet?" Bile rose in my throat.

"She means metaphorically," Trisha corrected. "I had to write a thousand-word memo of apology for my behavior and choice of work friends." She glanced up at Jane and me then averted her eyes apologetically.

I could tell Trisha had been crying. I liked her a lot, and she'd always had more tact than me. But seriously? "You're not going to do it, are you? He's just trying to humiliate you. All of us."

"She already did," Jane answered. "He made her send it to the entire office. 'Dear Unbalanced Poser Who Calls His Office a Dojo, I'm sorry I thought Vanessa and Jane were cool and hung out with them. I've learned from this and thought very hard about the kind of person I want to be.'"

"I think they want me to be some kind of Barbie," Trisha said. "Do they make Chinese Barbies?"

I looked back and forth between them, horrified. "No," I breathed. "I mean, yes, they make Chinese Barbies, but no, you can't become one."

Jane had dubbed a particular clique in the office *the Barbies*. There was Brunette Barbie, Bitter Barbie, Bad Barbie, Burned-Out Barbie... They dressed well, drank over lunch, and frequently used happy hour to talk about their wild nights out on the weekends. They all had the same smile (except Burned-Out Barbie, who never seemed too "with it"). Their faces had traded in and out as some left the company and new ones were hired, and I hadn't spent much time getting to know them. Or anyone, really, except Jane.

"What was I supposed to do?" Trisha asked, a little defensively. "I need this job."

I tried to check myself. Trisha was a single mom, and she adored her daughter, Claire. I understood but hated how Xavier was playing god with people's self-worth and livelihood.

"Rumor is we could have stayed, too, if we'd begged," Jane told me. She picked up a kitten and tried to settle it on her lap. The kitten let out a loud yowl and bit her index finger. Jane and I locked eyes for a minute while she nursed her finger and I considered her words. A mutual understanding passed between us. We didn't beg for anything. Except maybe food, if we ended up under the bridge.

A lot of good our pride did us, though. We were the two who would have to check the YES box after *Have you ever been fired?* on any application going forward. Next question: *Reason? Face.*

I shook my head. "Can I get you anything?" I asked them.

"Yeah. We got fired today. On a Thursday. Calls for shots," Jane responded as she leaned back and closed her eyes. A kitten got stuck between her and the back of the couch and squeaked. "Seriously, Nessa? These little floofs are everywhere."

"I know," I said apologetically. "It feels like so many more than five."

"There are at least seven," Jane said.

"Maybe six?" Trisha added.

"No, no," I told them. "Definitely only five. They're all calicos, so it just looks like more. I named them Unus, Duo, Tres, Quattuor, and Quinque. One through five in Latin. Thank God there weren't six. Sex the kitten is *not* okay."

I went to the kitchen to see if I had any alcohol. "Sex kittens always get adopted first!" Jane yelled from the living room.

I grabbed an unopened bottle of peppermint schnapps someone had left at my apartment a while back. I twisted off the cap and grabbed three glasses from the cabinet over the refrigerator. I wasn't a big drinker, so I didn't have a large selection. I brought the bottle and glasses back into the room.

"Which one is which?" Trisha asked.

I shrugged. "They all have long white fur with black and orange spots, you know? I have a checklist somewhere that specifies all their markings, but the only one that stands out to me is that one," I said, indicating the kitten that had gotten stuck behind Jane. "She has a beauty mark on her cheek."

Jane looked behind her on the couch. "She looks like Marilyn Monroe! But, you know, furry. Could've named that one *Sex*. Just saying."

I ignored her. "That's Duo. But the others all look the same. When I first got them, I tried labeling them with a Sharpie, but they just licked it off."

"You drew on them with a marker?" Jane asked, horrified.

"Just a little number inside one of their ears. That's what they do at the shelter," I replied. "That's another thing that sucked about Directis. They made it so hard to volunteer. I'm supposed to handle the promotional stuff for the animals, like the posters and advertisements, and I've barely been keeping up by working on them late at night. Which cuts into, you know, sleep." I swallowed. "I guess not now, though."

"Do they take people at the shelter?" Jane asked.

"That's not how human adoption works," Trisha told her.

Jane grabbed the schnapps from my hands and took a long swig straight from the bottle. She ignored the glasses I'd brought and passed the bottle to Trisha, who reluctantly took it with two fingers. "Uh, no, I'm good. Being sanitary is kind of my thing."

"Take a sip, Trisha. We had a bad day today," Jane said.

Trisha relented and took a long drag from the bottle. She looked a little sick. "Tastes like toothpaste. Gross." My stomach turned a little watching her. Trisha started to hand the bottle back to Jane but seemed to think better of it and took another long drink. "Actually, it reminds me of the mint baijiu cocktails my dad makes. Except for the aftertaste."

Jane squinted at her. "I used to work at a bar, but I've never heard of baijiu."

"It's like Chinese vodka," Trisha said. "My parents still prefer it over wine."

"My parents grew up in Illinois," Jane said. She reached back for the schnapps. "Wow, you just downed like half the bottle, Trish." She looked at Trisha with respect. "Nice."

She gave Jane an uncharacteristically large grin. "Claire's with my mom tonight, so bottoms up."

"I'm sorry this happened to you two," I told them. I swept two of the kittens off the couch and settled next to Jane. Trisha passed the bottle to me, and I also took a long swig and immediately gagged a little.

"It's not your fault," Trisha murmured as she held her hand out again for the bottle, and I gave it to her.

"But it is. I showed management I didn't respect them through my offensive face." I had staved off the tears all day, but I felt them prick my eyes as I leaned back into the cushions.

"Well, I got fired because I laugh inappropriately," Jane offered. She'd finally managed to get a kitten to settle on her thigh.

"And I got almost fired because I hang out with you two and need to think 'long and hard about whether or not I want to be a bad person or try to redeem myself,'" Trisha told us.

I hadn't known it was possible to feel worse. "This is all my fault," I moaned. "My dark soul is destroying your lives. I'm taking both of you with me to hell."

"We might be going to hell, but it won't be for this," Jane said sympathetically and took the bottle back. Some blond strands had slipped out of her messy bun. "Did you know we're just like that guy on the news who ran a drug ring out of the hotel he worked at? He was fired. We were fired. We're now in the same category as that guy." She let out a deep breath. "Do you think everyone there hates us now?"

"I doubt it," I said. "Xavier makes it hard to be on his side, you know?"

Jane looked up at the ceiling. "I just hope Marcus doesn't hate us. I don't care what anyone thinks but Marcus." Then she looked down at her hands.

"I'm sure Marcus doesn't think differently of you," I said softly. Marcus was the receptionist in the office. He was a few years younger than Jane, wore black hipster glasses, and had the tiniest man bun imaginable. She'd carried a torch for him since he'd been hired eight months ago.

Trisha let out a small hiccup. "You have a great face, Vanessa. Xavier is just jealous he's less beautiful-er than you are."

Jane and I looked at each other. Apparently, it didn't take long to get Trisha a little tipsy. Trisha reached for the bottle again, but Jane held it back.

"Maybe a break for you," Jane told her. "And if Xavier is firing people because they have better faces than him, that whole building is about to be out on their asses."

"That can't be why, though, right?" I asked. "There has to be some other reason."

"Who the hell knows," Jane said.

Trisha sighed loudly and dropped her head forward. Her long hair covered her face. "If I didn't have a kid, I wouldn't have written that memo, you know. Claire is counting on me. She's only four. I didn't do the best job picking her dad, so even if it means kissing the ass, or the ass feet, of someone like Xavier, I've gotta do what I've gotta do to take care of her."

My heart squeezed. "Trisha, we totally get it. Nobody's faulting you. I mean, Jane still lives with her parents. All our circumstances are different."

Jane flopped backward and dislodged the kitten from her leg. "Yep, and I totally lied to my mom and dad about all this. I told them our account got cut. So what're we gonna do? Like, I could waitress, but I can barely tolerate talking to people over the phone, let alone in person. Some of us weren't meant for customer service."

"Give me the bottle of toothpaste," I said. "I need some liquid courage to text my mom." I took the schnapps from her and had another sip. It was starting to taste a lot better. And I was definitely feeling warmer.

I pulled out my phone and sent a quick text to my mom. I got fired today.

OMG, are you okay? she texted back.

They were mean to me and Jane and they fired us and it sucked, I wrote back. I felt a rush of relief that I didn't have to lie to her like Jane did with her parents. My mom always took my side. Even if she still treated me like I was twelve.

I put the phone down on the coffee table. "I wish I could make Xavier feel as bad as he made us feel. You want to fire me, fine, but the insults weren't necessary. Someone needs to make Xavier understand that."

Trisha slid from her spot on the loveseat onto the floor before leaning her back against the faux-leather armrest. The kittens all made a beeline for her and started clawing at her pants. "I think I'm seeing double," she said solemnly as she ruffled a little calico's ear. "There's like a zillion cats in my lap. Hand me that bottle, Nessa."

I passed it over and thought about Xavier and Bobbert and Gary. "Calling three women into the conference room, one by one, criticizing us, not even letting us respond, then walking us out? It's just not right." As much as I hated being fired, I almost felt sorrier for Trisha, who had to go back in the morning. It all sucked, but Trisha was in for continuing humiliation. And so was anyone else who worked for Xavier if someone didn't stop him.

"They're horrible people," Jane said. "All of them. Bobbert was huddled in the corner like he was going to pass out. It's not like *he* was getting fired. Calm yourself and take a seat, Bobbert." She grabbed the bottle back from Trisha. "Once, when my cousin was tending bar, his boss made him work a lot of mandatory overtime. He got one of those little devices that makes noise like a smoke detector running out of batteries. He hid it behind the mini fridge under the bar and set it to go off every fifteen minutes. That thing went off for two weeks. They had to shut the restaurant down. I think they opened again once the batteries ran out, but they never found it."

"That's so badass. I wanna marry your cousin." My eyelids were getting heavy. "We should get one of those things for Xavier's office."

Trisha had slumped into a prone position on the floor, and the cats were pouncing and playing with her sweater. "Totally," she said. "We should do that." Her voice was really faint like she was about to fall asleep. "Is this what heaven is like? Kittens everywhere?"

"Maybe a listening device instead," I said. "It's just as small. Or, even better, a two-way transmitter. Then we could whisper creepy things or cause disruptions at the worst possible time." I grinned. My body felt nice and relaxed.

"Well, it's not like we have anything better to do," Jane grouched.

"You're not wrong," I told her. "We could probably learn all sorts of weird stuff about them. Like, how often do they talk about their feet in there?"

"Bare feet are a magnet for germs," Jane added. "I mean, you can literally get herpes from going barefoot."

"Oh my god, gross," I said.

From her spot under the kittens, Trisha piped up, "Wire the office. Herpes. Check."

"Wiring the office, okay, but no herpes," I protested.

"Maybe herpes," Jane said. She leaned over on the couch and sympathetically rubbed my back. "We could always share a street corner," she suggested.

"I've got my eye on a spot under the bridge, but there's room for two. Not that it counts as a roof, exactly."

"You'll have to keep these kittens on a leash, though, because they're going to peace out as soon as they have the chance," Jane said.

"So true," I agreed and tipped up the bottle to get the last drop. "My whole life I've been a little insubordinate, but that's the first time I've seen it in writing."

"Saaaaaame," Jane groaned.

Trisha hiccupped. "Saaaame," she added, eyes closed.

"There really is something shady going on over there. I want to know what it is," I said as I lazily grabbed a kitten from Trisha's pile.

We were all quiet for a moment until Trisha spoke again. "I've got this." Her slurred voice rose sleepily from her place on the floor. "We consult Sun Tzu. You cool with that?"

It didn't seem to me like any of us "got this." And was Sun Tzu that guy who wrote a war manual a million years ago? "Sure, Trisha," I told her and closed my eyes. Whatever was happening at Directis would have to wait until tomorrow.

Chapter 2

All warfare is based on deception.

—SUN TZU, *THE ART OF WAR*

I BLINKED BLEARILY. IT WAS FRIDAY MORNING, MY FIRST OFFI-cial day without a job. I'd forgotten to turn off my daily phone alarm, which had sounded at 6:00 a.m. like normal. The beeping pounded in perfect rhythm with my lingering headache. Jane and Trisha had stayed until after 2:00 a.m. the night before. It had taken us that long to sober Trisha up so she could drive. While it had been cathartic, I was going to pay for it today with a hangover. Trisha had to go back this morning, though, and see Xavier. Except for the whole paycheck thing, she had it way worse. As for me, I intended to allow myself a weekend of self-care (otherwise known as *wallowing*) before facing my new situation head on.

I checked my phone and sighed. Twelve missed texts from my mom. I vaguely remembered texting her I'd been fired. I'd have to deal with her at some point, but I didn't feel like talking about it now.

I settled into a morning of pajamas and not showering. I ate peanut butter straight from the jar and kept my TV tuned to the true crime channel. My living calico blanket made me too comfortable to move. This whole situation had hit me harder than I realized. I was usually pretty confident in myself, but now I felt like keeping a scarf over my face and my personality to myself. After a particularly upsetting episode of *Double Crossed in Dumpsters*, I vowed never to go out in public again.

I'd just started a new episode of *Swampy Deaths* when my email dinged. I pulled my phone up to scan the new messages, and my heart stopped.

From: Gary Gallard
Time: 8:42:03 AM EST
To: Vanessa Blair

Subject: Separation from Directis

Ms. Blair,
Your employment has been terminated. We are willing to provide you with three extra days of wages, to which you are not entitled, if you sign the attached severance agreement. This message also serves to remind you that you are not eligible for unemployment, as you were fired due to misconduct.
Regards,

Gary Gallard
Human Resources
ggallard@directis.com

Huh. I thought an employee only got severance when they were laid off. I didn't know anything about being fired, so maybe I was off base. Regardless, my bullshit meter went off.

I clicked on the attached PDF and skimmed through it. It had a surprising number of *therefore*s and *subsequently nonetheless*es mixed in randomly. Basically, it amounted to a request for me to admit wrongdoing, not sue the company, and not seek unemployment benefits.

All in exchange for three days' pay. My eyes narrowed. Talk about dangling a baby carrot. I wasn't going to sue the company. But to admit to wrongdoing? Hell no. Not in any universe.

I was chewing on my lip and mulling over the email when I heard a key turn in the lock. The kittens scattered. "Vanessa!" my mom called from the hall. "You don't have to let me in. I have a key!" As if I hadn't given it to her.

I sighed. "Hey, Mom," I yelled back. Goddammit. I should have responded to her texts; then maybe I could have wallowed in peace. I shoved the jar of peanut butter behind a couch cushion.

She walked into the living room, wearing her typical uniform of a crisp white button-down shirt, rolled at the sleeves, jeans, and a large beaded necklace. She set a brown paper bag on the coffee table. Her eyes, so much like mine, were filled with concern and a hint of disgust. I looked down at myself. There were smears of peanut butter on my pajama shirt that had attracted little tufts of cat fur.

"Honey, I'm worried about you. You never wrote me back. What happened?"

"They don't like my face," I said, not looking up and willing myself not to cry.

"Oh, darling, what on earth are you saying?" My mom perched on the edge of the couch and lifted my chin. "You have the best face in the entire world."

I rolled my eyes and pulled away. "You're such a mom," I said.

"Did someone actually say that to you?"

I nodded, and fresh waves of shame rolled over me. "Xavier Adams did. He also said I don't respect management and that I have a dark soul."

"Where were you working? Thunderdome?" she exclaimed and

pulled me into a hug. "I don't want you respecting anyone who would say something like that."

I nodded as she stroked my hair. "Is it okay if we don't talk about it?" I asked.

"Don't let these people make you doubt yourself. They're terrible, and they shouldn't have fired you, and I bet not a single one of them graduated from college with a four-point-oh average like you did, even if you majored in something useless."

"Mom—"

"I want to know their names, all of them, so I can call their mothers," she said. We'd moved north when I was a kid, but Mom had never really lost her accent or her Southern ways.

"No, totally not necessary, Mom," I told her. "I appreciate the support, but please stay out of it."

"I'm just saying, their mothers need to be made aware of the situation. What was the name of the main guy you said was mean to you? Excalibur? Excalibur Lincoln?"

I stopped for a moment and thought about her logic, which was usually a little off-center from mine. Where had she come up with that? Maybe a name with an *x* and a former president? I was *not* telling her his real name again, so I just nodded. "Yes, Mom, his name is Excalibur Lincoln."

"Well, I'm going to give Mr. Lincoln a piece of my mind. Then I'm calling Mr. Lincoln's mother and letting her know how Excalibur has been behaving." She reached over and smoothed my hair from my face. "I just want my baby to be happy. I raised you to be a strong woman, and your strength is written all over that beautiful face of yours. At least when you have minimal hygiene standards. You intimidated the heck out of Excalibur. That's why he fired you."

I leaned against her and let her stroke my hair. It was nice to be comforted. "I brought you a casserole, too, sweetie," she said. "And some snickerdoodles. I'd offer to let you move in with us, but you know your dad is allergic to cats. Is there anything else I can do for you? What about Jane? I can call her mother, too, and see what we can do for Jane."

"Thanks. And don't call Jane's mom." Why did she always want to talk to everyone's mom?

"I want to help. This is just a bump in the road." She pulled me into a hug. "It's not the same as Auntie Beatrice."

I stiffened and pulled out of the hug. "It's absolutely not!"

"That's what I just said. But maybe we could still learn a few things from her, if you get what I'm saying." She gave me a look.

Aunt Beatrice was my father's sister. She had been in trouble with the law a few times, and I hadn't seen much of her growing up. She'd committed arson and had been in prison for as long as I could remember.

"Different type of fire, Mom. Getting let go from a job isn't a gateway drug to actual fire. I'm not going to end up in jail with a string of burned-down houses behind me."

"I know you're not. I just said it wasn't the same."

"And you know Dad doesn't like it when we talk about Auntie Bea," I told her.

She put up her hands. "You're related to them; I'm not." She looked over my shoulder at the television, and her eyes lit up. "Oooh! *Swampy Deaths*! Are they having a marathon?" She grabbed the remote off the coffee table and checked the guide. "Yes! Time for a day of true crime with my ride-or-die." She winked at me.

Suddenly, I wanted to be anywhere but here. "I should probably spend the day looking for jobs. You know, be productive and stuff instead of watching reality TV."

I'd gotten my love of true crime from my mom, but she always took things a step too far, imagining perpetrators that didn't exist, insisting the police hadn't dug deep enough. She squinted at the screen. "I understand, sweetie. I've seen this one anyway. The husband did it." She looked at me conspiratorially. "It's always the husband, am I right?"

I shrugged. "I mean, yeah. Usually."

"Take the rest of the day to relax, sweetheart. Then you really should shower. And promise me you'll file for unemployment. It can hold you over until your next job."

"Yeah…about that. Directis just emailed me a legal document. It's jargony, but I think they're asking me to sign away my right to unemployment in exchange for three days' pay. I also have to admit I did something wrong, which I didn't. But I need money, and—"

My mother gasped. "Vanessa Leigh, don't you dare. Your integrity is not for sale. They really ought to be ashamed of themselves." She patted my arm. "If it were six months' pay, then…maybe we could fudge the integrity thing. But three days? That's not even a Coach purse; it's a wristlet. Don't sign anything." She leaned over and kissed my forehead. "So you promise you'll file?"

I nodded.

"Say it, Vanessa."

"I promise I'll file for unemployment."

Mom smiled. "That's my girl." She stood. "Okay, sweetie. I'll put the casserole in the fridge. It's your favorite: Alfredo and noodles. The cookies will be on the counter. I'm on my way to bridge club with the girls, but I'll check in on you again tomorrow. And don't you worry at all about Excalibur. It's under control."

I winced again. Awesome.

After she left, I shot Jane a quick text. Did you get an email from Gary?

Yeah, she texted back. Already signed that shit and sent it back. I need the money and I wasn't going to sue anyway.

I'd promised my mother I'd check out unemployment benefits, but maybe if I was super lucky, I wouldn't have to. I loved what I did for the animal shelter, and if I could get paid for it, it'd be a win-win. I grabbed my cell and dialed their number. It couldn't hurt.

When someone picked up, I cleared my throat. "Is Danielle around?" I asked. She was the shelter director. We weren't close, but I liked her, and we worked together on events.

"She's in the back with the new intakes," the voice answered. "Did you have a message?"

"My name is Vanessa Blair. I was checking to see if there were any staff positions available," I said. "I volunteer already and would love a more permanent—"

A sigh stopped me midsentence. "We don't have any openings. Not enough funding. I'll let her know you called, though. Thanks."

The phone clicked off. It had been a long shot, but it still bummed me out. Time to go online and try for another long shot— unemployment benefits. I didn't know anything about them, if I was eligible, or what to expect, but the weight of my situation was starting to bear down on me. I had a rent payment due in a couple weeks, and $47.86 in my bank account. But I'd be damned if I let my indefinite number of furry dependents starve because I'd looked Xavier in the face. At least I had one more check coming, though I wasn't sure how much it would be.

I pulled up my laptop and opened the Job and Family Services page. It was surprisingly straightforward. I lowered the sound on *Swampy Deaths*. It was just getting good. They'd found a body in (where else?) the swamp.

The first portion was all personal and demographic information, which was easy. Strangely enough, Directis wasn't showing up in the computer system under the list of employers, so I manually entered all the information I knew and checked the box for DISCHARGED under reason for unemployment. "I'm not going to let them make me feel like a criminal," I muttered.

A red box appeared in the middle of the screen, with the words NOTICE OF ELIGIBILITY ISSUE in bold. Awesome. *Here comes the fun part.* I clicked on the link in the box, and a separate questionnaire appeared on the screen.

What was the reason for discharge? My fingers hovered over the keys, but I typed it out. *I was told my face was unacceptable in the workplace.*

Did your actions violate any company policy? I doubted the handbook said anything about expressions, so I checked the NO box.

Had you received a prior warning for this conduct? Another no.

Were you aware you could be discharged for such an offense? A resounding no.

I finished the application, which included signing up for job matches, and hit SUBMIT.

The job market for my skills wasn't exactly popping. After college, I'd spent a year as an intern at a classical museum and then a couple years editing intra-industry travel reports, which was as thrilling as it sounded. When the economy took a dive, people stopped traveling, and the company I worked for closed.

I'd sent out my résumé to every place that was hiring, and Directis had been the only one that had called back. Telemarketing had kind of been my only option at the time. Turns out a degree in Latin wasn't the key to financial success. My education had emphasized other things, like *homo doctus in se semper divitias habet.* A learned person always has wealth inside himself. I certainly hoped so because it looked like that was the only wealth I'd have to live on for a while.

I put the laptop away and glanced up. The police on the screen were arresting the husband. I grabbed the remote and flipped off the television. Maybe I could take the weekend to figure out what I actually wanted to do with my life. Did revenge count as an occupation? How much did it pay?

Chapter 3

If you know neither the enemy nor yourself, you will succumb in every battle.

—SUN TZU, *THE ART OF WAR*

THE WEEKEND PASSED IN A CONTINUOUS LOOP. SLEEPING ON THE couch, not brushing my hair, eating cold casserole straight from the fridge, watching true crime shows on repeat. It was broken up by the occasional text from my mom or Jane and feeding the kittens. Mostly, I slept and felt sorry for myself. I also thought a lot about my face. It had never been a problem before, that I knew of, and I wore it every day. When Monday morning rolled around and I woke up again on the couch where I'd fallen asleep, it was time to get it together. Five furry bodies were nestled in a line down one of my legs. I'd been wearing the same clothes for three days now.

I had other obligations. The animal shelter had a fundraiser event coming up, and I'd promised to design the marketing materials and keep track of the donations. I had all the time in the world to devote to it now.

I gently removed the kittens and got up for a cup of strong black coffee and a hot shower. Then I opened Photoshop on my laptop and dragged my best shelter pictures into the brochure layout. I was rearranging them and fitting in the text when my phone buzzed. I didn't recognize the number.

"Hello?" I asked.

"Hello, I'm looking for a Ms. Vanessa Blair," a masculine voice said.

I immediately felt like a kid in trouble. "Speaking?"

"Hi, Ms. Blair. My name is Carter Beckett. I'm calling from the Madison Unemployment Office. We received your application for benefits, and I was wondering if you would have time to come by our office to clarify a few things."

My stomach sank further. "Anything I can answer over the phone?"

"Your application mentioned an unusual reason for your discharge, one I haven't seen before."

I sighed. "You and me both."

"If you have time today, we'd like to get all the issues squared away. We're located on Winchester Street."

I knew where that was…vaguely. "Okay, can I just drop by any time?"

"The sooner, the better," he responded.

An hour later, I found myself sitting in my car outside the unemployment office on Winchester. The sun was bright, but the air was still crisp, and the falling leaves had littered the sidewalk in yellow. I ran the lint roller over my clothes one last time and got out of the car. The office was in a strip mall, and there were only a few cars parked outside. I hurried to the door, the cold biting through my sweater and giving me goose bumps. I thought longingly of my fall-weather wool jacket I'd left behind at Directis. I opened the door and approached the front counter hesitantly. "I filed for unemployment on Friday," I told the woman sitting behind the desk. "I got a call from someone asking me to come in."

She looked at me over the top of her red cat-eye glasses with a frown. "You're supposed to file online." She then looked back at her computer screen as if dismissing me completely.

"I did," I told her. "I got a call from someone named Beckett, I think?"

She slowly rose in her chair. "You have a seat, and I'll go see if he's here."

"Thanks," I said and looked around me. There were no chairs. A headache had started to form behind my left eye, but at least I was out of the house and being proactive. I was caffeinated *and* clothed.

The waiting was starting to increase my anxiety when a man came around the corner and offered me his hand. His whole arm was sleeved in tattoos. He was wearing a black T-shirt and dark jeans. Clearly a far more casual work environment than I was used to. "I'm Carter Beckett," he said in the same voice I'd heard over the phone. Then he cleared his throat. "Are you—?"

"Yes, I'm Vanessa Blair," I answered as I shook his hand. "I'm here to answer some questions about my application."

When he didn't immediately answer, I looked up. He had dark hair and pale blue eyes, which were squinting at me.

I sighed loudly. Of course. He was looking at my face, deciding right then and there whether my firing was justified and if I qualified for benefits. I narrowed my eyes at him. "Stop looking at it."

That snapped him out of it. "Please, Ms. Blair, I won't take up too much of your time."

He cleared his throat again and gestured for me to come behind the counter. I followed him to a small office at the end of the hall.

He sat behind the institutional metal desk and motioned for me to sit in the folding chair opposite. The room was small and impersonal. There weren't any pictures or a million coffee cups and pens like my desk had had. There wasn't a lot in the office that gave away any information about the person in it, but it did have its own door, something I'd always wanted. I'd have given my kingdom for a door when I worked at Directis. He looked directly at me. "Please tell me a little about your situation."

I looked down at my hands and tried not to chew my lower lip. "I was fired from my job, and on advice from my mother, I filed a claim for unemployment benefits. I might not be eligible, but she said to file anyway to find out. I don't really know anything about this process."

"Your mom is right. You should always file, and the state can decide from there."

"She'll be excited to hear that. She'll probably want to call *your* mom to thank you," I muttered.

He looked like he was about to respond to that, then paused. "What was the reason you were given when you were terminated?"

"My face."

"I thought there must have been a misspelling or autocorrect error on the application. Were you actually fired for your face?" he asked.

"I wish I were kidding," I replied. "That was the main reason I was given." I was still looking down at my hands, but I could feel his eyes on me. "*Please* stop looking at it." In that moment I was very thankful for my long hair. I untucked it from behind my ears and shook my head a little, letting it come down over my cheeks to hide as much of my face as I could.

"What?" he said.

"I know you're looking at my face, and it's weirding me out. I'm already supremely self-conscious about it, given this whole thing." I gestured with my hands and snuck a look at him from under my lashes.

"I don't mean to come off as insensitive," he said gently. "When the reason involves appearance instead of performance, we look at the possibility of discrimination. If it could be related to a skin condition, facial anomaly, that sort of thing, you would have protection under the law."

Oh. Duh.

"Can you give me any more information about the circumstances?"

"The owner of the company called me into the conference room to tell me I was being terminated because of my face and the expressions it makes." I tried to keep a little snort from escaping. "I was a good employee, came to work on time, and had never been written up or given any warnings. I'm on the inside of my body, obviously, so I don't know what my expressions look like. I can assure you they were unintentional." I tried to keep my voice steady, but saying it out loud was so embarrassing.

"I see nothing wrong with your face," he said. "Since we've received your claim, the next step is to contact your employer and get their side of the story," he said. I cringed as he continued, "Once we receive that, a determination will be made as to your eligibility. If you don't agree with the decision, you're welcome to appeal it, which would lead to an informal hearing."

I nodded. A potential face-off with Xavier. No thanks. If it ever came to that, I made a mental note not to share that information with my mother. I could easily imagine her showing up and shouting, "I object!" after anyone spoke.

"Typically, you'd get about half of your weekly salary from your last job if you qualify," Carter went on. "More, if you have dependents. Do you have any?" he asked.

I thought for a moment. "Human?" I asked.

"Legally, you can't claim any other species as dependents," he said, leaning back in his chair.

"Okay, then, just myself."

"Was that *really* the reason you were fired?" he asked.

I glared at him, and he drew back.

"Oh," he said. "I see."

What was *that* supposed to mean? I pulled a few more strands of hair in front of my face and fought the urge to hide completely behind my hands.

He smiled politely and pushed a stack of forms toward me across the desk. On his tattooed arm, I caught a glimpse of a small inked cat nestled inside his elbow. "These are the standard assistance guides to follow when making weekly claims," he told me. "If you have any additional questions going forward, you're more than welcome to give me a call or stop by and see me again. Here's my business card as well. Carter Beckett," he reminded me.

I smiled and picked up the stack he'd given me. *Be normal, Nessa,* I told myself. *Don't be weird. Or be less weird.* "Thank you," I said. "I'll do that."

I'd just gotten back to my car when Trisha called. I hadn't really heard from her in the past couple days, only trading a few texts here and there. Same with Jane. I'd been too far inside my pity bubble to come up for air.

"Nessa," she said breathlessly.

"Hi, Trisha. You okay? Are you at work?" It probably wasn't a good idea for her to call me from work. Xavier's eyes were likely on her at all times.

"Yes and yes. We need to talk. Can you meet me at Starbucks this afternoon?" she asked. "The one on Covington Street, farthest from the office. We won't know anyone there. I'm calling Jane, too."

"Sure. Not doing anything else. But you're making me nervous."

"No need for nerves!" she said excitedly. "All good. So see you there after work?"

"Okay. I showered. Shouldn't let it go to waste. But what's up? Did something happen?"

"No spoilers!" she said brightly then paused. "We missed you at the Social Committee meeting today. This year's whirly ball tournament won't be the same without you."

My stomach squeezed. For the first time, I felt a rush of relief at being unemployed. The Directis Social Committee no longer had power over me.

Chapter 4

Eight weeks earlier

"IT'S TIME FOR ANOTHER OF OUR TWICE-WEEKLY WE MEETINGS. Is everyone on the line?" Xavier asked. We were all wearing our headsets, looking at Xavier as he pranced around the office. The satellite location was on the phone call as well. Those who worked in Xavier's main office, like me, were still required to dial in. That meant we could hear him in person, loud and clear...and over the phone line, on a three-second delay. The intro came out more like "It's—it's time, time for, for another anoth—of, of our, our..." I hated it so much. Bobbert was constantly keeping watch, though, for anyone who removed their headsets.

Ever since Directis had been bought by Trimaran Corp the year before, we'd had to add the conference line to the meetings. Xavier seemed to enjoy having an even bigger audience for his performance. Beyond the obnoxious echo, becoming a subsidiary of Trimaran hadn't changed things much for us. Management kept the inner workings of the deal a secret from us, but the only difference I'd noticed was that Gary seemed more stressed, but not Xavier: he was just as shoeless as ever. It still boggled my mind that any corporation would meet Xavier and think, *Yeah, this is the guy I want to invest in.*

"These meetings are a time for us all to be...we. We synergize our momentum and work in conjunctive with each other to improve ourselves," he said.

I perked up and looked over the heads at desks until my eyes found Jane's. "Conjunctivitis? Pink eye?" I mouthed at her. She shrugged back. Jane loved the We Meetings. It was basically free phone time, which cut into our productivity but also increased the amount of time our phones were dialed out. In the telemarketing world, the "dialed out" time was crucial.

I tried not to snicker and double-checked that my line was on mute. "Today's call is about nurturing and fostering the 'we,'" he went on. It took all I had not to roll my eyes. I didn't dare look at Jane. "As you are aware, when Directis was acquired by Trimaran, it allowed us to expand, and Trimaran has agreed to funnel the profits into that expansion." He paused dramatically. "The results of our most recent employee survey indicate that not all of you feel part of the Directis family." He cleared his throat, and I cast a furtive glance at the people near me. Why were they still filling out those stupid surveys? "I assume this is because we now have a parent company and not because of my leadership." He smiled again and waved at us. "In order to contravene this, we're going to step up our Social Committee activities."

There was rustling in the office. I tried not to groan. The Social Committee sounded like it came out of a teen movie, but it was more a form of sadism inflicted by management onto its employees to create a "pleasant" working environment. They already inflicted their madness on us for each holiday. We'd had to do a secret Santa gift exchange at Christmas time, and weirdly, more than one of us had drawn Xavier's name. On Valentine's Day, Xavier had given a speech about the importance of love and being nice to your wife, and then he'd insisted we hand-make valentine boxes and exchange little cardboard cards with each other. That one was particularly frustrating. I didn't have a wife, for one, and for two, I was no longer in grade school. Saint Patrick's

Day had involved a desk-decorating contest and the potential to be pinched by Bobbert if we didn't comply. He'd been a walking assault charge that day. For Halloween, Xavier had asked everyone to dress as Xavier. There had been so many rolled pants and bare feet, I'd dry-heaved most of the morning.

"Jenna, who'd been running this committee, is no longer with us," Xavier said, then clapped his hands. "Let's shake things up!"

There was a soft murmuring. Had she died? Quit? Been fired? I wasn't sure I could remember what Jenna looked like.

"The committee will now be run by…" His eyes narrowed as he searched through the faces in the room. "You," he said into the second row. "You are now in charge of the social committee."

Two employees in the second row looked at each other. "Did you mean her or me?" a short balding man asked, pointing first to himself then to the woman next to him.

"The one I'm looking at," Xavier snapped back.

The female employee, Cheryl, looked panicked. "He can't mean me, right?" she whispered loudly.

"You, I choose you!" Xavier yelled.

Cheryl shrank back and smiled weakly. "I'm Cheryl," she said. I didn't know her well, but she was kind of the office mom, so to speak. She left homemade cookies in the break room a couple of times a month.

"Cheryl will be organizing the next event of the Social Committee, which will be the Office Olympics," Xavier announced.

No… I shut my eyes tight. *Please say this isn't happening.*

"Teams will be chosen at random, and there will be an array of events, all based on actual Olympic sports."

Please, I prayed silently, *don't let there be a luge event.* I could picture us lying on wheeled platforms from Home Depot and being launched through makeshift rows of empty filing cabinets.

"Everyone will be required to participate. I will choose the country each team represents," Xavier continued. "You'll be expected to provide your own flags."

The entire office was quiet. Did everyone share my sense of dread?

Xavier smiled widely. "Of course, this will take place outside work hours so we can be as efficient as possible. Stay tuned for more information on this opportunity to coheese together."

Awesome. I rolled my shoulders to relieve some tension. I already had a grueling and mind-numbing telemarketing call schedule. I didn't want to *coheese* with anyone—it sounded sticky—and certainly not on a homemade luge hurtling through the office.

"As always, at the end of our We Meetings, I'd like to give you, the audience, the opportunity to ask me questions. You can ask me about anything! How I'm doing, how much you enjoy working here, your ideas for the future. This is a meeting for all of us. And…go!" Xavier stood back expectantly.

On the call, the other office was silent, like always. I figured they always kept their line on mute. I looked around my own office to find everyone staring down at their desks. Xavier always did this. He presented himself as open and approachable, but clearly, his employees felt otherwise. An older woman named Geraldine stood and cleared her throat. "It's time for the weekly refrigerator cleaning," she said aggressively. "Everything will be thrown out. It'll all be on the walkway outside if you haven't eaten it by 2:00 p.m., even if it's condiments or whatever. It'll all be outside." She droned on and on while I snuck a look at Jane. She was shooting a murderous look at Geraldine. She'd thrown out Jane's lunch at least a dozen times in the past couple months.

Geraldine seemed unconcerned that her militant refrigerator management had attracted the attention of the local wildlife. It used to just be birds, but now there were possums and at least one wild turkey who waited at the back door for the leftovers Geraldine provided. Jane's cold pizza always went first.

After Geraldine finished, we waited in silence until Xavier finally announced brightly, "Great! We can talk again in three days at our next We Meeting. Until then, Directis to successes! Say it with me. Directis to successes."

He pointed at us, and a small reluctant chorus chanted the words back at him.

What did that even mean?

Chapter 5

Spying is the sovereign's most precious faculty.

—SUN TZU, *THE ART OF WAR*

"Can I get something started for you?" the barista called to me from behind the counter. I gazed longingly at the menu over her head. It was a couple hours after Trisha had called, and I'd found a table off to the side to wait for her and Jane. Normally, I'd go for a grande cappuccino, dry, extra foam. Now, I was jobless and on my way to an unobstructed view of the river from my spot under the bridge. So I'd done what I would never have done before: I brewed my own coffee at home and brought it with me. To a Starbucks. Like the transient I would eventually become, seeking warmth from the cups of employed people's coffee. I sank my head into my hands. "I'm good," I told her.

"How far we've fallen," a familiar voice said. Jane took the seat across from me at the table and put her own travel mug down. "Ladies of leisure brew their own coffee," she told me.

"What if I don't want to be a lady of leisure?" I asked.

She paused. "You don't? I'm stressed, too, but aren't you a little glad we don't have to go back? We worked as telemarketers for a guy who wanted to be a trophy game hunter until he discovered the guns were too heavy. Isn't part of you happy that chapter of your life is over?"

"Yeah," I admitted grudgingly. "I just wish it had been on my own terms. Do you know why Trisha called us?"

"No. She was all breathless. Said she wouldn't tell me anything until we all got here." Jane took a sip of coffee. "How was your weekend? I applied to like forty jobs. Everything from doggy day care to lead architect. If it's posted, they have my résumé."

"Um, yeah, totally, same," I lied, my cheeks getting warm. I'd gone through all the listings, gotten more depressed, thought about how I would never work again, and wallowed further. I vowed to go home that night and put together a list of jobs to apply for first thing in the morning.

Jane looked at me closely. "Why're you flushed?" she asked.

"Constant embarrassment?" I suggested.

At that moment, the door to the outside swung open, and Trisha hurried through it. She brought with her a blast of cold air, and I wrapped my hands more tightly around my warm travel mug. She had on little black heels, an aqua sweater, and a pencil skirt. It perfectly accented her black hair, which was tied back in a low ponytail. Seeing her sank my heart even further. I had on something with less cat hair than normal, but it was still a sharp reminder that she was still employed, whereas I wasn't.

She sat at our table with a big grin. "The plan is in place."

Jane and I looked at each other. "What plan?"

"You know," she said and looked around furtively. "I wanted us to meet in a public place, but we still have to be careful." Then she winked at us.

A knot formed in my stomach. "What plan, Trisha?" I repeated.

She blinked. "Operation Destroy. Or is that too violent? Should it be something different? Operation…Expose? I don't know—that sounds a little wimpy."

Jane slowly reached across the table and put her hand on Trisha's wrist. "What did you do?"

"Only what we decided," she said a little defensively. "I didn't go rogue. But it was such a rush." She grinned at us again. "I felt, like, really alive. Is that silly?"

The ground seemed to be tilting. "I don't remember deciding anything." Had I been drunker than I realized? Or had Trisha?

"We did, too," Trisha insisted. "It was a whole twelve-step plan."

I looked at her blankly. "Plan for what?"

"To show them they messed with the wrong girls. To ferret out the underbelly of their corruption."

"What do ferrets have to do with—" Jane began, but Trisha cut her off.

"You were the one who came up with it, Nessa," she said. "Twelve-step programs are the path to healing. We couldn't come up with twelve full steps, though. I think we might have been a little bit drunk. Our twelve-step plan only has six steps. Step one: bug Xavier's office. Step two: give him herpes. Remember?"

Jane choked loudly on an ill-timed sip. "*Oh my god, tell me you didn't give him herpes!*"

Trisha shushed her immediately. "Keep your voice down, Jane. No, I didn't give him herpes. I don't just have herpes lying around. And I'm not paying for infectious diseases."

My head spun. Paying for diseases? How would you do that? And... how much would they cost?

"All I had handy was ringworm."

It was my turn to choke.

"Or maybe it's scabies," she added. "The neighbor's dog had something. I don't know what. Got it just in time, though, because they took him to the vet this morning, and it's mostly cleared up. You'd better believe I covered every inch of Xavier's Astroturf with it."

A vague memory surfaced. That sounded like Jane.

"Maybe mange?" Trisha paused for a moment. "Can people get mange?"

"Less hair on his toes would be good," Jane said weakly. "But how—"

"Shhhhh," I told her. "Don't ask questions you don't want answered."

Jane shook her head slowly. "And you said you did *what* to Xavier's office?"

Trisha looked around again to make sure no one was watching us. She leaned forward and whispered, "I bugged it. Well, I bugged the conference room." She flashed a big smile, beaming with pride. "Doing the conference room instead was my idea."

"This was *all* your idea, Trisha," Jane told her.

"No, it wasn't. It was Nessa's. We worked out the details Thursday night, but I modded it a little. I thought we'd hear more information this way since they have all their meetings in the conference room. And I took your advice, Nessa, and got a two-way receiver, so we can talk back if we want."

It *did* sound like me. "Did I say that?"

Trisha nodded. "You did, and it's genius." She reached into her bag and put two small black devices on the table. "One for Nessa and one for Jane. Mine's in the car. I think it's funny the company is indirectly financing their own sabotage through my paycheck. Don't you?"

Jane and I eyed the little boxes. "I might have suggested a listening device, but I *never* agreed to biological warfare," I told her. I picked up the transmitter, feeling the curiosity start to overtake me despite myself. It couldn't be legal, right?

"You'll be able to hear everything they say. Green light means it's receiving a signal. Blue light means two-way transmission. They also have a button to record. If you hear anything good, just push this." She pointed at a red button then flipped a switch to turn it on.

"The 'me-ness' is what makes the 'we-ness' work at Directis," Xavier's voice boomed out of the speaker.

I lunged across the table and turned it off, looking frantically around our table. There weren't a lot of people in the cafe, and only a few heads swiveled in our direction.

"There's a volume control on it," Trisha said meekly, "I just haven't found it yet."

"What's a weenus?" Jane asked.

I took a deep breath. "Did you say there were more steps?" I tried my best to remember more of that conversation. Was drunk me really a genius?

"You can't expect us to implement all the steps in the first couple days," Trisha protested. "You and Sun Tzu have so many ideas. I have more supplies coming through Amazon Prime."

I could feel my eyes widen, just as Jane's were doing. "Is Sun Tzu some friend of your dad's?" Jane asked.

"Honestly, Jane, didn't you ever take a business class or a history class?"

"Yeah, but I blocked it out. And aren't you worried about losing your job?" Jane said. "You're on permanent probation."

"None of them ever paid any attention to me until I fell in with the 'wrong crowd,'" she said. "I *am* the wrong crowd. Plus, I'm not going to get caught. We're not going to let them keep humiliating people like they did us."

"Yeah, but is this legal? Planting listening devices?" I asked.

"Of course it is. They do it all the time on TV," she assured me and then shrugged. "And if it's not, oh, well. I already did it. Ignorance of the law is a defense."

"No, it isn't," I said.

"Okay, but being drunk when planning a crime is definitely a mitigating circumstance."

"She's got a point," Jane piped up.

"You're the one who said it, Nessa. This is war. War always has casualties, but I have it under control." Trisha flashed us another smile then stood from the table. "I have to get Claire from day care. I'll text you," she said over her shoulder as she hurried off.

I was pretty sure Trisha had no idea what was legal, and it didn't seem like she cared. Like it or not, I was in this. I couldn't leave my friends to fight a war alone.

Chapter 6

Startled beasts indicate that a sudden
attack is coming.
—SUN TZU, *THE ART OF WAR*

LATER THAT EVENING, I WAS SITTING ON THE COUCH WITH MY KIT-
tens, trying hard to relax. It felt like I had an itch inside my spine that I
couldn't scratch. My eyes kept straying to my handbag, where I'd stashed
that little box Trisha had given me.

I looked down at the little balls of fluff. "Remind me not to drink
with Trisha," I told them. One chirped in response. The rest ignored me.

I didn't want to be complicit in any sort of crime and wind up like
Aunt Beatrice, and I didn't want to do anything that might destroy a
chance at a new job. But…I had to admire Trisha. She was the only one
of us left in the office, and she was trying to right a wrong. She was brave.
Potentially unhinged, but definitely brave. While I, apparently, talked
a big game, Trisha had actually done something. I'd meant it when I
said something was going on at Directis, and here was Trisha getting the
ball rolling.

I snuck another look at my bag. Would it hurt anything if I switched
the receiver on for a few minutes? Would anyone even know? It was like
Pandora's box: thrilling and a little scary. If I turned it on, there was no
telling what I might unleash.

I reached over and pulled the zipper open then gently removed
the device. It wasn't a big deal to flip a tiny switch. It was after 8:00

p.m. anyway. Surely no one was still at work. It would just be a little white noise.

I took a breath and did it.

Suddenly, the apartment was filled with music… Was that Journey? The kittens all ran for cover. "What on earth is happening?" I asked out loud, fumbling for the volume switch. I couldn't find one.

Then I heard it. Over "Don't Stop Believing," there was a voice I recognized. "She thinks she can win against me? No one wins against me," Xavier mumbled.

I felt like I'd been doused with cold water. Did he mean Trisha? Me? Jane? A random *she*?

I could hear his feet flapping against the hardwood floor in the conference room. It sounded like he was pacing. "I said I was going to consult with legal, but the joke's on her. I don't *have* legal."

In my imagination he was alone, walking the length of the conference room, his voice growing louder and then fainter as he moved toward and away from the transmitter.

"I wish I could see her face when she realizes I took the cat. She can kick me out, but she loves that cat. Makes it all worth it." The foot flapping slowed. Then I heard a rustling. It was followed by a loud feline hiss and a little scream from Xavier. My heart immediately went out to that poor creature. The cat, not Xavier.

Were he and his wife not getting along? I knew he was married. I'd met her several times at office events and once at the Christmas party. She was one of those people who looked through you instead of at you. The smiles and the graciousness always seemed insincere. She also asked for my name every time. I hadn't liked her very much, but she'd chosen to spend her life with Xavier, so I hadn't expected to like her anyway. For the first time, I felt a small pang of sympathy for her. It probably took a lot to put up with Xavier. And a cat custody battle had to suck.

An image of their wedding suddenly bloomed in my mind. Her in a 1980s gown with huge, puffed sleeves and a beaded headdress, him in a tuxedo with a crisp pleated shirt, cummerbund…and trousers rolled to the knee to show off his bare feet. I dry heaved a little. No. He had to have been wearing shoes. Right? She couldn't have known he was a shoe-optional man then. It was the only thing that made sense.

The flapping resumed, and I imagined him continuing to pace the conference room. Suddenly, it stopped again. "Who is that?" he asked, as if surprised. "Handsome, assertive… Is he real? How does he have so many natural gifts?"

Who could he possibly be talking to? I stopped. Had I been wrong to assume he was alone? Was someone else actually in the room with him? Was he…serenading Bobbert? Surely not the cat? Oh my god, I needed to turn this off.

I reached toward the switch when I heard, "It's Xavier!" come from the speaker. "He doesn't stop believing; he's the man in charge," he said. Was he talking to his own reflection? I suddenly felt dirty, like I needed a shower. He'd always seemed arrogant and a little on the extreme side of "quirky," but this was a whole new level. Was this really what he did when he was alone?

I could picture him in front of the framed mirror that stretched from one side of the conference room to the other. I had thought it was there to reflect the light from the windows. Was it Xavier's personal stage? Was he standing barefoot on the conference room table, flexing and admiring himself? I used to put my muffins on that table.

I reached again to turn it off, but my cell phone buzzed with an incoming call. Jane.

"*Are you hearing this?*" she screeched through the line.

"Yeah, I just turned it on, and I *can't* anymore—"

"Are you kidding?" she asked. "This gives me life. I've been listening all evening. Earlier, he sang 'I Will Survive' and he knew all the words. There were some foot sounds, too, so I think he did the choreography, but that's just a guess."

"All evening?!" I said.

"Whaaaat?" she shot back. "This is the most entertainment I've had in a long time. I need to know more about why he's sleeping in the office with some random cat."

The music stopped, and there was a frantic scrambling over the wire. "Bob! What're you doing here so late?"

Bobbert's voice answered, "I just stopped by to pick up my computer. You okay? You're bleeding."

Xavier cleared his throat, and I imagined him straightening his suit. "Just a scratch. There's a cat visiting. His name is Haiku. We're doing some breathing exercises, you know, to stay grounded."

"That's a cat?" Bobbert asked tentatively. There was a pause, and I visualized Xavier nodding as…Bobbert saw a cat for the first time? "Now that we're weeding out the negative energy, that should be easier," Bobbert said.

I felt immediately cold again. Did he mean Jane and me? Bastard.

"Yeah, bitches be loco," Xavier said.

I'm sorry, *what*?

"Yeah, uh, loco," Bobbert replied.

"You have stuff for Trisha to do tomorrow, right?" Xavier asked.

"We've got her emptying the dumpsters, and she's on kitchen duty."

Jane growled into my ear. "They're still trying to humiliate her, Nessa. We can't let them get away with this. I don't know what in the world is wrong with them, but they need to be knocked down a few pegs."

She was right. My heart ached for Trisha. I might not have any money or career prospects at the moment, but at least each day I got further and further from the humiliation. They were pouring salt into Trisha's wound.

"I'll see you in the morning, Xavier. Don't stay too late." Bobbert's voice got fainter as he moved away from the transmitter.

"'Night, Bobs. See you in the morning."

There was some more rustling, and things grew quiet. Jane and I listened to the silence together for a few moments before Xavier spoke again.

"Remember you're in charge, Xavier. No one is going to catch you. Ever."

My eyes narrowed. Besides being an ass, what, exactly, *was* Xavier doing? *Catch* implied honest-to-goodness illegal activity.

"They're going to put Trisha on trash duty," I mused. "I've been watching a *lot* of *Double-Crossed in Dumpsters*, and you wouldn't believe what they find in the trash. It's legal too: if they throw it out, it's fair game."

"Ooooh, good call. I'll text Trisha right now. We can listen *and* dog their trash! Only misdemeanors, no felonies," she said. "Wait, which ones are the more serious ones? I get them mixed up."

We listened for a while longer but didn't hear him leave. The silence was punctuated with the occasional hiss. Jane happily assured me she would take one for the team and listen throughout the night to make sure we didn't miss anything. I'd told her to get some sleep, but she sniped, "Oh, hell no," and disconnected.

I switched the device off, brushed my teeth, and put on clean pajamas. I got into my bed for the first time in many nights and snuggled down in the blankets. I did my best to shake off all thoughts of Xavier and his insanity.

I must have fallen asleep quickly. I woke up disoriented, my hair stuck to my cheeks. I'd been sweating. I checked the clock: 2:13 a.m. Then I heard it. Murmuring coming from the living room.

I grabbed a can of hair spray from the bathroom table and stealthily walked into the living room. The room was dark, except for a blinking blue light in the middle of the living room floor. The receiver.

"Shit!" I cursed. I distinctly remembered turning that thing off.

"Who said that?!" a voice shrieked over the receiver.

I froze immediately. Had he heard me? How?

Then I saw the little calico crouched next to the device. Her eyes were huge, and her fluffy rump was high in the air, wiggling in kitten attack mode. Oh no. Unus or Duo or whoever must have flipped the switch to allow for two-way communication.

There was a slow meow through the speaker. Duo or Tres came bounding over and responded with a high-pitched meowing. They all started to meow in tandem.

Not good.

I heard what faintly sounded like whimpering coming from the speaker. "Where are you? I've searched this entire office, and I can't find any more cats. Am I insane? Why do I keep hearing them? Someone's trying to drive me crazy." Xavier's voice had a hysterical edge to it.

Shit, shit, shit. I tiptoed very quietly over to the receiver, my finger over my lips to shush the kittens. One looked at me with dilated eyes. We stared each other down. This particular kitten had that small black spot above her lip. Duo, this one had to be Duo. Then, before I could stop her, she defiantly picked up the receiver in her mouth. I grabbed for it, but she wouldn't let go. I managed to thumb the switch to the left, turning the light to green. Receive only. Before I could push the switch all the way to OFF, Duo shook her head and, receiver still in her mouth, took off. Horrified, I watched her run away. This couldn't be happening. I ran after her as Duo bounded into the laundry room and squished herself between the washer and dryer.

I stood in the laundry room, breathing hard, weighing my options, when I thought I heard my phone vibrating in the living room. I ran back and picked it up. Jane.

LMAO I definitely heard more than five kittens, she'd texted.

This is NOT funny, I texted back.

Xavier thinks he's going insane, so I'd call this one a win, she responded.

Echoing slightly from the hollow space between the washer and dryer, Xavier's voice sounded again. "Are they gone? Have you called off your fellow demons, Haiku?" There was a hiss and a low growl in response. Duo's fur puffed up like a snowball, and she added her own small growl.

We really were all going to hell. Trisha, Jane, and me. But if we were going, we were taking Xavier with us.

Chapter 7

The onrush of a conquering force is like
the bursting of pent-up waters into a chasm
a thousand fathoms deep.

—SUN TZU, *THE ART OF WAR*

THE NEXT MORNING, I WOKE UP SLOWLY, ENJOYING THE FEEL OF THE sun streaming through the bedroom window. A purring kitten was curled up under my chin. I stretched my arms over my head and felt an ache in my shoulder. My eyes popped open. The events of last night came flooding back in a horrifying rush. I'd spent hours trying to get the receiver out from between the washer and the dryer before finally giving up and going to bed.

"Don't try to cozy up to me, Quinque. You guys are in trouble." The kitten gave a squeak as I sat up and went to the kitchen for coffee. I distinctly heard male voices coming from the hallway.

I stomped to the laundry room and peered between the washer and dryer. Sure enough, the receiver was still there. Two kittens were curled up next to it in the tiny space. One was trying to sit on it while the other was batting at it with a fluffy paw. I again tried to force my arm between the washer and dryer, but it wouldn't fit. The yardstick I'd tried earlier wasn't long enough. The kittens must be made entirely of fluff.

I put all my weight on my shoulder and pushed the dryer as hard as I could. My shoulder ached, but still nothing. It didn't budge, but the kittens scattered. Maybe the landlord had the machines bolted to the floor. I grabbed a coat hanger and unraveled it before jamming it into the space.

Meanwhile, the Bobbert and Xavier Show droned on. "Our

quarterly goals haven't measured up to what we had envisioned," Bobbert said. "With this type of quarter, we'll have to tighten up training and orientation."

Both were already nonexistent, so I wasn't sure how he planned to do that. The tip of the stretched-out coat hanger barely brushed the receiver. *Please, please, please still be set to one-way transmitting*, I begged silently. I used my phone light to brighten the gap. The kittens were back, blinking owlishly at me. Relief nearly made me weak when I saw the green receiving-only light.

Thankful for small favors and not for kittens, I swung my phone light over the crack under the dryer. "Dammit," I muttered under my breath. The washer and dryer *were* bolted to the floor and possibly the wall as well.

There wasn't any way I could reach the transmitter without help, and I wasn't going to let anyone but Trisha or Jane know about it. I had to leave it for now.

I set about my typical morning routine—coffee, hot shower, quick makeup—and then settled in for some serious online job hunting. From the laundry room, I could hear Bobbert talking about numbers and percentages. I rolled my eyes and only half listened. Whatever was actually going on at Directis wouldn't be discussed at a public meeting. *Asinus asinum fricat.* Mutual admiration among donkeys.

When he seemed to be wrapping up at last, Xavier interjected with, "We should call everyone in for the We Meeting. I'd like to introduce the staff to my new emotional support cat, Haiku Adams." Bobbert, or someone, must have reached toward the cat because Xavier snapped, "Don't touch him! He bites."

One of the best things about having been fired was that I no longer had to go to We Meetings (more accurately, Xavier's Me Meetings). Even if I couldn't get that receiver out from behind the dryer, I was *not* going to attend another one, even virtually.

Earlier that morning, I'd gotten an automated email from the unemployment benefit service, letting me know I needed to provide a copy of a pay stub for eligibility. Apparently Directis wasn't showing up correctly in their database of employers. I had just under a week to drop it off, but now suddenly seemed like the best time to get that errand out of the way.

I quickly packed up my laptop and phone and headed out. It was another bright day, but the air had a chill in it that made me run to my car. The windshield was covered with fallen leaves, so I threw my stuff in the car and set about pulling them off. By the time I finished, I was shivering, and my teeth were chattering. I'd asked Trisha about my jacket, but she'd said it hadn't been there when she'd looked for it. Now it was a matter of principle. I didn't need it, and I didn't need Directis.

I got in the car and blew on my fingers to warm them, then started the engine. It wasn't really *that* cold yet, but I'd always been a bit of a weather wimp. I blamed it on growing up in the South.

It was a short drive to the unemployment office. Once I got to the little strip mall, I walked briskly across the parking lot, through the front door, and up to the desk. Cat-Eye Glasses was working again. She glanced at me over the top of the rims. "Yes?"

"I got an email that I need to provide a pay stub from my last employer. It's not showing up in the system. Can I give that to you, or do I need to give it directly to Mr. Beckett?"

She shook her head and took the paper. "Name and last four of social?" she asked in a bored tone.

"It's on the paper," I answered.

She looked at me again. "Name and last four of social," she repeated.

"Vanessa Blair, fifty-three thirty-one," I answered.

She then pulled me up in the computer system and went through my record, turning the screen at each interval to verify the information.

Once everything was squared away, I leaned across the counter and asked, "Is there a coffee shop nearby? Preferably one with Wi-Fi?"

She squinted at me. "Two blocks down on Main. It's the closest. Steam Room, I think."

I thanked her and left the building. I found the coffee shop easily, and when I pulled up outside, my phone buzzed. Jane. She'd texted:

> Service cat bites my hand
> He puts the "wee" in meeting
> Funny and so sad

I snorted. Jane was enjoying this way too much.

The coffee shop was styled in black and white with accents of bright red and had a modern and slightly funky style to it. Artsy photos of typewriters and coffee mugs lined the walls. I liked the atmosphere immediately and made my way to the counter.

A young woman with green-tipped hair grinned at me. "What can I get you?" she asked.

I opened my mouth to order my usual, then stopped. "I'm kind of broke," I confided. "Could I just, like, get a regular coffee and use your Wi-Fi for a while?"

She nodded sympathetically. "Of course. We get that a lot here. Are you looking for work?"

"Yeah," I answered. "I had to drop something off at the unemployment office, and I need to submit some applications and go through new postings."

She grabbed a red mug and turned around to pour my order. "Stay as long as you like," she said over her shoulder. "Also, we're hiring here, if you'd be interested in working as a barista."

I paused to consider that. "Do you like your job?" I asked her.

"Yeah, I do," she said. "I mean, it's customer service, so you're dealing with the public, but the Steam Room is independently run, and the owner is pretty cool. His name is Tom."

"Does he wear shoes?" I asked. I'd been burned before. I wasn't taking any chances.

She looked at me weirdly. "Uh, yeah, he does," she said. "It doesn't pay well, but we do get tips."

"I come from telemarketing, so I have experience with the public, but not as a barista, so I'm not sure how qualified I'd be. I love coffee, though, especially dry cappuccinos with extra foam."

She handed me the mug. "Espresso drinks are all the same basic ingredients, just in different quantities. You'd catch on pretty quickly. And you get two free per shift."

I gave her a smile and paid for the coffee. "Thank you. I'll definitely keep it in mind." I dropped the nickel she'd given me in change into the tip jar, vowing that, once I was a contributing member of society again, I'd come back and leave a much bigger tip.

I took the mug to a booth in the farthest corner of the shop. There were only a handful of people there, so it was nice and quiet. Unlike my apartment. I sat and felt my shoulders slump. I needed work, and fast.

I opened a career-finder website and chewed my lip. Where to start? A lot of telemarketers transitioned into recruiting. Both required phone work and people skills, and there was usually more room for career growth. That would be a dream come true right now. I searched the openings, but only two really fit the criteria. One was a position at Monarch Recruiting that sounded pretty cool, and the other was recruiting security guards for a local hospital. I applied to Monarch right away, then hesitated on the other. Did I want to do that? Did I want to do either? Did it matter? Beggars couldn't be choosers. I copied and pasted my résumé, then hit SUBMIT.

I stretched my shoulders and clicked open a new tab on my browser.

While I was being productive, I figured I'd apply for some financial grants for the shelter. They were struggling like I was, and I knew they didn't have enough funds to implement all the programs they needed. Every little bit helped both of us right now.

I was deep in the form process when I suddenly smelled something warm and frothy and wonderful. I looked up to see a steaming cappuccino placed next to me on the table. My eyes followed the hand holding the cup up to the tattooed arm, complete with a little cat nestled in the elbow, to the black T-shirt, then to the lightest blue eyes I'd ever seen since, well, the last time I saw them.

"Carter Beckett," he said. "I heard you tell the barista your favorite drink was a dry cappuccino with extra foam."

"Thank you, that was very nice of you." I looked over toward the counter. The girl with the green-tipped hair gave me a wink and a thumbs-up. "Would you like to join me?" I asked him.

He settled into the seat across from me. He had his own cup of coffee. It looked to be straight brewed and black. "I come here a lot over my lunch break for some quiet time," he told me.

"I can see why," I answered. "It has a nice atmosphere." I took a sip and closed my eyes. "This is amazing." Even pity cappuccinos were better than none at all.

"Good. Applying for jobs?" he asked.

"Yes," I said self-consciously. "My Latin degree isn't the most marketable. I should have probably picked something else."

He took a sip of coffee and looked at me thoughtfully. "You majored in Latin? I didn't even know that was a thing."

"It is and I did." I smiled. "But *cogitationes posteriores sunt saniores*. Second thoughts are wiser."

"How in the world did you end up in telemarketing?"

"There isn't a huge demand for translating old texts." I shrugged.

"I worked as an industry editor after college, but the company closed when the economy took a downturn. Telemarketing was something I fell into afterward. That 'field' is usually hiring, and I have a knack for cold-calling. Altogether, I guess it makes for a weird job history. Or at least one not focused on financial gain. But enough about that. How did you end up working for the unemployment office?"

"I wanted to help people, and I moved through a few different state agencies. I worked in the foster care system before taking this position. My degree is in social work."

That squeezed my heart a little. I couldn't imagine the strength and patience a job like that would take. "That sounds hard."

"I got compassion fatigue. Right now, I'm able to help individuals with unemployment, but long-term, I want to make more of an impact, you know? Maybe work on the investigative side, preventing companies from hurting employees before they even end up at the unemployment office."

My hand slowed on its way toward the cappuccino. Was that why he was sitting with me now? To get information on Directis? I shook off the thought. "Are you hiring?" I asked.

He laughed. "Not at the moment, but I'm sure we'd be lucky to get you if we were. Can I ask you another question? Just out of curiosity?"

Just curiosity? I nodded.

"Your boss *really* fired you because he didn't like your face?"

"Cross my heart," I replied. "Those exact words. Which, sadly, isn't the craziest thing he's ever said." I tried to keep my voice lighthearted and studied the foam on my cappuccino. "My face led him to the conclusion I have a 'dark soul.'"

He sat back and shook his head. "This is a little hard to wrap my head around. We haven't had any claims come through from Directis before, which is kind of strange. Do they have a lot of turnover?" he asked.

"Yeah. I haven't really been keeping track, but it seems like it." I shook my head. That really *was* kind of weird. Something to listen for over the receiver. "Unfortunately, you would never be able to work there. They prohibit the hiring of any employees with visible tattoos on the neck, face, or hands because they can't be covered with long sleeves."

"But I just have a little bit on my neck," he said, touching his T-shirt collar. The black edge of a tattoo extended a quarter of an inch above his collar.

"Nope, still speaks of poor life choices," I told him.

"Too bad. That was going to my next career move. But, seriously, I don't understand what any of that has to do with telephone work."

"You and me both," I said. "Tell me about your cat tattoo."

He grinned widely. "I got it to honor Johnny Super Punch, a kitten I found when I was a kid. We lived pretty far out in the country, and one day she showed up on the porch. She was in bad shape. I snuck her inside and tried to feed her and give her a bath. I begged my mom to let me keep her and ended up getting a paper route to help pay for her vet bills. She passed away this summer. I had her for eighteen years."

There was so much awesomeness in that story. "Johnny Super Punch?"

"I can't be held responsible for that. I was ten. It was also long before I learned that all calicos are females."

"I'm no better at naming," I said. "I foster for the Humane Society and currently have five long-haired calico kittens wreaking havoc on my life. Unus through Quinque."

He raised an eyebrow at me.

"One through five in Latin," I said.

"You have calicos? Seriously?" he asked, his eyes bright. "Are any of them spoken for?"

I shook my head. "They won't be available for adoption for another couple of weeks. They need a final vet check and spay surgery first."

"Johnny Super Punch was a long-haired calico. I've been thinking about getting another cat for a few months, but I haven't been back to the shelter since she died. Do you know Danielle? I used to walk the dogs for her, and I drop off supplies whenever I have extra income." He sat back in the booth and grinned at me. "Can I meet them?"

I hesitated. I did know Danielle, the shelter director, but I didn't know Carter. Was it smart to invite him back to my place?

"Um," I said, "Just a second…" I trailed off. I pulled my phone out of my bag and quickly shot a text to Danielle. Hey, do you know Carter Beckett? Serial killer or nah? I texted.

I got jumping gray dots almost immediately then heart-eyed emojis popped up in the text box. Nah. Carter's great! she wrote back.

I looked up at him and smiled shyly. "Sure—" What about the receiver? I quickly checked the clock. It was nearing one in the afternoon. Xavier usually took long lunch breaks and often did his Tai Chi or whatever the hell it was on the lawn at this time of the day. We might be okay. Maybe I could get Carter in and out of my apartment without Xavier babbling loudly from the laundry room. "Do you mean now?" I asked.

"Is that okay?" he asked and smiled at me again. "I don't have to be back at the office for a while. I came in early today," he said.

"Yes. But be warned: this litter is a handful."

"I expect nothing less. Where do you live?"

"I'm on Brighton, in the Woodland apartment complex."

"Great." He pushed back his chair and stood. "I'm ready to meet some kittens."

I took my mugs to the dish return and gave the girl with the green-tipped hair a small wave. She grinned back at me. Carter and I walked to the parking lot together. "This is me," I said, stopping in front of my Jeep. "You can just follow me over there, and I'll see you in a few," I said.

"Great," he said. "Thanks, Vanessa. I appreciate this."

"Anything for a fellow rescuer," I told him and tried to steady my nerves. The receiver between the washer and dryer felt like an albatross around my neck.

Once in the car, I immediately called Jane. "Is Xavier in the office right now?" I asked frantically.

"He and Bobbert just stepped out," she responded. "Why, what's up?"

"Thank God. Those kittens stole the receiver, and I'm taking Carter back to my place, and—"

"Hold up! Who's Carter? Why's he going to your place?"

"He works at the unemployment office. He's interested in adopting a kitten."

Jane snorted over the line. "You're taking some old dude back to your apartment to see the kittens?"

"He's not old. He's average-aged. *Anyway*, the kittens stole the receiver Trisha gave me, and now I can't reach it to turn it off. Wanted to make sure the coast is clear."

Jane started to say something but took pity on me. "You should be good. The Xavier Show won't start again until at least two. I expect a full report."

"Perfect. Oh!" I said before she hung up the phone. "Have you talked to Trisha? I haven't been able to get ahold of her."

"Just a few texts here and there. She mentioned maybe hanging out tonight, though. You can tell us both about this guy."

"Bye, Jane."

A few turns later, I pulled into my parking lot and waited while Carter took the spot beside me. We got out at the same time.

"I live just in here," I told him as we walked inside the apartment lobby. He gestured for me to go forward as he held open the door to the hallway.

Just as I was turning the key in the lock, my phone started buzzing. I let Carter into the apartment but could immediately hear angry voices from the laundry room. I put my handbag and keys on the entryway table before reaching to check the messages. My heart was thumping like crazy.

ABORT ABORT XAVIER IS BACK, Jane had texted.

"I don't have time to make an appointment," Xavier's voice rang through the apartment. "The skin on the bottom of my feet is crusted, and there's pus everywhere. Can't you just diagnose me over the phone?"

Oh my god. The herpes/mange/ringworm/scabies had taken hold. I ran into the hallway and closed the laundry room door. "Sorry about that!" I said brightly to Carter. "I leave the TV on in the laundry room so the kittens don't get lonely. Take a seat on the couch," I told him. "I'll round up the litter so you can meet them." I flipped the radio on as I went toward the bedroom. Van Morrison was playing, and I turned it up a little louder than I normally would. *Please drown out Xavier*, I prayed.

Carter gave me a strange look but didn't say anything. The calicos were sleeping in a big fluffy pile on the bed. I picked them up one by one and nestled them in the crook of my arm. I took them out to the couch for Carter to see.

His face immediately melted. "Look at these little poofs," he cooed. "You are all so cute," he told them. The kittens were stretching and yawning from their nap, except Duo. She stalked over to Carter's lap and began to climb up his shirt with her sharp claws. "Ow," he muttered as she made her way up to his neck and settled into a sitting position on his shoulder. Her huge tail curled around his chin and over his nose. "I like this one," he said through her fur.

"Full disclosure," I said. "That one is a problem."

"I like her," he said again. She started purring and began to groom his eyebrow.

Over the kittens and the music, I heard Xavier yelling, "I can do the biopsy myself. I'll cut off a piece of the crust and have my employee drop it off at your office. I told you, I'm very busy. I don't have time right now to make an appointment."

Carter stroked Duo's fur and stared at me. "Are you sure you don't have someone locked up in your laundry room?" he asked.

I weighed my options. Admitting to that was probably better than admitting to the truth. "Yep," I said. "Got a dude tied up in the laundry room."

He chuckled and shook his head while disengaging Duo from his shoulder. "Maybe you should change the channel," he suggested.

If only…

"I should be heading back to work. Save this one for me." He passed Duo to me, and she immediately took off toward the laundry room, clawing at the closed door.

"Okay, thanks for stopping by," I said and walked him to the door as fast as was polite. I opened it, and he stepped out into the hall. "You know how to find your way back?"

"Yeah, I'll be fine," he said. Then he paused, looking directly into my eyes. "I don't understand how someone could object to your face," he said then turned and walked down the corridor.

I closed the door after him and leaned against it, but I could still hear Xavier. "I didn't ask you whether or not I should wear shoes—I asked you to diagnose my feet," he said angrily.

I sighed and closed my eyes. Even after being fired, I couldn't get away from him. But at least I wasn't in a conference room battling coworkers for a plastic Office Olympics trophy. I held tight to the thought.

Chapter 8

Seven weeks earlier

WE WERE ALL GATHERED IN THE CONFERENCE ROOM. EARLIER THAT day, Marcus—the receptionist—had taken apart the long table in the middle of the room and removed it. He had also covered the walls with pictures of maps and magazine cutouts of food from different countries. The five Olympic rings had been recreated as huge coffee-stain circles printed on simulated notebook paper and hung as a banner that spanned the length of the windows. The perfect atmosphere for the first annual Directis Office Olympics.

I stood quietly with my group, staring at the floor. By this time, I had the floor memorized, square by square. As Team North Korea, I had been grouped with Geraldine, Trisha, Gary, and a few other coworkers. If I could keep staring at the floor, maybe I could make this whole thing go away.

Unfortunately, looking at the floor allowed a direct sight line to Xavier's newly fancy feet. He'd dressed for the occasion by rolling his dress pants to the knees and donning a pair of high gladiator sandals. Still sockless, his toes peeped around the straps in the sandals and spilled out on the sides. He was wearing his suit jacket and tie. It gave the impression of business from the waist up, Roman circus from the waist down.

"The Office Olympics allows us a rare opportunity to be competitive with each other in a bodily sense," Xavier announced.

Why does everything he says have to be so weirdly gross?

"I know we post your telephone times on the board to publicly shame those who don't measure up, but we rarely get to best each other physically as well," Xavier went on. "This will help coheese us as a team and raise morale."

I shook my head a little to clear it. Was this a guy thing or, like, a management thing? Did beating each other really bond people? I thought about all the close friends I'd had and the groups I'd been a part of over the years. Granted, there weren't many since I wasn't exactly a joiner. But in every instance, I couldn't find anywhere regular shaming and… "bodily" competition increased our love for each other.

"Our first event will be the Desk Chair Race," he told the room. "One member of the team will sit in a chair while another pushes it as fast as they can around the perimeter of the room. Then they switch. Whoever gets back to the starting point first wins."

I heard a squeak and looked over in time to see Bobbert grab Jane's arm and forcibly push her toward the wheeled office chair. "I'm not a good choice for this event," she pleaded at him.

"You're the lightest on the team, and we're going to win," Bobbert growled back. I sent up a silent thanks that I hadn't been put on Team Iraq with Bobbert.

Once everyone had paired up and given Xavier their full attention, he blew a whistle to start the race.

All hell broke loose. The room filled with grunting and scraping sounds. Grown adults everywhere were diving for a seat, like musical chairs in elementary school gone horribly wrong. Geraldine and Gary pushed past me, almost elbowing me in the jaw in their haste to get to the chair first. I shrank back against the wall and glanced anxiously at Xavier's feet. One rolly chair accident and he could lose a few toes.

From the back of the room, I had a good view of the contestants as they started pushing their chairs as quickly as possible. People were bumping into each other and falling, and I could swear I saw Geraldine casually trip another team member as they rolled by. "Dear God," Trisha whispered.

I hadn't heard her come up beside me. I reached out and touched her arm. "We're dreaming, right?"

"If that's what gets you through, Vanessa," she said softly.

We shrank against the wall as a bunch of middle-aged adults wearing dress pants and jackets scooted dangerously close to us. When you're young and you imagine your future, you don't picture a short man wearing gladiator sandals and gripping a whistle forcing you to run around a meeting room to stay employed. Over your lunch break. In order to buy toilet paper and coffee. Why, again, had we all wanted to be adults so badly?

I had zoned out thinking about the sadness of our existence when Xavier blew the whistle again. "The winners are Team Iraq!" I looked up to see Jane and Bobbert had toaster-caked the other contestants. They'd won by the length of a conference table.

Bobbert was flexing and stomping and grunting as Jane made her way over to me.

"Good job, Iraq," I murmured to her as she came to stand beside me. "You kicked North Korea's ass."

"I only won so it would be over sooner," Jane said. "And so I don't have to compete in the next Hunger Olympics event—"

"Office Olympics," I corrected her.

"It's always over lunch, and it reminds us that we're powerless. *Hunger Olympics* is more accurate."

Once the chairs were moved back, I saw Cheryl was still sitting in the middle of the floor, her foot twisted oddly. I went over to help her up. "Are you okay?"

"I think it might be broken," she told me, her eyes shiny and large. "I tried to get out of the way, but someone landed on me, and I guess I broke their fall—"

"Then you'll be perfect competing in the three-legged race, our next event. It will take place outside," Xavier interrupted. I looked at my watch. We only had fifteen minutes left in our lunch break.

"Maybe she should sit this one out," I said to Xavier.

He looked at me darkly, and Cheryl immediately interrupted. "I'm excited about the next event!" she said brightly then snuck me a warning look and hobbled after the rest of the group to the doors.

This wasn't the future I'd been promised in grade school.

Chapter 9

Be subtle! be subtle! and use your spies
for every kind of business.

—SUN TZU, *THE ART OF WAR*

ABOUT AN HOUR AFTER CARTER LEFT MY APARTMENT, TRISHA
texted me and Jane: Girl's night tonight at Nessa's? So much progress!

The word *progress* made me more curious than I'd like to admit.
Come over whenever, I texted back.

Great! I'll come after work. Is seven okay? Trisha asked.

I'll be there. Jane.

At seven exactly there was a light rapping on the door. I opened it,
and Jane brushed past me down the hall. "Leggings are now pants," she
informed me. "I never thought I'd say that." She slumped next to a pile
of sleeping calicos on my couch.

"We need jobs," I sighed. "We're wearing pajamas as clothing."

"I don't know. Now that I know leggings can be pants, I feel very
free. Like I'm about to do Pilates, but all the time."

"How's the job search going?" I asked her.

"I have an interview at a bar on the west side tomorrow," she
said. "I have applications in at a bunch of places, but I can't wait
anymore. I had to let my Sephora membership lapse, and it physically hurt me."

"Yeah." I sat next to her. "A package of hot dogs and buns breaks down to about seventy-five cents per meal. As long as I only eat one. It's so hard to eat only one," I admitted.

"I can't even be a vegetarian anymore," she griped. "It's so much cheaper to eat meat! I'm totally over being poor. It's not at all boho chic. You holding up okay?"

I shrugged. "I guess. I've been sending out applications and working on shelter stuff. Keeps me from crying in the bathroom."

She touched my shoulder. "We don't work there anymore, Nessa. You have a whole apartment to cry in now, not just the bathroom."

"It still feels that way, though, with Xavier and Bobbert living in my laundry room."

"Whatever. Xavier mangling seventies rock is my favorite. It still sucked seeing our jobs posted yesterday, though."

My stomach flipped over. "Directis posted our jobs?"

She nodded. "At two dollars less an hour than they were paying us."

"You're kidding."

"Nope." She opened her mouth to say more but she was cut off by a howl from the laundry room. A couple of kittens scattered, but Duo and maybe Quinque remained on the couch.

"All I did was walk by," Xavier's voice echoed from the laundry room. "You don't have to bite me every time. I hate you, Haiku."

Jane grinned and counted on her fingers. "*I hate you, Haiku. You bite me all the damn time…*" She paused. "Five more syllables."

"No more haikus about Haiku," I groaned.

"I've been doing this all day! I'm like a poet now." She stopped. "Wait, is there money in that? Can I maybe write haikus for people about their cats?"

"I seriously doubt it," I said. I took a deep breath and stared at the ceiling. The receiver had been quiet for an hour or so. The silence was nice. "You've got to help me get that thing out of my laundry room," I said. "I need to be able to mute Xavier and Bobbert when people are here." I rolled my neck on my shoulders, trying to release some tension. "I know someone's going to complain to the landlord eventually."

"But it's fascinating," Jane argued. "Have you really listened to what they're saying? There's some shady shit going on over there."

"Like what?" I perked up. I *had* been listening, but all I'd heard so far was idiocy.

Just then, Xavier interjected over the intercom, "What do you want?"

"You busy?" we heard Bobbert ask. "Gary and I wanted to speak with you for a minute."

We heard some shuffling, and I imagined Bobbert and Gary walking into the conference room and taking a seat at the table. One of them cleared his throat. "Uh, we received notice of Vanessa Blair's application for unemployment benefits," Gary said.

I sat up immediately. Jane and I looked at each other.

"She's the one with the face," Xavier answered.

"Yeah," Bobbert said, and there was an edge in his voice. "The one who majored in Latin and thinks she's better than us."

I flushed in anger.

Jane covered her mouth with her hand and whispered, "Oh no he didn't…"

"I *am* better than them," I huffed. "At least ninety-five percent of the population is better than them."

"No, no, no, no, no," Xavier stated. "She signed the separation agreement. She can't take any legal action against us, ever. She agreed not to apply for unemployment."

"Actually," Gary broke in, "she didn't sign."

"*What?*" Xavier roared. "Why didn't anyone tell me this?! They all have to sign, Gary. You know this."

Jane and I stared at each other. "Why?" I mouthed at her, as if they might hear me.

She shrugged. "Beats me."

"I was following up. I didn't think she could get an application in so fast," Gary protested.

I felt a perverse pleasure that something I'd done was causing them such annoyance.

There was a loud thump, like someone, likely Xavier, had banged his fist on the conference room table. "You should have caught this sooner, Gary," Xavier said lowly.

"I'm aware of that," Gary said. "They've asked us to fill out a questionnaire as to why we fired her."

Bobbert snorted. "Because she thinks she's smarter than the men who run this whole office," he griped.

"And her facial expressions were unacceptable," Xavier argued. "Insubordinate. Remember?"

I heard Gary sigh uncomfortably. "I think it's probably better if we don't contest it. I let the unemployment office know we're consulting with a legal representative and will get back to them."

"Do we have a legal representative?" Bobbert asked.

"No," Gary said. "We most definitely do not."

"But if we don't contest it, they'll think we're admitting fault. That would be worse," Xavier stated.

"I disagree—" Gary started, but Xavier cut him off.

"What about the other one? Janet? Did she file?"

"My name is Jane!" Jane yelled at the laundry room.

"She signed the separation agreement," Gary responded.

"Send the questionnaire to me," Xavier said. "I'll look at it later."

There was a pause. "Okay," Gary finally said, "but no one responds before they run it by me."

Was that a growl? From Xavier or the cat?

"Have you looked through any of the applications from today?" Bobbert asked.

There was some paper shuffling and chair moving. Then Bobbert cooed, "You're such a round kitty," which was followed by a yelp then quiet crying.

"Told you not to touch him," Xavier said smugly.

I ran to the laundry room and closed the door most of the way, muffling their voices slightly. Then I flopped back on the couch next to Jane.

"Why are they so upset about unemployment?" I asked. "They weren't even in the database until I filed."

"Um, I think it raises their taxes or something," Jane offered.

"It must be more than that. We should talk to Trisha. Maybe there's something in the trash about it," I said. "And their resentment is weird. We did their monkey dance. We swiveled our goddam chairs. We never told Xavier what an idiot he is."

Jane chewed on her fingernail thoughtfully. "Well...this is a common theme I've been noticing. I listened to them all day. They seem to find strong women intimidating."

I rolled my eyes so hard, it actually hurt. "Really? We're in a new century, for God's sake."

"I know," Jane agreed, "but they aren't. They're upper-class older white dudes. They have their heads literally inside each other's asses."

"Not the right way to use the word *literal*, Jane."

"Sorry. That's just how it looks in my head." She shrugged. "They've been interviewing our replacements all morning. The more qualified and well-spoken the candidate is, the quicker they move her out the door."

"That's absolutely insane. Now I feel insulted that they hired me in the first place."

She nodded. "Me, too, but this might be a newer thing. I've been noticing the IQ level in the office has dropped a little. I think they don't like your face because they're intimidated by it."

"You sound just like my mom," I groaned as I felt a rush of love for Jane. Then I stopped for a second. "Am I, like, actually intimidating? Or, like, rude looking?" A fresh wave of self-consciousness washed over me.

"Of course not! But I'm not a sixty-year-old man who thinks it's 1870. I mean, you do have an are-you-fucking-kidding-me face, but that's a compliment." She squeezed my shoulder. "They found a replacement for me, though. Hired a former frat guy. He used the word *bruh* twice in his interview."

I put my head in my hands. "Why does this still surprise me?"

"I have no idea. Xavier's not the best guy. Do you remember Mary-Anne? Mom jeans, beaded glasses chain? Her desk was covered in Precious Moments figurines, and she always had a Diet Coke."

I thought back. "Oh yeah," I said. "The one Marcus replaced. Whatever happened to her?"

"We're friends on Facebook, and she's had it rough ever since they let her go."

"Why did they fire her?" I asked.

"I think I heard she was too slow. But I got the impression they meant in the relay races, not in her work speed."

I almost choked. "What?"

"She had trouble finding another job because she was honest that she'd been let go from Directis—something I never intend to be."

"Honest?" I asked.

"Absolutely," she said. "I'm not telling anyone what happened. It's not like you can send a picture of Xavier in with your application."

"Can you just lie like that?" I asked. The thought was so appealing.

"Don't know. I'm going to find out. Let Mary-Anne be a cautionary tale for you, too. It's been almost a year, and she's still unemployed.

Last I saw she was worried they were going to foreclose on her house, and her kids had gone to live with their dad. I had to unfollow her, it was so depressing."

"Wow," I said softly. "That's awful."

"Right. So we lie our way through it."

"*That's* what you got out of that story?"

"Yep. That's not happening to us. Also, Xavier's a total asshole."

We were quiet for a minute as I thought about Mary-Anne. It wasn't an uncommon story, but maybe the unfairness part was. And maybe it wasn't.

"I hope it works out for her," I said. "I hope we don't find her under the bridge." I could imagine a Directis reject colony joining me under that bridge by the river. Former employees milling about, trading stories, burning shoes. And me, trying to prevent them from turning to the only thing they knew: rolly chair competitions.

"I've applied for a few jobs," I told Jane. "Only one sounds great."

"Maybe they'll call," Jane said. "Stay positive."

My phone buzzed and I jumped, but it was only Trisha. I answered it and pushed the button for speaker.

"Hey, why aren't you here?" I asked.

"Hey!" Trisha called back. Her voice sounded slightly muffled. "Am I on speaker?"

"Yep," I told her. "Jane's here, too."

"Hi, Jane!" she called. "I don't think I'm going to be able to make it this evening. I'm so sorry!"

"Everything okay?" Jane shouted into the phone.

"Yeah, it's just that Xavier gave me a piece of his foot today, and I'm supposed to do something with it. It's in a ziplock bag on my passenger seat," she explained.

My eyes met with Jane's over the phone. "You don't know what to do with it?" I asked.

"No! I mean, it looks like what my neighbor's dog has, so I think we succeeded, but why would he give me a piece?"

"He mentioned a biopsy earlier, I think," I told her.

"They have to take their own samples. The dermatologist said they won't accept a baggy of foot crust. Who would? I understand he's mad about the scabies or mange or whatever, but he wasn't making a lot of sense. Plus, Haiku piddles on his Astroturf now. So, technically, he could have a cat bladder infection for all I know."

"He can't have a cat bladder infection," I said. "He's not a cat."

"He's not a dog either, but he definitely caught something," Trisha argued.

Jane grabbed the phone from my hand. "So you're driving around with a dime bag of foot disease?" she yelled into the speaker.

"Well, yeah." Trisha sounded defensive. "He gave it to me. I don't know if I should throw it in the dumpster or bury it."

"Why would you bury it?" Jane exclaimed.

"Because it's human remains, Jane. That's the proper thing to do." We could hear what sounded like her car accelerating. "I've been checking the trash, too, Nessa. Only problem is getting the papers to my car without anyone seeing."

"Hm." I mulled it over. "Could you create a diversion? Like, pull the fire alarm or something?"

"Yeah, totally. I can handle that," Trisha answered. "I also typed out some things and have a document I think you both should read. I'll send a PDF later tonight."

"No!" I said. "I don't want anything in my email that police could find later. At least print it instead!" I grabbed the phone back from Jane.

"I'm always careful what I put in writing, Nessa!" Trisha called out. "I know that email can be intercepted, so don't worry. Gotta go. Sorry again about tonight!"

The call clicked off.

"Well, I, for one, am very excited to see what Trisha has come up with," I announced. "Even if we all end up sharing a cell with matching life sentences."

"This is Trisha we're talking about. She's not going to do anything too illegal."

"Well, that went out the window when she bugged the office. Also, the legal system is pretty black-and-white. Things are legal or illegal."

"Oh, it's fine. But before I go, tell me about this guy you had over."

I looked at the ceiling. "He's an animal lover, he wants to adopt my craziest kitten, and he's the one looking into my unemployment case."

"And he's cute?" Jane asked.

I shrugged. "I guess. Yeah."

She nudged me with her shoulder. "You have a crush, don't you?"

"No!" I protested. "We have a professional relationship. He mentioned he wants to be an investigator instead of a claims officer, so he's probably just hanging around to get the deets on Directis." I caught her looking at me and felt my bravado crumble. My shoulders slumped. "And I'm not in a good place to date anyone. It's just so embarrassing, Jane. Getting fired was, like, the most mortifying thing I've ever been through. And that's what he knows me for."

"Not me," Jane stated. "I took a swimming class in college and lost my suit during a high dive. It's all up from there."

"That would suck," I agreed.

"Haven't been in a pool since. Then I took a yoga class. I didn't have my 'core engaged' during sun salutations and fell headfirst into the person in front of me. Everyone in the class was bent over, and they all went down like dominoes, face to butt. I also don't do yoga anymore."

I felt a quick rush of love for Jane. "Thanks," I said.

"I'm sure this guy doesn't think less of you," she told me. "At least he won't if he ever sees Xavier. He practically comes with a visual warning label."

I nodded and sighed. "One look at his lower body gives you the sense he might need medication and therapy."

She glanced over at me. "Have they decided yet on your case? I thought unemployment was only an online thing and you never talked to a person. I was pretty sure there were no humans involved at all, just a massive computer that spits out denials."

"Guess not," I told her.

She hesitated then glanced at me from under her lashes and tried to look casual. "Have you, you know...heard from Marcus lately?"

I shook my head. "Maybe you should reach out to him."

She snorted. "Nah, probably not the best idea. Even if getting fired wasn't my most embarrassing moment, it still wasn't great. The office is probably gossiping about me. I bet Geraldine threw a party when Gary walked me out. Before, you know, she fed my lunch to the wild turkeys."

"I'm sure he doesn't care about that. He's probably neck-deep in survivor's guilt."

She shook her head. "I was too big a coward to ask him out, and now I'll never have the chance."

"He's not dead, Jane," I said.

"He might as well be. He's still stuck in Xavier's tower, like Rapunzel or something, and I'm a free agent on the ground." She sighed dramatically. "Marcus, Marcus, untie your man bun!"

"Or just text him," I suggested.

She buried her face in one of the soft kitten bellies on the couch next to her and yelped as the cat rabbit-kicked her in the chin. "Kinky or whichever cat this is has no sympathy for my pain," she complained. She lowered her face until she and the kitten were eye level. "I'm going to be living with my parents forever without my true love, and you deny me the comfort of your furry belly."

The kitten stretched upward and sniffed Jane's cheek before delicately biting her on the tip of her nose.

"Ow! This is why I don't do cats. That's my cue." She stood up and rolled her eyes. "Kinky says to take the pity party elsewhere."

"Quinque," I corrected her.

"That's what I said."

I shook my head. "You're always welcome to pity party here. Don't listen to them."

Jane grinned as she gathered her handbag and slipped on her flats. "Thanks, Nessa. This evening has me wishing I'd applied for unemployment, on so many levels."

Chapter 10

He will win who knows when to fight and
when not to fight.

—SUN TZU, *THE ART OF WAR*

THE NEXT MORNING, I AWOKE TO MURMURING OUT IN THE LIVING room. The kittens were nowhere to be found. I sat up and rubbed my eyes, my hair a mess, and looked around the bedroom. What was I hearing? More Xavier nonsense?

I stood and stretched, then padded to the bedroom door in search of coffee.

I stepped into the living room and blinked. I was not alone. My mother was perched on the loveseat, and seated around the room were three other women about her age. They all stared at me expectantly.

"Vanessa, do you have a moment?" my mother asked.

I blinked again. "Mom? What're you doing in my apartment? Is everything okay?"

"It's fine, sweetie. I wanted you to meet my friends. From bridge, remember?"

I tried to shake off the cobwebs. "Is Dad okay?"

"I imagine he is," she answered. "That's Linda." She pointed to a woman in her late fifties with obviously dyed bright red hair, who grinned at me and waved from the couch. "That's Tammy." She gestured to a woman sitting next to Linda on the couch, with long blond hair and unmistakable false lashes. "And that's Sharon." A third woman was sitting on a floor pillow in the corner of the living room, under the windows. Sharon had long braids and was wearing a tunic, no makeup, and leggings as pants. Piled in her lap were all the kittens. I liked her immediately.

"I need coffee before we do...whatever this is." I waved my hand vaguely. "Anyone want any?" I asked the group.

"Oh, we helped ourselves, honey," Tammy said and pointed to their coffee cups. Of course they had.

I walked into the small kitchen to brew a cup and was greeted by the sight of casseroles and baked goods on every surface. I spotted a plate of my favorite food of all time: chocolate chip muffins. The coffee was immediately forgotten as I stuffed a whole muffin into my mouth and munched in bliss. I swallowed quickly as I made my coffee extra strong in the single-cup server. I grabbed another muffin and went out into the living room to sit on the loveseat next to my mom.

"This is an intervention," she announced.

"Wait, what?" I said and swallowed a huge gulp of burning coffee. I needed that caffeine.

"No, no, Kathy," Sharon said in a low, smooth voice. "This isn't an intervention. Vanessa isn't on drugs. Is she?"

"No!" I protested. "I'm not!"

"Nothing wrong with a few drugs," Tammy interrupted. She flipped her blond hair off her shoulder and winked at me. "Legal ones, of course. Just saying."

My mom gave her a look. The kittens stirred in Sharon's lap, and a couple of them lazily swiped at her braids. I kept my eyes on them as I waited for the coffee to kick in. I'd burned the hell out of my tongue.

"I told my bridge group about your employment situation," my mom said.

"Thank you," I said, genuinely touched and a little embarrassed, as I dove into my second muffin. Was that customary? Did people bring you food when you were fired, like they did when someone died? I didn't like to cook, and my bank account was dwindling, so I wasn't complaining, but still… "Is that why you're here so early?"

"I also filled them in on what's going on with Excalibur Lincoln."

I groaned internally. I'd forgotten about that.

"Linda over there"—my mom pointed—"is our computer expert. She can't find any record of an Excalibur Lincoln being born, well, ever."

I nodded. Unlikely anyone had been cruel enough to name a child that. "I guess we should give up, then," I said hopefully.

Linda leaned forward on the couch, her bright red hair clashing with her purple lipstick. "An assumed name. Maybe one of many. What do you think he's hiding? Who do you think is looking for him? Did he kill one of his wives? Was he in the Mob?"

"Any additional pictures of him?" Tammy cut in. "I don't know if facial recognition is really a thing, but—"

"Oh, it is," my mother insisted. "It's even on the Facebook."

Additional photos? How many did they have?

"We can always do a reverse image search, like on *Catfish*," Linda said. "I always watched those guys on *Catfish*."

The muffin stuck in the back of my throat, and I felt like the air was squeezing out of my lungs. Doing recon with Trisha was one thing. Doing it with my mom and her friends was something else entirely. "Mom," I pleaded, "Let it go. People get fired all the time. It doesn't mean you need to form a Bridge Brigade."

Tammy and Linda's eyes lit up. "Bridge Brigade!" Linda cried.

"Vanessa Leigh," my mom admonished. "All I wanted was to speak with his mother, but now we've discovered he's not who he told you he is. Someone needs to alert the police."

"Not yet," Sharon interrupted. "Be cool, Kathy. We're in the research phase."

The truth was almost never the best course of action with my mother, but what choice did I have? "Mom." I took her hand and forced her to look at me. "His name isn't Excalibur Lincoln."

The women exchanged conspiratorial glances. "We know," Mom said. "We think it's Xavier Adams. But is *that* even his real name? We found him by googling your old company. Why is he using both names?"

"He's not. I just didn't correct you." I sighed. "Mom, I'm not in middle school. I'm an adult. I'm looking for another job, and I don't want anything to mess that up for me. Do you all hear me?" I looked at each one individually. All of them, except Tammy, looked sufficiently contrite. Tammy had pulled out a compact and reapplied her lipstick, the exact shade of orange sherbet. "I don't want any of you within twenty feet of that building. And no more googling." I looked my mom directly in the eye. "I appreciate the support, and I love you. But leave it alone."

"I am too big a gift to the world to waste on those who don't see my greatness," resounded from the laundry room. I covered my face with my hands. Of course. Morning platitudes with Xavier.

Tammy immediately perked up. "Do you have a man in your bedroom, honey?"

I thought quickly, again faced with the impossible choice of which option was better, the insane truth or an outlandish lie. His voice was a little more strident than usual. Of course, he had to pick this morning to shout.

I chewed on my lower lip. "So I have an affirmations recording that comes on in the morning to give me a self-esteem boost?" I tried to keep my voice from rising at the end but failed.

All the women were now looking at me with extreme interest.

"Other people are stepping-stones I must tread on to the path of my dreams," he continued.

"That doesn't sound very affirming," my mother said. "I taught you better than that."

Time for option two. "There's no man in my bedroom. Just in my laundry room."

Linda and Tammy were on their feet and headed to the laundry room before I could even blink. Sharon stayed comfortably on the floor.

"Wait for me!" my mom yelled after them.

"There's no one in here, Kathy," Linda called back.

"I'm a very attractive man. My self-worth doesn't depend on the love of a selfish animal. Or a spouse." He just wouldn't stop.

Linda and Tammy filed back into the living room. "It appears Vanessa's dryer has a very high opinion of itself," Tammy announced.

My mom locked eyes with me. "Vanessa Leigh, explain yourself this instant."

"One of my former coworkers bugged the office and gave me a receiver. It's stuck between the washer and dryer because of the kittens. I don't want it there, but every part of me is too wide to reach it." It all rushed out at once, and I felt my usual blush heat my cheeks.

"Is that Excalibur talking?" my mom asked.

I nodded.

"He sounds like an ass," Sharon stated.

"This is noth—" I started to respond when my mother shushed me loudly.

Then she put her finger to her lips and motioned for all three women to follow her. I sighed and trudged after them.

"The lining of my cloud is silver, and it's full of money..." Xavier trailed off as we all made our way toward the laundry room. The kittens scampered after us.

Duo immediately tried to squish herself in between the washer and dryer, but only managed to get her head through before she got stuck, back legs and potbelly thrashing. She jerked her head free then shook off, looking surprised.

Even the kittens were getting too big to fit in that crevice.

All five of us crowded into the tiny room, and Sharon immediately began folding the clothes in the clean-laundry basket next to the washer. Tammy leaned against the wall, and Linda and I propped ourselves against the dryer. My mother stood still in the center, staring into the distance.

Just then, we heard a knock over the speaker. "Xavier, are you free?"

"Who's that?" my mom hissed.

"Sounds like Gary, the HR guy—" I started, but she shushed me again.

"What do you want?" Xavier.

"Bob and I wanted to touch base about some recent events," Gary said.

"Fine," Xavier growled. There was what sounded like bare feet thwacking, then Xavier snapped, "Bobs! Get in here!"

There was some shuffling then a hiss that ended in a short hacking sound.

"Did Excalibur just spit at his employee?" my mother whispered. "What a disgusting man."

I shook my head. "I think he stole his wife's cat—" I got out before she shushed me again.

"Morning, Bob," Gary said. "Xavier, we wanted to mention the whiteboards out in the pit," he began.

"Where all the peons sit?" Xavier asked. Maybe they were nodding.

"The pit," my mother gasped. "Peons? Is there some BYOB stuff going on there?"

"It's BDSM," Tammy interjected and glanced over at me. "Right?"

"No and no! That's what Xavier calls the main room where the employees sit," I said but stopped before my mother could shush me again.

"What about the whiteboards?" Xavier asked. I heard shuffling, and in my mind, Bobbert was sweating and still trying, against better judgment, to pet the cat.

I tried not to groan. I had hated those whiteboards with every fiber of my being. Each account, or team, had one, and they used them regularly to shame us for our phone times, sales, and whatever else they could think of. Each day they put up the name of the employee who did the worst in each category the day before. It was an awful way to be greeted each morning.

"When I got in this morning, someone had changed them. There were no 'last place' employees listed. Every name had a star next to it," Gary told him.

You could hear the anger in Xavier's voice when he responded, "What? Are you serious?"

"It's okay," Gary assured him. "No need to get worked up."

Someone had actually changed the board? Trisha? I had wanted to so many times but had never risked it.

"I was meditating when you interrupted me," Xavier griped. "We need to find out who did this. Clearly it's not humiliating them enough."

"Oh, it is," Bobbert replied. "In fact, I just spoke with Geraldine and Nancy. Their account is just the two of them, so every day their whiteboard has one of their names on it.'"

"They complained about the board?!" Xavier yelled. "I don't care if there's only two of them on that account, one of them is still the *worst* each day!"

"Well, Nancy was just saying it wasn't motivating for them—"

"Then Nancy can pack her things," Xavier growled.

Gary cleared his throat. "Xavier, let's not be rash. We've already let a few employees go recently who were good producers, and—"

"I'm not sure she was the one who messed with the board—" Bobbert interrupted.

"Do I look like I care?" Xavier's voice was low. "I don't like being questioned by them."

I couldn't remember exactly which one was Nancy, but my heart went out to her. We had all wanted to bring up the issue. In my imagination, Xavier was angrily tapping his (probably swollen and crusty) naked feet on the floor and Bobbert was holding his hand out for Haiku to sniff, still not getting the hint.

"We can let Nancy go at the end of the day. But I'm thinking we might need to send out a daily email that logs exactly what each person did the day before, so it can't be altered in any way. And find out who was being insubordinary with the board. Maybe we could even have an Underperforming Employee of the Week certificate for those who need the most improvement."

"Maybe we could try a permanent probation for Nancy, like the one Trisha is on," Gary offered. "Since the account only has two workers, we could give her an opportunity to improve."

"I'm sorry, is Gary in charge of Directis?" Xavier sneered. "What are your thoughts, Bob?"

Well, clearly Bobbert would be an idiot to disagree with him. I looked at the bridge club all crowded together in the laundry room. Linda had unnecessarily pressed an ear to the dryer. Tammy looked pretty zoned out. Sharon was still quietly folding the laundry in the clean basket, but her lips were pressed into a thin line, and my mom was standing still with her eyes narrowed.

"You got it, Xavier," Bobbert answered. "I'll have Marcus start putting together the certificates, and we'll fire Nancy."

"You're both dismissed," Xavier replied.

"Hey, real quick, the girl with the face, Vanessa? Whatever happened with that?" Bobbert asked.

"Who?" Xavier snapped. "The Loch Ness Monster? None of your business."

There was an audible four-person gasp in the laundry room. No one had called me that since elementary school. I wondered for a second if it was possible to die from embarrassment.

I tried not to look up, but I could feel the weight of the bridge club's eyes on me.

There was a loud warning meow, which I took to mean Bobbert once again couldn't keep his hands to himself, before the sound of a door closing. I assumed they'd both left. But, after a pause, Xavier began the platitudes again.

My mom inhaled a deep breath and marched us all back into the hallway near the kitchen. She drew me into a hug. "I can't believe my baby girl had to work for such a bony-eared assfish."

I tried not to snort as she hugged me. My mother hardly ever said anything overtly negative about anyone; her favorite go-to phrase was the subtle Southern insult: *I'll pray for you.*

"That's nothing," I told her. "Don't even get me started on the unattainable sales goals just to deny everyone their bonuses."

"Well, at least we have someone on the inside." Linda grinned. Their faces all brightened. Then she glanced over at me. "Trisha, right?"

I looked back and forth between them. "No," I said forcefully. "No, *we* do not. No. This was all the kittens' fault."

Mom glanced down at our feet, where a flock of calico floofs weaved around our legs. "I told you fostering was a terrible idea."

"You can't blame those sweet babies," Sharon cooed.

"I can blame them," I said. "I do. Working for Directis was also a terrible idea." Though it would have been kind of cool to see Xavier's face when he found out about the whiteboard.

"We just want to help," Linda said. "No one deserves what you went through. Whiteboard shaming! Have you ever heard of such a thing? This all seems pretty sketchy."

"Maybe there's more going on here than just assfish," Tammy added.

I shot them a pained smile. "Thank you, but I'm fine."

"We absolutely understand," Sharon said a little quickly. She gently scruffed the kitten who was trying to climb her leg. "We're headed out for breakfast. You're welcome to come, Vanessa."

"Thanks, but I'm probably going to keep hitting those muffins pretty hard," I said.

"We could stay, if you want," Linda began, but Sharon elbowed her sharply.

"All right!" Tammy said, a little too brightly. "We'll all catch you later!"

She, my mother, Sharon, and Linda all headed for the door, but my mom hung back for a second. "I just love you, sweetheart," she said. "We'll behave."

"I'm serious," I told her. "*Non progredi est regredi*. Not to go forward is to go backward."

She rolled her eyes at me and kissed me quickly on the cheek. "That's what a college education gets you. Random sayings no one understands."

"Goodbye, Mom," I said as I closed the door behind them. She wasn't wrong, though. A four-year degree in a dead language spoken only in the Vatican and a job as a telemarketer. Scratch that. Ex-telemarketer.

I closed the laundry room door then wandered back to the kitchen and grabbed yet another chocolate chip muffin. There was so much good food on the counters that it almost softened my feelings toward my mom. She had never once questioned whether I'd deserved to be fired. On the other hand, she'd turned into a detective to track down my former boss's mother. I guess they kind of evened each other out.

But…had my mother used the food as a distraction? She knew I couldn't resist those muffins. Did she want to keep me complacent so she could play out her fantasy as Jessica Fletcher? Could Xavier have been doing something similar? If so, what was he trying to keep his employees from discovering?

Chapter 11

Let your plans be dark and impenetrable
as night, and when you move,
fall like a thunderbolt.

—SUN TZU, *THE ART OF WAR*

ONCE MY MOM AND HER FRIENDS WERE GONE, I GRABBED A SHOWER. My hair still wet, I fired up my laptop to do some serious job hunting. I planned to dedicate the entire day to finding the perfect job and parsing real information out of Xavier's nonsense. I quickly clicked on my email browser tab to find the mailbox downloading an extremely large file. As soon as I saw the subject line, my heart jumped. *War is an Art Form.* From Trisha, obviously.

From: Trisha Lam
Time: 2:05:18 AM EST
To: Vanessa Blair, Jane Delaney
Subject: War is an Art Form

Hey ladies,

So I know you've both heard of The Art of War by Sun Tzu. He's got a lot of important ideas (and some weird ones— skip over those), but he believes in spying (check!), irritating the enemy (check!), and not letting him rest (foster kittens for the win!).

Anyway, I've attached a copy to this email for you both to refresh your memories. There'll be a quiz. LOL

Make sure you two "attend" the next We Meeting in the morning at 10!

Sic semper tyrannis!

Take the bitches down!

(That was for you, Nessa! I googled it.)

XOXO,

Trisha

PS—I decided it would be best to save you-know-who's foot pieces. I doubt they'll come in handy later on, but they're in my freezer just in case. Also, we got another shipment from Amazon (yay!).

Trisha had sent me an honest-to-God war manual. I vaguely remembered having read it in a business class, but I hadn't realized Trisha had meant the war thing so literally. Between her, my mother, Jane, and now a dead war general, how could we lose?

I clicked on the attachment. The PDF expanded on my screen, and the first line I saw was, *In crossing salt-marshes, your sole concern should be to get over them quickly, without any delay.* What?

The muffins were sitting like rocks in my stomach, but that didn't stop me from wanting another one. It had already been a lot with Xavier, and Trisha now seemed to be connecting a conference room and a salt marsh. I was resisting the urge to go back to bed and pull the covers over my face when my phone buzzed.

How are things on the outside? Marcus.

I paused, suddenly alert. I hadn't expected to hear from him again.

I liked Marcus, but we weren't close, and we hadn't spoken since I'd been fired.

I've been better. You? I texted back.

I settled down onto the couch with Duo, and possibly Uno and Tres, as I watched the little jumping gray dots on the phone screen.

It sucks here even more than it used to, he wrote back. You and Jane holding up okay?

Yeah. I've got muffins. I'll tell her you said hi, I texted.

I heard murmuring from the laundry room and reluctantly opened the door to hear the 10:00 a.m. We Meeting, per Trisha's instructions.

"Is everyone on the line?" Xavier whined through the speaker. "As you all know, this is a time for us to conjoin our goals and work together to endure Directis's vision." There was some rustling, then Xavier snapped, "Why is it so stuffy in here? Marcus! Fix the air-conditioning!"

Got to go, our esteemed leader calls, Marcus texted. Keep in touch, okay?

Hm. Could Marcus possibly be an ally? He'd certainly been one to me once, on the "inside."

There were a few moments of silence, followed by mumbling and some stomping. Then Xavier continued, "Let's begin by discussing our goals—"

His voice cut off, and I could hear a loud whir of the air-conditioning then a lot of gasps and nervous laughter followed by screaming. Uh-oh.

I grabbed my phone and pulled up the group text with Trisha and Jane. WHAT DID YOU DO? I texted.

Sun Tzu told me to forage off my enemy. I hit the supply closet before the meeting, Trisha wrote.

Who's Sun Tzu? Jane responded.

Check your email. Trisha.

Is a million-year-old guy talking to you? Jane texted back. You guys aren't friends.

I groaned. It was impossible to keep them focused. WHAT HAPPENED, TRISHA? I could still hear lots of commotion and cursing coming through the receiver.

I created a diversion, just like you told me to. Remember all that glitter we got for the Office Olympics but didn't use? I turned the air off and put it in the ducts before work this morning, Trisha texted. It's so beautiful. It's like a unicorn exploded in here.

I stared down at my phone. Trisha had glitter bombed her supervisors and colleagues?

LMAO Pics or it didn't happen!! From Jane.

An image downloaded onto my phone screen. At first it was hard to tell what it was. It was blurry and taken at an angle. In the bottom corner of the screen, I could barely make out Xavier, his graying hair turned almost completely electric blue. Part of the ceiling was visible in the upper right, and there were lots of blurred blue figures in the background. And lots of sparkles.

Jane wrote:

Glitter glitter everywhere
And all the boys did shrink
Glitter glitter everywhere
Too bad it wasn't pink.
Whoa, I really am like a poet now.

There was so much noise coming through the speaker.

I think I was overzealous, Trisha texted. We got a little sweaty with the air off. It's sticking to my skin like glue.

I cursed my vivid imagination. I could see Bobbert and Xavier in my head, covered in glitter, looking like rejects from a rave. Oh god, and Geraldine. I bet she was not pleased.

There was a lot of blustering and coughing coming through the speaker. The calico zoo had already scattered from the noise, and I could hear Xavier wheezing, followed by a loud painful-sounding thump.

Xavier just bit it. Slipped in the glitter. His feet have been oozing a little lately. I almost feel bad, Trisha texted.

He has a bladder infection on his feet and he's STILL not wearing shoes?? Jane asked.

"Everyone out!" Xavier roared through the receiver. "I'm going to find out who's responsible for this!"

It suddenly felt like the muffins were coming back up. I suggested a fire alarm, Trisha! They go off all the time and it doesn't look like sabotage, I texted.

Everything's better with glitter, she wrote back.

Even vampires! Jane added.

There was a huge commotion with lots of rustling and the sound of chairs moving, and I was trying to absorb the horror when the phone buzzed again.

Are you still there? It was Trisha. I got some in my contacts. I knew it was coming, and I still looked up. Can one of you pick me up?

I'm headed into my interview now, Jane wrote. Don't blink, you'll scratch your cornea.

Last thing I wanted to do was go to the Directis office, but I couldn't leave Trisha there. On my way, I texted.

It took me about ten minutes to get there, and the chaos was visible even from the road as I drove up. I parked in the fast-food parking lot next to the office and awkwardly slumped in my seat to make myself less visible.

Everyone was out on the lawn, shaking out their clothes and hair, taking off suit jackets and shoes and socks, and dumping clothes out in the grass. I caught sight of Marcus, who had pulled his hair free from its bun, releasing sparkling rain onto his shoulders. Geraldine was just sitting in the grass, staring at nothing. Bobbert was hopping up and down. It was way too cold to be stripping on the front lawn. No one looked happy, and I hadn't caught sight of Trisha or Xavier. The grass, however, was gorgeous. It had a fairyland sheen, and I took a moment to appreciate the power of glitter.

I reached for my phone to let Trisha know I'd arrived when a movement near the car caught my eye. I looked up and let out a yelp. A beautifully glittered face stared back at me through the window. I put my hand over my racing heart and tried to relax as my body finally caught up with my brain. Trisha. An alternate universe Trisha that brought back so many memories from the Office Olympics. I felt a quick pang of nostalgia. *Forsan et haec olim meminisse iuvabit.* One day, it may please us to remember even these things. I was nowhere near there yet, but I had the feeling all the same.

"Sorry I scared you." Trisha panted as she opened the car door. "Are you okay with me sitting in here? It's never going to come out of your seats."

I patted the black fabric seat. "Hop in. That glitter is stunning," I said.

She gave me a huge grin. "It is! They're going to have to firebomb the office to get rid of it."

"But it looks like sabotage, Trisha, not an accident. Don't get caught, okay?"

She waved her hand dismissively as she slid into the passenger seat. I caught sight of her red eyes. They were tearing up, and her eyeliner was smudged down her cheeks.

"I didn't have a choice, Nessa. I needed a longer diversion. I found a raccoon in the bin the other day, so who knows what else is in there. Had to break out my gloves and mask before I got the bags in my car."

"Be careful," I said, a little queasy. "Kind of a bummer. I was stoked to see what was in there."

"Right now, maybe only mice," Trisha said brightly. "I'll take it to my mom's garage and fumigate it. Then we can all go through it together." She paused. "I'm sorry to make you come back here. It's insensitive. My eyes are too irritated, and Xavier said we all had to leave immediately. He's making us come back this afternoon and work straight through the evening."

"It's okay, Trisha, really. That was probably not wise, but I admire your dedication. I mean, you were always so quiet at work. I honestly didn't think you had it in you." I passed her the little bottle of eye drops I'd brought with me.

She tipped her head back and put a couple drops in each eye, sighing with relief. "I'm an introvert. I just don't have the energy for small talk at work after all the team-building crap they make us do. It's exhausting. I already have to chitchat with the moms in Claire's play group. But you and Jane are fun. That night when we hung out in your apartment was like the first time in a long time that I had real friends." She shrugged. "And I'm enjoying myself. I found out I'm a total badass."

"You definitely are," I agreed. "But I don't want them eating away at your self-esteem."

"Sun Tzu says to appear weak when you're strong. They have no idea what I'm capable of." She glanced over at me. "Did you reread *The Art of War* yet?"

"I'll look at it," I promised. "Is that why you changed the whiteboards in the office?"

She shook her head. "I didn't touch the whiteboards. I don't know who did that. It was a great idea, though. Xavier has been losing his mind over it. This will probably redirect his attention, though."

I looked at the blue sheen now covering the black seats of my Jeep.

I ran a finger over the fabric, watching as the glitter sank farther into the creases. "This stuff is the consistency of powdered sugar," I murmured.

She nodded. "It's ultrafine grain; you don't even need glue."

I opened my mouth to reply when a flash caught my eye. I scanned the edges of the parking lot. "Did you see that?" I asked Trisha.

"See wh—" she started to respond when I saw it again.

"Over there!" I said. "Is someone taking pictures? With a flash? In the daytime?"

She turned her head to look. "I think I see some movement over in the bushes."

I quickly glanced at the lawn where the Directis employees had been shaking out their clothes. Most of them had already gotten into their cars, and a few had left already.

We looked at each other. "Should we check it out?" I asked reluctantly.

Trisha bounded out of the car before I could blink. I looked around furtively to make sure none of the employees could see me then followed after her. My adrenaline kept me from feeling too chilly in the autumn air as I took off.

She sprinted over to the edge of the parking lot, and a head popped up from the evergreen bushes, a head I immediately recognized. Even with the dark glasses, hat, and trench coat.

I jogged the rest of the way over. "Seriously, Mom?" I asked.

Three more heads popped up. Two of them were dressed like my mother: dark glasses, hats, and trench coats. I could see Tammy's long blond hair escaping from under her fedora, and Linda's purple lipstick gave her away immediately. Sharon was dressed as she had been earlier, in a tunic and leggings.

"This is not real life," I said to myself.

My mother heard me anyway. "You said to stay twenty feet from the perimeter of the building," she said defensively.

"I measured," Tammy volunteered, holding up a retractable tape measure.

Linda reached over and touched Trisha's wrist. "I don't know you, dear, but you look lovely."

Trisha smiled. "Thanks." She glanced over at me. "Are you friends with Vanessa?"

"That's my mom," I grouched. "And—"

"The Bridge Brigade!" Linda interjected brightly. "We were doing recon, and then all these blue people started pouring out of the building."

I couldn't stop myself from groaning.

"I'm Trisha," she answered.

Sharon's eyes lit up. "The one on the inside!" she crowed. "Did you do this?"

Trisha nodded delightedly.

"You go, girl," Tammy said.

Before I could separate them, my mom pushed her way through and took off her sunglasses. "We've heard so much about you, sweetheart," she said. "I'm Vanessa's mother, Kathy, and this is Linda, Tammy, and Sharon." She gestured to the other women. "We're not sure your boss Excalibur is on the up and up," she said, her voice pitched low.

"She means Xavier," I mumbled, "and you need to go."

"We're following the rules," my mother protested. "And where is your coat, Vanessa? It's too cold for you to be wandering around out here like it's summer. It's September, and you're going to catch a cold."

"I lost my jacket," I said, exasperated. "And time for new rules! Why on earth are you dressed that way?"

"We're undercover," she said.

Sharon shook her head. "I told them camo was better. They have zero chill."

Trisha kept a smile pasted on her face but murmured in my direction, "What's happening? Shouldn't we be coordinating our efforts?"

"Can we discuss this somewhere else?" I asked them. "First new rule, Mom: no less than twenty miles from the perimeter of the building."

"That's not fair," Tammy argued. "My esthetician is four miles away, and I have an appointment."

I felt my left eyelid twitch, and a headache formed behind my eye. I turned to Trisha. "They're vigilantes just like you," I said. "Righting wrongs."

Trisha smiled at them. "It's so nice to meet you."

"You too!" My mother beamed at her then gave me a dark look.

"Take any good pictures?" Trisha asked.

"We've only been here a couple of hours," my mother confessed, "so we're not really sure. We have pictures of everyone entering and exiting the building. Maybe we can all meet up this evening and go through them together."

"Mom," I barked. "No coheesing."

She blinked. "Is that Latin?"

"It's a 'we' word," Trisha added helpfully. "Something *Excalibur*," she said hesitantly, "made up."

"We should all get coffee, Trisha," my mom said. "It sounds like we have a lot to talk about."

"That sounds wonderful. Another time? Excalibur wants us back at work as soon as everyone is cleaned up, and my eyes are still irritated."

"I don't get it," I said. "So many times, he made us look ridiculous just for fun. Why does he care if everyone is covered in glitter?"

"That was *him* subjecting *us* to humiliation. All bets are off when it's the other way around," Trisha told me matter-of-factly. "It's, you know, *insubordinary*."

"And it's the second *insubordinary* thing today," I mused thoughtfully.

"The people in the pit are restless!" Trisha said.

"Well, it was lovely to meet you," my mother said. "I'm sure we'll see you later this afternoon." Then she winked.

"Nope," I objected loudly.

"Don't worry, Vanessa, we're leaving," Linda interjected. "We need to go through everything we've collected so far. We can touch base later."

My mom swept Trisha and me into a quick hug. "See you later, darlings!"

I waved weakly as she and the Bridge Brigade ducked and ran across the street to where a burgundy minivan was parked. Subtle.

On our way back to the car, Trisha turned to me and grinned. "Your mom is so cool."

I squeezed my eyes shut tight. Not the word I would have used. I glanced at the sparkly blue grass and thought back to the Under the Sea synchronized dance that had caused Trisha to order all the glitter in the first place. I tried not to get lost in the memory but failed. Some things imprint themselves onto your soul, whether you like it or not.

Chapter 12

Six weeks earlier

I WAS STUCK ON A CALL WITH A CUSTOMER. SHE WAS IN THE MIDDLE of telling me why her son was getting a divorce, and I didn't see any way off the call anytime soon. I added the appropriate "oh" and "that's too bad" while I organized my pens in order of color. Normally I would try to wrap it up, but for what? Just so I could call another one?

Then my work email dinged. A message from Bobbert, sent to the Directis office distribution list. *Surprise!* the subject read. Like with every message from management, dread pooled in my stomach. Still adding the occasional "aww," I opened it.

> From: Robert Ruddy
> Time: 9:03:39 AM EST
> To: Directis Office Distribution List
> Subject: Surprise!
>
> Good morning esteemed colleagues,
> It's your lucky day! Our survey results from our first Olympic event indicate that our employees *still* don't feel part of a "team" environment. I've decided to assist Cheryl with the Office Olympics in order to put the "we" back in "team."

We will meet in the main room today at 12:00 noon. Please cancel any lunch plans you might have and wear comfortable shoes. Attendance is mandatory.
Thank you,

Robert Ruddy
Account Manager
bruddy@directis.com

I put my head in my hands and quickly disengaged from my phone call. I wanted to shake the management team. This was NOT how you made employees happy or kept turnover to a minimum. How about paid vacation days? Or better health insurance? Or maybe an occasional "thanks for your hard work"? Or even letting us eat lunch in peace. Was that so difficult? But no, we had to wear comfortable shoes and do God knows what during the only time we had to ourselves. There was an audible sigh a few rows over then the sound of a potato chip bag opening. My guess was Cheryl.

I hunkered down at my desk and tried to focus on my work. When noon finally rolled around, Jane and Trisha came over to get me. "Time for tweam building," Jane said.

"The what?" I asked.

"Bobbert put the *we* in team," Trisha answered.

"Goddammit," I sighed and followed them into the main room.

Bobbert was standing next to the door, grinning stupidly in a gray suit. His chest was puffed out proudly. Marcus stood next to him, not daring to look any of us in the eyes. "Marcus has assisted me in clearing the space. I'm going to divide you all into groups. It's time to practice."

Bobbert stalked around the room, herding employees into different corners of the room like a sheepdog. Everyone backed away from him quickly, leading to several distinct groups of employees.

"I have lunch plans," he told us. "I'll be leaving now, but Marcus will explain the rules, and I look forward to your final performances."

Performances? And why did he get to have lunch plans?

He gave us all a wave and exited the room. We all turned to Marcus expectantly.

He looked at us briefly then shook his head. His little man bun flopped back and forth. "I'm sorry about this, everyone. The event is synchronized office-chair dancing." He glanced down at the piece of paper in his hand. "There will be extra points for level of difficulty in choreography, costumes, and creative use of a chair."

"Like pole dancing with chairs?" Cheryl asked hesitantly.

"Do we have to strip?" Jane blurted.

Marcus looked at her, then Cheryl. "Honestly, I'm not sure. I don't think so. I think it's more like synchronized swimming but with chairs."

"Then, like, bathing suits?" Geraldine interjected.

Marcus closed his eyes for a few beats. "I don't think the exact nature of the costumes has been specified," he said.

"How do we swim in chairs?" Gary asked from somewhere behind me.

Marcus was getting visibly flustered. "Routines should be five to ten minutes long, and on Friday, you'll perform in front of a panel of judges with scorecards. Since today is Monday, you'll have all week to practice in your downtime. I would like to reiterate that this was not my idea."

I quickly looked around me. Jane and Trisha were standing with me, along with Bitter Barbie, Geraldine, and a few others. Costumes? Choreography? Synchronized swiveling?

Everyone started murmuring at once. Geraldine immediately corralled us in the corner. "We only have four days to practice. How late is everyone able to stay after work?"

Bitter Barbie started counting on her fingers. "If we use each lunch break and all stay after for two hours each day, we'll have roughly twelve hours to work out our routine. That's not a lot of time. Does anyone object to 'Wrecking Ball' by Miley Cyrus?"

Jane and I immediately put up our hands.

Bitter Barbie rolled her eyes. "Fine. How does everyone feel about Eminem?"

"I don't like candy," Geraldine said. "Let me grab my measuring tape. If I can get all your measurements before lunch is over, I can get the costumes started tonight. Who's going to order the glitter?"

Everyone scattered. "We're going to need a lot of glitter," Trisha whispered then grabbed my hand and squeezed. "It's going to be okay, Vanessa."

"I don't believe you," I said.

"Yeah. It's written all over your face," Jane broke in.

"Geraldine is going to be touching us, and there will probably be sequins, and we have to learn a routine—" I protested.

"Don't forget sacrificing every lunch break and our personal time after work," Jane responded.

"I don't know if I can do that," Trisha said. "I'll see if I can have someone pick up my daughter."

Geraldine came rushing back with her tape measure. She immediately grabbed Jane and spun her around. She wrapped her sewing tape tightly around Jane's neck. "Just measuring your collar," she said sweetly.

Jane made a choking sound. "Isn't it enough you toss my lunch every day?" she asked.

"If you didn't use the company refrigerator as your trash can, I wouldn't have to," Geraldine snapped back. She spun Jane back around and reached for her crotch. "Inseam!" she barked.

"Wait." Bitter Barbie jogged back with a portable speaker hooked up to her phone. "Do we want to wear, like, mermaid tails? We're going to be sitting anyway, so it might really add some depth to our performance."

Wasn't it enough that I had to come here every day and provide zero value to society? Was my dignity now also for sale? Oh, that's right, I was giving it away for free, during my "free" time.

Chapter 13

No ruler should put troops into the field
merely to gratify his own spleen.
—SUN TZU, *THE ART OF WAR*

THE NEXT MORNING, JANE HAD VOLUNTEERED TO TAKE A SHIFT
listening to the transmitter, so after making a cup of coffee, I reached
into the plastic drugstore bag that I'd thrown on the floor after getting
home last evening. It had a nice, new, weirdly purple set of earplugs in
it. I squished one into each ear and set about my morning: checking
email, combing the job boards, updating the shelter's website, checking for new grants, finishing the fundraising brochure, and wasting a
chunk of time on Facebook and Instagram. I planned to relieve Jane
later, but for now, it was blissfully quiet with the earplugs in. I thought
longingly of a time when I didn't need them in my own apartment,
where I'd lived alone without Xavier. Granted, I'd also been working
for the jackass, so it's not like I'd had a full day of not hearing his voice.

A little while later, I glanced up at the clock and realized with a start
that it was almost noon. I had to get the kittens to their wellness check
at the animal shelter. My weather app said it was supposed to be a little
warmer today, which was good, but I was guaranteed to still find it cold.
I wound my long dark hair into a knot then went to look for the kittens.
I found them in a large fluffy pile on the floor cushion and stuffed them
one by one into an oversize carrier. I grabbed my laptop and was just
heading out the door when my phone buzzed.

I considered not answering it, but it was from a number I didn't recognize. I clicked the button. "Hello?" I asked.

"Hello, is this Vanessa?" a familiar voice asked.

"Yes?" I answered.

"Hi, Vanessa, this is Carter Beckett. We met at the unemployment office and at the coffee shop. And again at your apartment."

I couldn't help but smile. "Yes, I remember," I said.

"I thought it might be worthwhile to speak with you over the phone to evaluate whether or not facial expressions would have any relevance to successful telemarketing."

"Seriously?" I asked, suddenly annoyed.

"I'm picturing the expression on your face right now. Not acceptable."

"But—" I began.

"No, not seriously." I could hear the grin in his voice and felt some of my annoyance slide away.

"I was calling to check on Duo," he said a little hesitantly.

"I was just taking them to the shelter for their wellness check," I told him. "Do you still want to adopt her?"

"Very much," he answered.

"I can let them know she's spoken for, but it'll help if you can go over and fill out the application. Little calicos go fast, even if they're hellions."

"I'm just coming up on my lunch break. How about I meet you there?"

I quickly checked my makeup in the mirror next to the front door. Eyeliner on point. The hair knot wasn't the best, but it wasn't terrible. Wearing my hair down was usually a liability with kittens anyway. "Sure. I'm leaving now," I told him. The kittens had started screaming in the carrier. "I'm not torturing them, I promise," I said.

"I definitely need to see them to make sure," he answered.

I rolled my eyes. "See you in a few."

A little while later, I pulled up outside of the Walter Green Animal

Shelter and parked in the shade of one of the large trees at the edge of the lot. It still had a few leaves left on it, and I hoped it would keep the car from heating in the sun. Even though it was cool outside, Uno through Quinque screamed like banshees if their seat was too warm. I lifted their carrier out of the car, the underside now covered in a blue sheen. I held it away from my body as I hurried to the front door. The last thing I needed was more glitter on me or the kittens.

When I got to the door, Danielle, the shelter manager, opened it and gestured for me to come in. Her curly brown hair was highlighted blond and pulled into a messy ponytail. She was about twenty years older than me, but I was at least a head taller. "Hey, Vanessa! It's so strange seeing you in the daytime!"

"Yeah." I lowered my eyes. "I've had a change in my work situation, so I'm looking for new opportunities," I said neutrally. "Would you keep me in mind if anything opens up here? In a non-volunteer capacity."

"I got your message," she said. "If only. I'd hire you in a second."

I let out a breath. "Thanks."

"You're what this place needs. We might have some opportunities in the future, but you know nonprofits. No promises."

I nodded. "I know things are tight. I've been applying for additional grants for the shelter to ease up some assets for the fundraising program. If we could just get it off the ground, I think it would pay for itself."

She grinned. "Bless you. And I think you're right. If we could get a position started, the right person could turn it into something." She waved a hand toward the intake room. "Feel free to check out the new ones while you're here. They're not on the web yet, so if you have time to take some glamour shots of them, that would be awesome. A couple of them are pending adoption, so no pictures there, but their cages are marked."

"Sure. I sent the completed brochure layout for the fundraiser to the board yesterday."

She gave me a warm smile. "I saw it; it's perfect. Already sent it to print." She gestured to the carrier. "How're the little calicos doing?"

"They're driving me crazy," I told her flatly.

She smiled. "That's what happens when you live with a bunch of kittens."

"Somehow it's worse this time," I said as I handed them over to her.

She turned to take the kittens to the back room when the door buzzed, signaling someone else had entered. She grinned past my shoulder. "Hi, Carter! What's up?"

Carter stepped into the tiny front hall of the shelter, filling the space behind me. "My friend Vanessa has talked me into adopting one of her little monsters."

Danielle's eyes lit up. "Wonderful! I'm going to get these guys looked at while you fill out an application." She handed him a clipboard, whispered, "Way to go, Vanessa," and went into the isolation room.

Carter grinned at me. "Sit with me in the cat room while I fill this out?"

I nodded, glad to get out of such a small space.

He led me through the double doors into an airy room with windows along one wall. There were cats on all the counters and window seats. A few of the regulars came over to greet me as I sat on a patio chair and felt my shoulders start to relax. This was my happy place.

He sat opposite me on a bench. I was scratching a white, bi-eyed cat's chin when I looked up and caught him staring at me. He gave me a grin.

"How're things going?" he asked as he filled out the questionnaire. "You look stressed."

"I am," I confessed. "The other day at the café, I applied for a lot of jobs. And…there are other things that are bugging me."

"I'm sure." He put the pen down and looked at me thoughtfully. "Have you heard anything from Directis since you left?"

"They asked me to sign a separation agreement stating that I wouldn't seek unemployment benefits and that I wouldn't sue." I rolled my eyes. "I didn't sign, obviously."

"Interesting." He tapped the pen against his cheek. "I double-checked. We've never gotten any requests for benefits from a Directis employee before you."

"Really? Is that weird? Because they fire a *lot* of people."

"Yeah, it's a little weird. Especially because the company is so large."

"It's not, though." I looked at him. "It's telemarketing with a personal touch. Small company, big personal impact. Or words to that effect."

"Hm. Their website indicates they're expanding pretty rapidly."

I blinked. "They were bought out last year by Trimaran. Maybe their employees are going into the unemployment system under that name? But, if anything, it seems like they were losing people and not filling all the positions, even before they fired Jane and me."

"I haven't seen an application come through from someone named Jane. I'll have to check on Trimaran."

The white cat had settled into my lap and was purring loudly. I petted his back absently. "Jane took the severance. She agreed not to put in a claim."

He put the clipboard to the side and leaned forward in his chair, resting his elbows on his knees. "I hesitate to mention this, but you're going to get a copy of it at a later date anyway, so it doesn't change anything."

I immediately stiffened. "What?" I asked.

"Directis contested your claim."

I felt cold. "And?"

"And, well…" He paused for a minute. "Honestly, I've never seen anything like it."

All the relaxation I'd felt from being around so many cats was instantly gone. "What did they say." It wasn't a question.

"It states that you were a bad influence on the other 'young women' in the office because of the inexacceptive"—he stammered a little—"expressions on your face."

"Come again?"

He shook his head. "There were a lot of creative words in the statement."

I sighed. Of course. Xavier would much rather make up his own words than learn the ones that already existed. And damn him for *still* talking about my face.

"It also discussed that you weren't a team player. That you refused to put the *we* in"—he almost choked on the word—"tweam."

My whole body got hot. "I wasn't a team player?"

"You weren't a *tweam* player," he corrected me.

I could feel the anger start to bubble up in my throat. "I participated in trust falls in our office break room. I sang karaoke with the tech department for a mandatory contest. I tied my leg to another employee's and hopped around the lawn while people came out of nearby businesses to watch. I participated in a scavenger hunt where I had to go into stores and repeat riddles to people who weren't being paid nearly enough to listen to our bullshit. I personally had to dress as the office Christmas tree because my boss didn't like the smell of pine. I not only put the *we* in tweam, I put *every* letter in tweam." By the end of my tirade, all the surrounding cats had backed away from me, even the one previously on my lap.

Carter was still staring at me thoughtfully. "How did any of you manage to get any actual work done?"

"That's an excellent question," I snapped. "Most of this happened on our 'own' time."

I sat next to Carter on the bench and whipped my phone out of my pocket. I opened a social media app and pulled up the Directis page. I tilted the phone toward him so he could see the screen and tapped on the icon labeled PICTURES.

"They put a star on your head and everything," he murmured as I flipped through the photos from the Christmas party. I kept flipping through the images, past the ones of our escape room "adventure," the toe-wrestling championship, and the unfortunate water polo fiasco. I stopped when I came to the Halloween party and gazed at a picture of Jane, Trisha, me, and five other women all dressed as unicorns.

"You're really rocking those hooves," Carter observed as I squinted at the picture.

"This picture was taken less than a year ago. With the exception of her," I pointed to Trisha, "who is on permanent probation, everyone in this photo has been fired."

"That's significant," Carter said as he looked closer at the picture. "You're not exactly having the best time in these pictures. Your face…"

I looked at him sharply. "What about my face?"

He held his hands up. "Sorry. I just mean you don't look happy."

"Would you?" I asked.

"Absolutely not. I would rather staple my fingers together than do *any* of the things you just showed me."

I sighed. "It wasn't enough, though. I still wasn't *tweamy* enough."

"Hey." He bent his head down and caught my eye. "I know losing a job can be devastating to your self-esteem. It can shake your confidence and leave its mark on how you see the world. I never want to belittle that. I hear people break into tears every day when I talk to them on the phone. But I also want you to know none of this is your fault. Based on everything I've seen, you tweamed the hell out of that job. You didn't deserve what happened to you. Not being a tweam player is not grounds for termination."

He paused and leaned back against the bench. "I shouldn't be saying any of this, but I know employment law, and I've never seen an employer response like the one I received from Directis." He looked down. "One of the reasons I wanted to see you today was to let you know I've turned your case over to one of my colleagues for review. I won't be handling it going forward."

"What? Why?" I asked.

"Because I'm adopting one of your dependents. Because we've sort of become friends. Because I can't stop thinking about your face, Vanessa."

I felt the flush bloom up my neck and onto my cheeks. No way he just said that. I was still asleep, maybe losing oxygen from a calico kitten blocking the air. "You're not serious."

"I'm completely serious. I should also be going. I have to get back to work." He stood and touched my shoulder lightly. "It was nice seeing you again. I'm going to drop off this application with Danielle." He reached into his pocket and pulled out a card. "Text me and let me know how Duo's wellness check went, okay? Carter Beckett."

I nodded silently and watched as he walked out the door. I turned to the white cat who had returned to my lap. "What was his name again?"

The cat gave me a slow blink and licked its tail. I stayed in the sunny cat room for a few minutes longer before going to the intake room to meet the new arrivals.

When I got back to my apartment building, I hoisted the kitten carrier up onto my hip while I slid my key into the lock. Uh-oh. I could hear voices coming from inside, spilling through the door and into the hall-way. A neighbor poked his head out of his apartment. "You've got some obnoxious roommates," he said. "Tell them to keep it down, okay?"

I nodded, embarrassed. "Sorry. Grampa drinks," I told him and hurried inside.

Xavier and someone else (possibly Gary) were yelling. I opened the door of the carrier so the kittens could escape then grabbed the last chocolate chip muffin off the counter and headed for the laundry room. I hopped up onto the dryer, already furious with Xavier and Gary, and settled in to listen to the show.

"You need to confer with me when you do these things." Definitely Gary.

"Which one of us is the boss?" Xavier yelled back.

"You are, but God knows why," Gary shouted.

I immediately perked up. I'd never heard Gary angry before. I'd also never heard anyone shout at Xavier like that. Everyone handled him with kid gloves.

"Don't you dare talk to me like that!" Xavier roared. "I pay your salary!"

"You're right. I'm sorry." Gary immediately backed down. In my imagination he had deflated and was cowering at the end of the conference room table. "I shouldn't have questioned you. It's just that, legally, you can't say things like that to the state. We shouldn't contest Vanessa Blair's unemployment benefits."

I stopped, the last bite of muffin halfway to my mouth.

"She doesn't deserve them," Xavier snapped back. "If we don't fight it, we're admitting we were wrong to fire her. That makes us look guilty."

"It's better for everyone if we don't invite them to look into it further," Gary answered. "She didn't sign the severance, so we let it go and keep moving forward."

"You know how much I hate it when people question me," Xavier said irritably.

"I do, but there's a bigger picture here," Gary said persuasively. "One slipped through."

"She's making us look guilty, and it's going to end up costing us money," Xavier stated.

"Her benefits will cost a lot less than any consequences that come from fighting it."

Xavier mumbled something, but I could tell he was starting to calm down.

"We're doing fine," Gary continued. "Just give me a heads-up before you fire anyone else so we can prepare better. We can make sure this doesn't happen again. We'll make them sign before we let them pack up their belongings."

"About that. I'm firing Trisha."

My legs banged on the side of the dryer as I stood. Oh, hell no.

"Maybe you should reconsider. We've let a lot of people go, and we want to keep attention away from that. You fired Nancy without consulting me, and our staff is lean as it is. Trisha is doing fine on permanent probation, and she's still meeting her call times. She's also doing a good job of cleaning and managing the break room."

"I don't like the energy in the office," Xavier stated. "There are shenanigans going on, and I won't tolerate it. I saw her talking to some spies earlier. And she's still friends with that Vanessa person. My spiritual side tells me she might have something to do with it. I want her out by the end of the week."

I stood there in my laundry room and stared at the pile of dirty clothes in the corner, shaking with anger. They had to be stopped. I needed to warn Trisha.

Chapter 14

The sight of men whispering together in small knots
or speaking in subdued tones points to disaffection
amongst the rank and file.

—SUN TZU, *THE ART OF WAR*

I got to Starbucks long before Trisha or Jane did. I looked at
the espresso menu longingly but took a sip from my travel cup and pulled
out my phone. I also grabbed a notebook covered in embossed cats and a
matching pen from my bag.

I opened the pictures from the Directis's social media page again
and scrolled to the Halloween party. Unfortunately, the women in the
picture weren't tagged, and I was blanking on their names. One was
Abbey something. Another was…Chloe? And the most recent one.
Nancy something. I wrote the only two names I was sure of at the top
of the list. Jane Delaney. Vanessa Blair. Then Mary-Anne something. I
looked through a few more recent pictures, stopping on one particularly
unflattering picture of Jane, Marcus, and Geraldine from the Under the
Sea chair dance. Oh! Bitter Barbie. Damn. What was her real name?

I tapped the pen against my lips, once again struck by how little I'd
been paying attention over the past couple years. In the margin I wrote,
Bitter Barbie, Burned-Out Barbie, Brunette Barbie… Was there also a
Bored Barbie? Their faces had changed in and out, and I hadn't taken the
time to get to know any of them personally. Jane had been the only one
I'd gotten close with, and then later, Trisha.

I was lost in thought when Jane slid into the seat opposite me. She had on a tailored white blouse and slim black pants. Her blond hair was waved down her back.

"You look great," I told her.

"Thanks. So do you," she said.

I smirked and looked down at my sweater. It was a heather gray, but that white cat had turned it mostly white. "I'm a mess."

"A hot mess," she answered. "I had my interview earlier."

"And?" I asked.

"And I have the job if I want it. Do I want it, Nessa?"

"Do you like eating?" I asked her.

"Yeah. A lot."

"Then I'm going to say yeah, you want it."

She slumped forward in the chair. "I know, I know," she groaned. "And I've been thinking about going back to school, so the hours would work better for me. I didn't get a lot of responses from my other applications."

"Same," I agreed. "The job market sucks right now. I even applied to a few jobs on Craigslist earlier today." I shuddered. They sounded legit, but who knew? It was desperate times.

"That's where the killers hang out," Jane said. "I'm still mad at Xavier and Bobbert for dumping us out on our asses. And if you get killed, it'll be their fault. Have you listened to them today?"

"Yeah. That's actually why I asked to meet tonight."

Jane opened her mouth to speak when Trisha hurried into the café, still in her work clothes, black laptop bag slung over her shoulder. She sat at our table, out of breath, and Jane gave a low whistle. "That highlighter is better than anything you can get at Sephora."

Trisha's makeup was classy and subtle, like always, and drew attention to her large dark brown eyes. All of it was earth toned and on point, except for an electric-blue sheen that brought out her cheekbones and shone brightly on her forehead.

Trisha shook her head and a few sparkles fluttered onto the table. "I've showered a dozen times. I think it's just a part of me now."

"Then it must be a part of Xavier and Bobbert, too." Jane grinned. "Bobbert drives that manly luxury truck; sparkles are just what it needed."

"Sorry I'm late," Trisha said. "Xavier made us stay past five and was kind of picking on me this evening." She fanned herself, and still more glitter shimmered to the floor.

"What do you mean?" I asked.

"I've had good phone times all week, and my sales record has been good, but Xavier called an impromptu We Meeting before he let us go home to present me with this...certificate." She reached into her bag and pulled out a slightly crumpled piece of paper.

Jane took it from her and spread it out on the table. "Underperforming Employee of the Week: Trisha Lam. This document is hereby given to Trisha Lam for not reaching her goals this week." She looked up incredulously. "Are you freaking kidding me?" she asked.

Trisha nodded. "And I *did* reach my goals. At least the goals I was aware of. But then Xavier said that my sales goal had gone from sixty units to a hundred and ninety per month. Would have been nice to know that, but even still, that number is impossible."

"That was the *worst*," Jane groaned. "When they doubled or tripled your monthly goals and then said you weren't entitled to the sales bonus. That happened to me like every single month."

"Me, too," I said. "I heard them talking about that earlier over the transmitter. They're trying to humiliate you, Trisha. It's some sort of weird display of power to keep the employees in line. I guess the gold stars on the whiteboards are making him even more sadistic than normal," I said.

Jane picked up the certificate to look at it again. "I know I shouldn't be surprised at this point, but the effort they put into making people feel bad and worried about their jobs is insane. Do they do any actual work themselves?"

"*Oderint, dum metuant*," I murmured. "Let them hate, so long as they fear. You'd have to be a tiny man to get all your validation and power from belittling others."

"He *is* a tiny man," Jane told me.

"I meant emotionally," I said.

"Oh. That's what I meant, too," she said, averting her eyes.

"Xavier said the next one on their list to be fired is…" I cleared my throat. "You, Trisha."

Trisha looked at me with big eyes and nodded. "Totally. I'm next on the list. It's like he wants to get as many digs in as possible before he does it."

"I wanted to let you know so you could be prepared," I said.

Trisha gave me a beautiful big smile and reached across the table to touch my hand. "You're so sweet, Nessa. But of course, that little shit is going to fire me. Directis is a sinking ship, and I've been on borrowed time since Gary walked you two out. Actually, since I started, I guess."

"But you need this job, Trisha," Jane broke in. "You have Claire to worry about, and—"

"I need *a* job," Trisha corrected her. "But not this one. It was only ever supposed to be a stop along the way, right? For all of us. We're way too cool to be telemarketers forever."

"Yeah." Jane nodded. "We weren't going to 'find' ourselves there."

"But we found each other." Trisha grinned.

I nodded. Something affirming in all this lunacy.

"Xavier's been real testy lately. I don't know if it's his bladder disease or all the glitter stuck in his foot crust, but he's on a short fuse. The way he walked Nancy out…" She shuddered. "It was exactly like it was with you. Except he had more of a limp this time. And she knocked the whiteboard off the wall before telling Gary and Xavier she was jealous of all the people who had never met them."

Jane blinked. "So…nothing like when we got fired."

"Damn," I said. I wish I'd heard that exchange.

"Who is Nancy again? She sounds cool," Jane added.

Trisha reached into her bag and pulled out her laptop. She sat it on the table and flipped it open. Glitter puffed into the air. It was everywhere between the keys. "I can't imagine how much of this stuff I have in my lungs," she muttered as she pulled up the Directis home page.

"They fired Nancy yesterday afternoon, so they probably haven't taken her picture down off the website," Trisha told us as she clicked on the MEET THE STAFF tab at the top of the screen.

The Directis staff page loaded slowly. When it finally popped up, Jane read the banner aloud: "Directis is a fast-growing company with a high moral drive to succeed. We give back the personal touch! Would you like to become part of our *tweam*?"

I rolled my eyes. "Seriously? Even on the website?"

"I've never looked at it before," Jane said. "Someone really should be editing Xavier. He's body slamming the English language daily."

Trisha put her finger on the track pad and started scrolling down the page. There were a lot more pictures than I'd been expecting.

"They probably just haven't had time to update it yet," Trisha said. "I'm not sure who in the office takes care of that."

"Maybe Marcus?" Jane asked.

Trisha kept scrolling until we made it to the *d*'s when suddenly Jane cried out, "Wait! There's me!" Hers was a bathroom selfie, her head cocked, a puppy Snapchat filter over her face.

Both Trisha and I turned to look at her. "What?" she asked. "I look adorable."

I shook my head and looked back at the screen. "Hold up. We're in the *g*'s, and we're not even a third of the way through. How are there so many people on here?"

"That's weird," Trisha said. She scrolled quickly, rows and rows of pictures with no end in sight.

"Who's that?" Jane pointed to an unfamiliar face.

"No idea," I said.

"She's new," Trisha said.

"What about her?" Jane asked, pointing to another.

"Some of these people just started," Trisha told her. "New employees are going on, but it doesn't look like they're taking anyone off."

"Why would they do that?" Jane wondered. "It makes no sense."

"Maybe whoever is updating the website isn't told when people are fired," I offered. "It's not like they announce it. There was usually just an empty chair the next morning. But if Jane is still on there, then I should be, too, right?" When I'd first started, Gary had insisted I provide a photo for the employee directory. I had taken it at my desk and was trying to look professional, no peace sign or duck lips. Not like Jane's.

Trisha began scrolling back up, and we combed through the *b*'s. No Blair. I wasn't on the website. "Why would someone take down my picture but leave everyone else's?"

Jane grinned at me and opened her mouth to say something. I quickly cut her off. "If you make a single comment about my face, I'll smack you."

She sighed. "It was kind of too easy, anyway. What I was going to say is one of these things is not like the other."

I sat up straighter. "I filed for unemployment."

"But we're still not sure why that's important," Jane said.

Trisha was still intently studying the photos and stopped on a picture that immediately stood out to me. "Bitter Barbie!" I cried. "Her name is actually…Caitlin Ferrin? Never would have come up with that." I quickly scrawled her name in my notebook.

"The Barbies all look the same," Jane groaned. At that moment, the door to the café jangled, and Jane inhaled sharply.

Marcus stood in the doorway to the café, looking windblown and tired, with circles under his eyes, visible through his thick-framed glasses. He had on a wool coat and dress shirt, and stray strands of hair had escaped from his bun. He was also carrying a cropped black jacket. Was that *my* jacket? Bless him.

I waved at him. "Hi, Marcus," I said. "Come join us."

He waved back at us, and I noticed he, too, had a blue shimmer on his skin. "Give me just a second," he said and motioned toward the counter.

I nodded as Jane elbowed me sharply and Trisha swatted my hand.

"Did you know he was coming? You could have given me a heads-up," Jane hissed under her breath. "Like, prepare me for the shock."

I widened my eyes at her. "I knew you were coming from an interview so you'd look great. If it were pajama day, I totally would have warned you."

She flipped her hair back over her shoulder. "I guess. But what is he doing here?"

Trisha glanced around furtively. "I mean…can we trust him? Sun Tzu says we can't enter alliances until we are acquainted with the designs of our neighbors. Are you sure, Nessa?"

"He asked how we were doing after, you know." I fluttered my hand. "I just mentioned we were meeting here after work and he was welcome to stop by. He's not our neighbor, and he's not a designer."

Trisha nodded reluctantly. "Okay, but everybody be cool."

Jane cough-sneezed nervously and glanced behind her. "Oh my god, I suck at this. I can't be normal."

Marcus walked up and set four drinks on the table. He pushed a tall dry cappuccino in my direction, then he opened a straw and slid it into a grande caramel almond Frappuccino with extra whip. He pushed that one toward Jane. The fragrant mint mocha went to Trisha. He kept the iced macchiato for himself.

"How did you know?" I asked. Our drink orders were perfect.

"I pay attention." He smiled as he slid into the seat next to Jane. "You practically mainlined the stuff when we all worked together. It didn't look like you were going to order."

Trisha lightly brushed her arm against mine to get my attention. "I changed my mind; I'm fully in support of the new addition," she whispered loudly and gestured in his direction.

Marcus reached across the table and handed me my jacket. "I rescued this the day you left."

I took it gratefully. "You're the absolute best."

Marcus snuck a look at Jane. "It's nice to see you again."

She kept her eyes focused on her Frappuccino but managed to mumble, "And also with you."

I inhaled the smell of the cappuccino. "You rock, Marcus," I said. "We were just talking about when we worked at Directis."

He wrapped his hands around his cup and sighed. "It hasn't been the same since you left. I know the company has always had a lot of turnover, but...the temperature in the office is different now."

I squinted at him. "Is that why you messed with the whiteboards?"

He shook his head. "I didn't. Geraldine did."

"What?" I asked, stunned.

"I think she might feel bad about it now, because of Nancy, but even Geraldine is getting restless," he said.

"*Even* Geraldine?" Trisha asked hesitantly.

"You haven't noticed the subterfuge going on in the office?" he asked Trisha.

She took a long sip of her coffee and avoided eye contact. "No, I haven't."

He rolled his eyes and leaned back, one of his arms coming to rest on the back of Jane's chair. Her whole body shrank inward, and her eyes got huge, but he didn't pull away. "So you're not the one who glitter bombed the office?" he asked Trisha. As he spoke, a few stray sparkles fluttered down to Jane's shoulders.

Trisha choked a little on her long swallow and cleared her throat. "Me?" She blinked.

"It had you written all over it," he said.

I held up my hands. "Trisha has a unique way of interpreting suggestions."

"Which we fully support," Jane added. She looked at the flecks of glitter on her white shirt, and her cheeks got pink.

"But it's not just that," Marcus said. "Someone mixed catnip into Xavier's organic herbal tea, so Haiku knocks over every cup and rolls around in it. His desk is always wet. Someone also signed him up for a foot fetish magazine." Marcus shuddered. "It comes to the office every week, like clockwork. And I deliver it to him every time. He told me to stop, but it's *mail*. You're not supposed to mess with mail."

"We didn't do those things, I swear," Trisha murmured. "I wish I had. I can't imagine there's someone else trying to sabotage Directis."

"You can't?" Jane asked. "They're the worst."

"I know," she said quickly, "it's just that…everyone tries to keep their heads down. I know I did. We scrambled so hard just to keep our jobs. I mean, Nessa even danced as a paper dragon for the Lunar New Year."

I swatted Trisha's arm. "We don't talk about the Lunar Dragon incident."

I turned her laptop screen toward Marcus. "Do you know what's going on with the web page? Do you update it?"

Marcus shook his head. "I think Gary does."

I pointed to the MEET THE STAFF page. "Jane is still on there. So is everyone. It looks like people go on, but they never come off. Except me, apparently."

He squinted at the screen. "I don't think I've ever looked at the website."

"Same," Jane said.

He took control of the track pad and scrolled through the photos, just as we had earlier. "There are a *lot* of people on this page," he mused. "Why would there be so many people?"

"That's what we were wondering," I said. "They couldn't all be at the other office, could they? Could they be employees from Trimaran?"

"No," he murmured, still squinting at the screen. He scrolled farther down before looking up at us. "I've boxed up the stuff of at least a dozen of these people, not counting Jane."

"So fired employees aren't being removed?" I asked.

"But why?" Trisha asked.

Marcus shook his head, and his bun flopped. "There has to be a reason."

I thought about what Carter had said at the animal shelter, that Directis was expanding rapidly. As far as I could tell, people just switched out cubicles. An awful little thought occurred to me, but surely even Xavier wouldn't be that ballsy. "The only reason I can think of to keep fired employees on the site is to make it look like they have more employees than they actually have," I said softly, tracing the lid of my cappuccino.

Marcus leaned forward. "For whom? Clients or the parent company?"

"Both maybe? But my mom made me watch *All the President's Men* a dozen times when I was a kid. She calls Robert Redford *my Robbie*." I rolled my eyes. "And if I learned anything from that movie, it's to follow the money. Could Xavier be trying to convince Trimaran he has all these employees?"

Trisha fiddled with the cardboard sleeve on her mocha. "He always talked about how Trimaran was giving us money to grow, remember?" she asked.

"No," Jane answered.

"It was in the We Meetings," Trisha told her.

"Never listened to those," Jane said.

"If Xavier didn't actually have the staff, he would have to work his employees into the ground to cover the difference," Trisha said slowly. "Hence my little certificate."

"So if he doesn't expand, he pockets the extra salaries?" Jane asked.

Marcus shifted again in his seat, his arm resting against Jane's. Her hand jerked, and she almost knocked over her drink. "But to fool the parent company, it would have to be more than staff pictures on the web," he said.

"He doesn't want any outside attention from any organization," I said, mostly to myself. "Ex-employees filing for unemployment might trigger an investigation. Gary said something like, 'One slipped through.' That was me, the one who filed. So maybe there's some sort of payroll fraud going on."

"But all this is too risky, even for Xavier," Jane argued.

"This man connects to the universe through Astroturf," Trisha reminded her.

I shook my head again. "This could all just be Gary being lazy. The only way to know for sure would be to look at the financial records."

Trisha's eyes lit up. "Good idea."

"No!" I protested. "It's too risky to look in actual files. We should stick to the stuff they throw out. The last thing we want is for you to get arrested."

Marcus nodded. "And Gary might not know faux-fu like Xavier, but I wouldn't want to mess with him. Pretty sure he's straight-up evil behind that suit."

"Ew," I said. "Also, listen to Marcus. For your own sake."

Trisha slid a glance at Jane, who grinned, then Trisha turned to Marcus. "So you're not going to tell anyone that we were behind any of the…adventures in the office lately, right?" she asked.

He looked offended. "Of course not. I'm on your side. This is bigger than us, Trisha. I don't know what all is going on at Directis, but I know the employees are restless. I don't want to get in the way of the momentum."

Even if Trisha and Jane were a little nervous about letting Marcus into the "inner circle," I wasn't. Marcus had bailed me out once when I needed it the most and had been wearing a fish tail when he did it. I would be forever grateful.

Chapter 15

Five weeks earlier

IT WAS LUNCHTIME, AND THE LIGHTS IN THE OFFICE WERE DIMMED. Geraldine was rushing around, making sure everyone's mermaid tails were fluffed and tiaras were centered perfectly. The office chairs had been decorated with seashells and fishermen's nets and were arranged in a V in the otherwise empty conference room. A judge's table was off to the corner, complete with scorecards.

"Hey," Jane whispered at me. "Get your bikini top on, and use my glitter eyeliner." Jane's mermaid tail didn't make it easy for her to walk, so she small-step wiggled her way over to hand me a sparkly blue tube. "The Hunger Olympics waits for no man."

"Office Oly—" I started to correct her.

"I know, I know," she said. "But we're grown-ass adults wearing mermaid tails. Survival of the sparkliest. Get dressed."

I walked out of the conference room, passing Trisha on my way. Her mermaid makeup was on point. "Have you seen Bitter Barbie?" she whispered.

I stopped for a moment. "No," I said. Come to think of it, I hadn't seen her for the past few days. My anxiety over this event had numbed me completely to everything else.

"Weird," Trisha murmured. "It looks like everyone is ready except you. I put your costume and tiara in one of the spare offices for you to change. Go get dressed!"

"I had to wrap up a call. I was working. Because that's why we're actually here," I huffed then walked along the hall, glancing in each room as I passed. In the second spare office, I saw a blue-and-green mermaid tail covered in sequins, along with a seashell-shaped bikini top. A sparkly crown of crystal fish sat on top. I stared at it for a long moment then looked down at the glittery blue eyeliner in my hand. My outfit for a synchronized office-chair dance set to a Beyoncé song. In front of judges Xavier and Bobbert.

No. Fucking. Way.

Everyone had their limits, and I'd just reached mine. I threw the eyeliner at the wall and sat on the floor in a heap. I'd always been a bit of an internal rebel. I'd never liked anyone bossing me around and had always gotten a perverse pleasure in doing the opposite of what I was told. My mother referred to it affectionately as a slight case of defiance disorder.

I put my head in my hands. My high school self would be ashamed of me. I thought about the girl I used to be, in ripped jeans and Converse sneakers, low-key antagonizing authority figures. If she could see me now, about to dance in a fish tail for the Man, or in this case, the Men…

"Hey, you okay?" a soft voice asked behind me.

I turned to see Marcus, leaning in the doorway. We weren't close, but I had always thought he seemed like a cool guy.

"No," I said honestly. "I'm not." I gestured to the costume draped over the chair. "I have to wear that. In public. And swivel. Do you ever feel as if you're in Hell, but Hell looks exactly like our office, so people haven't noticed yet?"

He nodded sympathetically. "I wonder that literally every day."

"I don't know if I have it in me," I told him. "But I can't let my team down. We already lost Bitter Barbie—"

"Who?" he broke in.

"Ahhh…" My cheeks flushed pink. "That girl. You know. We call them the Barbies." I tried to hide my embarrassment.

"I always referred to them as the Bratz Pack," he said thoughtfully.

"I think we're best friends now," I said.

"We totally are," he said and grinned at me. "I don't think they announced it, but they let…Barbie go. I don't know the circumstances. They asked me to clean out her desk yesterday."

That pulled me up short. "Really? I wonder what happened."

He shrugged and tugged on his man bun. "How's Jane doing with the whole thing?"

"Well, she's a mermaid already, so I guess okay."

He crouched next to me on the floor. "Tell you what. I'll take your place in the synchronized swivel dance. I've seen you practice it enough that I see it in my nightmares."

"Don't tease a desperate person, Marcus," I stated.

"Just do me a favor. Let Jane know I played the hero, okay?" He grinned.

"Absolutely. One hundred and ten percent. Marcus saves the day," I agreed immediately.

He gestured toward the door. "Now get out there and pretend you sprained something while I get dressed."

I limped back to the conference room where Jane and Geraldine were waiting for me. "Where's your tail?" Geraldine snapped.

"Marcus has it." I focused my attention on Jane. "I sprained something, so I can't perform. Marcus agreed to take my place. He saved my life, Jane. Marcus is a true king among men."

Just then, Marcus turned the corner wearing my costume. Even I did a double take. He was doing the same strange waddle Jane was doing. He'd left the seashell bra and crown in the spare office along with his glasses. He was shirtless, wearing only the tail and some of Jane's sparkly eyeliner. He had taken his hair down from its little bun. It hit just below his chin and somehow made his cheekbones look chiseled. The whole effect was really working. God bless him.

"Who is this Neptune, god of the sea?" Jane murmured as he came toward us.

"And look how he rocks that fish tail," I said to her. "He could wear that to the club."

"Be cool, Vanessa," he muttered at me as he shimmied by. "Don't overdo it."

Jane didn't take her eyes off him as she toddled over to her chair.

As the music and strobe lights kicked in, I breathed a huge sigh of relief. I'd dodged a big one.

Chapter 16

Ponder and deliberate before you make a move.

—SUN TZU, *THE ART OF WAR*

After the meeting at Starbucks with Jane, Trisha, and Marcus, I tossed and turned in bed, unable to sleep. The cappuccino in the evening had been a bad idea, no matter how good it had tasted. Every time I moved, a kitten attacked my feet.

When I finally fell asleep, I had another of my recurring Directis dreams. Every few nights or so, especially in the early morning dream time, they'd hit me. I was working there again, but Xavier had forbidden anyone to speak to me. In the dream, I was always struggling to do my job, but it was next to impossible with everyone treating me like a ghost. Then they fired me, but I didn't have anywhere else to go, so I kept showing up at Directis like an idiot. I woke up feeling humiliated, sad, and guilty all at once. The guilt was the worst. I still couldn't completely shake it. Even though I knew I hadn't done anything to deserve the face speech, being stared at like a criminal as I grabbed my coffee cups and pens, or being walked out of the office, I couldn't fully accept that it wasn't somehow my fault. My job had been unapologetically parasitic, draining me emotionally and physically, destroying my relationships and taking all my free time. And *they* had told *me* I wasn't worth the sacrifice I'd made.

Did horribly unfair things ever get easier to accept?

My feelings were all jumbled, and I lay in bed staring at the ceiling, allowing them to pass through. Was Xavier really trying to defraud Trimaran? Even if I doubted whether *I* had deserved his treatment, I knew Jane hadn't. And neither had Mary-Anne, or Nancy, or likely any of the others.

I leaned over and grabbed the laptop from the bedside table then logged into my account on a job-search site. It was set up to send my résumé automatically to any position I had favorited. I searched for all positions within fifty miles, filtered out telemarketing, and then starred any job that came up. After I'd sent my resume to about seventy openings, I closed the computer and put it back on the bedside table. Maybe now I could let myself sleep.

I focused on slowing my breathing and felt myself relax. One by one, little furry bodies nudged against me, settling into fluffy, warm spots all along my legs and one right by my ear. The purring started, loud like only kittens can be, and I felt the last of my stress melt away as I drifted back to sleep.

I awoke to the sound of voices coming from the living room. I recognized the sound immediately. I rolled to the side and stared into Duo's wide, unblinking eyes. A couple of the other kittens were piled on top of her, a fluffy tangle of legs and bellies. "Can't you guys be better guard dogs?" I asked them. "You just let anyone in. Next time I'm fostering a pack of large rabid dogs," I grouched. "Maybe *they* can dissuade my mother from coming over unannounced."

I stretched slowly and took my time getting out of bed. I wasn't sure if I was awake enough to face what was sure to be another "intervention," but I couldn't avoid it forever. I resolved that today's agenda would focus on changing the locks and took five minutes in the master bathroom to freshen up and make myself presentable. Then I made my way to the bedroom door. There wasn't enough coffee in the world for the sight that greeted me. My mom and her friends had moved my couch over in front of the windows. The open space where it had been was littered with brightly colored catnip mice. So that's where all the cat toys had gone. My gaze traveled upward, and my body went numb.

A full-on serial killer wall. In my own living room. A candid 8x10 photo of Xavier Adams was in the center. He appeared mid Tai Chi, with his hips stuck out like a duck and his arms over his head. Underneath was an index card label that read EXCALIBUR LINCOLN, A.K.A. XAVIER ADAMS, A.K.A. WHO KNOWS. Thumbtacked to the card was honest-to-God red yarn that spider-webbed across the whole wall, ranging from picture to picture, capturing all my former coworkers at the most inopportune times. Bobbert's photo might have been the worst; his eyes were closed and his mouth open, like he was caught mid-sneeze. While I stood there, Linda teetered on a stool, adding two more pictures to the psychopathic display. One was Trisha, looking over her shoulder and winking at the camera. Obviously, she'd posed for her photo. The last picture was of me. It was my high school senior photo. Curled hair, black drape, soft smile. The index card under my picture read VANESSA BLAIR, INNOCENT VICTIM.

I couldn't hold in the strangled sound that came out of my mouth. Four heads turned and looked at me. Sharon, who had moved the floor pillow to a spot near where the couch had been, gave me a bright wave. She was holding a stack of photos with at least two kittens in her lap. She handed a photo to Linda, who grabbed it while tacking down a strand of yarn.

"Morning!" Linda called over her shoulder happily. Tammy wiggled her fingers in my direction from the loveseat, cradling a large camera in her other hand.

My mother, who had been lounging on the newly moved couch, quickly averted her eyes and shuffled off to the kitchen.

"Mom?" I called after her, my voice cracking. I cleared my throat. "Mom! You'd better get back here," I said loudly.

She came back a few seconds later, carrying a steaming mug of black coffee and a plate of fresh, warm chocolate chip muffins. She was blushing a little and still wouldn't meet my eyes. "Here's some coffee, sweetheart, and we made you a batch of muffins. I've been keeping them warm in your oven." I looked from her face back to the food, wavering a little. Then I remembered the wall behind me, complete with yarn (had they gone to the craft store just for that?), and my resolve came back full force. I crossed my arms. "Did you call Trisha? Or Jane? This is not okay, Mom."

She blinked in surprise, and I could tell she hadn't. "I wish I had gotten that Trisha's phone number. That's my bad. But you're absolutely right, Vanessa. It didn't look so murdery when we started." She smiled apologetically and pushed the mug and plate toward me anyway. It smelled so good. I took the food, deciding I could still be mad while I was eating it. I sat heavily on the couch under the windows and breathed in the smell of coffee.

"Should I even ask what you're doing?" I sighed.

"They do this on all the detective shows," Linda volunteered.

"Who does?" I asked. "The detectives or the serial killers?"

Linda hesitated and glanced down at Sharon for help. "Mainly detectives," Sharon assured her. Then she nodded at me. "But Vanessa's right, all the yarn might give the impression that, you know, a serial killer created it. But we're nonthreatening," she rushed on. "Like *A Beautiful Mind*, not like the Zodiac Killer. For the most part."

I downed half my mug of coffee in one swallow. "Mom, I rent this place! I have a landlord. And what about potential adopters? What am I supposed to tell people who stop by to meet the kittens?" The thought of Carter seeing it gave me hives.

"Well, what do you want me to say?" Her hands fluttered up to her neck, and she straightened the impeccable collar of her white button-down. She had the audacity to look personally affronted. "Do you know what your father would say if we did this at our house? Honestly, Vanessa Leigh, you need to think of others from time to time."

I almost choked on the too-big bite of muffin in my mouth. "That should tell you something," I sputtered. "When *Dad* is the voice of reason, maybe rethink what you're doing." I glared at the ceiling. "He's the one with the massive gnome collection, for God's sake," I muttered.

"Just because he has a whimsical side doesn't mean he thinks creatively," my mother reminded me. "He doesn't have the mind to solve crime like we do. Besides, I'm sure we get more visitors than you do anyway. And didn't we agree to call it a strategy board?" she asked the women in a stern voice.

What had they all been doing before my unemployment situation? I was pretty thoroughly convinced at this point that it *wasn't* bridge. "Are you all the world's worst photographers?"

"Hey!" Tammy protested. "You try taking photos through a telescopic lens from twenty feet away. We had to be stealthy. Plus, they move. Like all the time." She brushed a long blond curl off her shoulder. "If they could be still for like five seconds, it would really help me out."

Sharon gently reached up to grab a kitten who had begun to climb the yarn on the wall. She disentangled its claws. "We wanted to sort all the pictures we have from our intel gatherings. We thought this was the best place to use as our headquarters."

"Kathy gave us all keys." Linda winked then looked back to the wall.

I turned to my mother sharply. Her lips were pursed, and she was closely examining the remaining yarn, humming a tuneless melody to herself. "Mother," I said darkly.

"I should have checked with you, I agree," she said then nodded toward her bridge club. "But we're the ones who can break this open."

I threw up my hands, almost knocking the rest of my coffee onto the floor. "I got fired! We live in a right-to-work state. That means anyone can be fired at any time for any reason. It happens to people every day."

"But you're too good for them, sweetheart. Why were you a telemarketer in the first place? Nobody likes them. And it has nothing to do with dead languages." She paused. "No offense."

That stung, but she wasn't wrong. I'd taken the job because it had been open. Just like every other job I'd ever had. I'd never had the luxury of going after something that would *fulfill* me. But I hadn't tried either. "You can't always pick, Mom—" I started.

Tammy spoke over me as if I hadn't said anything. "My husband thinks I'm getting my nails done. He would be so worried about me if he knew I was doing recon." She batted her lashes. Sharon and Linda both muttered noncommittally.

"So, see?" my mom said. "We didn't have any other choice."

"Right. You had no choice. Your only option was to come to my house and build a conspiracy wall while I was sleeping." I took a deep breath. It was hard enough wrangling Trisha and Jane. There was no way I could work with my mother. My throat felt tight.

"Vanessa," my mom said as she sat down next to me on the couch and gently gathered my hands into hers. "It's been a week and a day now since you had a job. I know your savings are probably getting a little thin," she said soothingly. "I would offer to loan you money—" I started to protest and pull my hands back, but she held on tighter and talked over me. "But I know you wouldn't allow that. You're too proud, sweetie. But I wanted to let you know I've been decorating the basement, and you're welcome to move back in with your father and me. I remember how much you love florals." She grinned at me.

I pulled away from her. For one, I *hated* florals. For two, moving back in with my parents? They were trying to be supportive, but it felt like the ultimate failure. I tamped down my resentment. She was only trying to help. "I really hope it doesn't come to that, Mom," I said, holding my voice steady.

"Of course, we'll have to rehome your cats," she said briskly. "You know your father's allergic, and they'll destroy your new flowered curtains."

My cats? They were all I had left. Before I could respond, my phone buzzed. I held up a hand to my mother to let her know the conversation wasn't over then checked the number. Restricted. I took it into the bedroom and closed the door.

"Hello?" I asked.

"Hi, I'm calling for Vanessa Blair," came a pleasant voice.

"Speaking."

"Hi, my name is Justin. I'm calling from Monarch Recruiting. I'm following up on the application you submitted last week."

My heart jumped, and I quickly thought back through all the applications I'd submitted. This was the one I'd been most excited about. Except for the creative ones, which were pipe dreams anyway. "Yes! Hello."

"We've looked through your application, and we're excited to talk to you about your interest in the role. You have a great background in customer service that would translate well to a recruitment setting. Would you have time for a brief phone interview?"

"Of course," I said. "I appreciate the opportunity."

"Great!" Justin replied. "Does now work? Can you tell me a little bit about your background?"

I sat on the edge of the bed. "Now is perfect," I said and gave him a brief summary of my education and the jobs I'd had since I'd graduated. When I finished, he asked a few quick questions about my sales goals at Directis and how I handled the stress of quotas. I answered as neutrally as I could, sticking only to positives, but I figured it would be a good idea to brush up on my interview skills. Justin seemed nice, though.

After a few more perfunctory questions about my future career goals, which I answered vaguely while praying no one would come into the bedroom to interrupt, he cleared his throat and said, "Okay, Vanessa, since it's already Friday, would you have any time next week to come in for an interview?"

Thank God. "Yes, my schedule is open on Monday, if that works for you."

"Perfect," he responded. "How does 10 a.m. sound?"

"I'll be there," I said. An interview at Monarch. I tried to squelch the hope that bubbled up inside my stomach. If I could land this job, my mom and her friends might be so happy for me, they would forget all about Excalibur and recon and revenge. Maybe they'd focus on something else and leave my house. Maybe if I was good at recruiting, I could get Jane and Trisha jobs, too. Maybe I could stop eating hot dogs for dinner. Maybe no floral curtains. Maybe there were extra-dry cappuccinos at the end of this tunnel...

"Great. You'll be meeting with me and another member of the team. If things go well, you'll also interview with the on-site manager, so be sure to set aside up to a half day. I'll send you an email that confirms the date and time, along with an address and general directions."

"Thank you for your time. I look forward to seeing you on Monday."

I clicked the phone off and flopped backward onto the bed. After scooping up the only kitten left on the pillow, I held her over my head. "Did you hear that? An interview!" The kitten thrashed and tried to bite my fingers. "Shh, let me celebrate with you," I told her. Her claws dug into my skin, and I let her go, a smile blooming on my face. *Dum spiro spero.* Where there is life, there is hope.

Chapter 17

One may know how to conquer
without being able to do it.
—SUN TZU, *THE ART OF WAR*

I PULLED UP OUTSIDE OF A BRICK TWO-STORY HOUSE IN THE HEART
of suburbia. I double-checked the house number and turned the key
in the ignition, killing the engine. 597 Gardenia Court. Jane's parents' house.

I'd never been to Jane's house before. Sometimes it had felt like we
lived at Directis and never went home, but even when we did hang out,
it was always at my place. As far as I knew, Jane had never lived away
from home, though she'd been ready to move out on her own when
losing her job had stalled that plan.

I walked up the path to the front door, marveling at the little
orange flowers that lined the way to the porch. Someone had clearly
planted them and cared for them as well as decorated the porch with
potted plants, patio chairs, and a large welcome wreath on the door.
I would never be as adult as that. I rang the doorbell. A small blond
woman in sweater and slacks answered the door. She looked so much
like Jane: same cheekbones, same tilt to the mouth. She smiled warmly
and gestured for me to come in. "You must be Vanessa," she said.

"It's nice to meet you, Mrs. Delaney," I said, smiling.

"Call me Vikki," she said, as she waved me inside. "It's nice of you to
come visit Jane. She seems kind of down, since... You know."

"Uh—yeah," I stammered, trying to remember what Jane had told her parents.

"But let me tell you how proud I am of both of you," she went on. "To do what you did shows character and strength."

Uh-oh. "You think so?" I asked nervously, stalling for time. Hadn't she told them we'd been laid off?

"Don't be modest, Vanessa," she told me, patting my arm and leading me into the living room. It was decorated in soft taupe tones, with an area rug and hardwood floors. "The way you two volunteered to be cut from Directis in order to keep the jobs of the parolees working there, with only months to Christmas? It's noble. Stupid, too, because careers don't reward the nobly unemployed, but still, you two are very sweet. Honestly, though, I wasn't comfortable with you working alongside felons anyway."

"Felons?" I asked weakly. My voice sounded higher than normal, even to my own ears.

"I think it's weird that Directis has a convict rehabilitation program in the first place. Seems unreliable and risky, but I saw that boss guy one time, and I didn't get the sense that he made the best choices. Maybe he used to be in the Big House himself? Maybe that's why he likes convicts."

"I have no idea," I said. I glanced around nervously, feeling a trickle of sweat on my back under my sweatshirt. Where the hell was Jane? "Jane offered to help me prep for an interview. Is she here?"

"Congratulations on the interview! Jane told me all about it; she's so happy for you. She's upstairs in her room, last door on the left. Feel free to go on up."

"Thanks," I called over my shoulder as I hurried up the stairs and down the hall, toward the sound of Bon Jovi. I knocked on the door.

"Come in," she called, and I opened the door. Gone were the shades of brown from downstairs. Jane's room was an explosion of color. It was large, with a canopied bed in one corner and a loveseat and a papasan forming a sitting area on the other side of the room. There were photographs of sunflowers on the walls, millions of string lights, and a floor mirror dominated with Polaroids of Jane and her friends. There were a couple pictures of her and me together, dressed as fireworks for the Fourth of July party at the office. Another showed us as narwhals on Dress as Your Favorite Sea Creature day. We'd half-assed that one and reused our unicorn horns and mermaid tails. I couldn't help but smile a little sadly; the pictures brought on a weird mix of nostalgia and revulsion. Actually, the whole room did.

I found her crouched on the floor in front of the loveseat with several canvases and brushes, an array of acrylic paints in front of her. She'd covered part of her canvas in yellow.

"I didn't know you were an artist," I said.

She stood and gave me a quick hug. Then she sat back down and motioned for me to join her.

"I'm not," she said breezily. "I suck, but I don't let it stop me. You backed me up with Mom, right?"

"You didn't really tell her we sacrificed ourselves for felons, did you?" I asked as I settled next to her on the floor.

"I absolutely did," she said. "And I regret nothing."

I squinted. "You're not serious."

"Hey, it's not my fault my mom believes whatever I say. She still believes my high school science teacher gave me the option of either dissecting a rat or bringing it home as a pet. I had Scabbers for two years."

"Gross!" I exclaimed. "They don't make the kids actually kill rats!"

"I know," Jane agreed. "Can you imagine a high school bio class doing that?"

"I can't believe she bought that," I said in awe.

"I take full advantage of her naivety, and I'm not ashamed. Sometime

I'll have to tell you a few stories about stuff I got away with in college." She grinned widely.

I shook my head and looked back at her canvas. "What're you painting?"

"Dots," she said. "I can't draw to save my life. That's why I do abstract—if it's not any good, it's just because people don't get it."

She slid a small blank canvas and a tube of purple paint toward me. "Give it a shot." I pulled the canvas into my lap and squirted a little purple paint onto Jane's palette. She handed me a brush. "So do you really think Xavier is fudging things so it looks like he has like hundreds of employees?" she asked.

"I don't know," I said. "Maybe? Maybe he's trying to come off as, like, a Steve Jobs or Elon Musk to the guys at Trimaran, but we need proof. Preferably without more law breaking."

"Nothing more illegal than wiretapping," she replied earnestly.

I squinted at her. "Debating degrees of legality with you is a prime example of why we have to be careful."

She averted her eyes and shifted, adopting a businesslike look. "So tell me what you learned when you worked at Directis," she said.

I drew a purple upside-down V on the canvas. "That maybe they teach dystopian novels in high school to prepare you for working in an office. Like Orwell's Thought Police works just as well with a tiny dictator in a tiny office fiefdom as it does with the government. *Nineteen Eighty-Four* isn't science fiction if your future can be impacted by what you *don't* say, or"—I gestured to her—"by what your laugh might actually mean."

She blinked at me. "I think you're the only one in high school who read that book." I opened my mouth to respond but Jane cut me off. "But I know what you mean, because the Capitol pushes down the districts with things like the Hunger Games, so yeah. But anyway," she said as she put down her brush and straightened, giving me a haughty look. "Jane

Corp doesn't like the comparison and isn't going to hire you. Hard pass. Try again. What did you learn when you worked at Directis?"

I also put down my brush, accidentally smearing purple paint on the side of my hand. "I learned how to work in a high-stress, pressure-driven environment with constant interruption. It allowed me to hone my concentration skills."

She nodded and flashed me a grin. "Can you name a situation you've had in an office that you should have handled differently?"

We sat there for several minutes staring at each other. "So many," I finally muttered.

"Yeah, that one wasn't fair. I found a bunch of questions on Google to ask you. How about this one: tell me a little about your past supervisor."

"Am I supposed to lie?" I asked her.

"Yep. You'd better," she said. "Or just avoid the question altogether. No one wants the whole truth in an interview anyway, especially about how you feel about your former boss."

I nodded and let out a slow breath. "I work well with little supervision, and my former manager was very hands-on. However, I get along with others and can adapt to many different management styles."

"Excellent." Jane beamed at me. "You told me your former boss is a jackass, but you said it well."

I grinned at her. "Go me!" I said. "But it feels like a minefield, answering questions about Xavier and Bobbert."

"Then get ready for this one," she said as she picked up her brush and added several black dots along with the yellow. "Why did you leave your former position?"

I sighed deeply. "I've been wrestling with that. I don't want to talk about being fired, but I also want to be honest."

She nodded sympathetically. "When I interviewed for the bartending job, they didn't ask any of these questions. They were mostly just happy to have me since I'd worked there before. I have zero problem making something up, but I get it, you're not into that." She rolled her eyes and grinned. "But in any case, it's best to be vague. So what did you hate the most about Directis, aside from Xavier?"

"The stupid office culture," I answered immediately. "And the impossible sales goals. And how boring it was. Like my brain got more and more atrophied every day."

"So…you moved on due to personal differences? Not the best fit for your skill set? Lack of career growth?"

"That sounds way better," I said. I painted another upside-down V and connected them to form cat ears. "And it's not even completely off base." I drew a heart nose and looked back up at Jane. "I wish we still worked together."

"Me, too," she said. "But we really *are* better off. I actually registered for classes next term. You know that's why I live at home, right?"

I shrugged. I hadn't asked because I didn't want to make her uncomfortable.

"I've been saving money to go back to school. Rent is nuts around here. And I'd saved enough to start, but there wasn't any time to take classes, with all the Frisbee golf and other bullshit. I don't know when I would have gotten around to it if they hadn't kicked us out."

"Wow," I said. "Proud of you, Jane. What do you want to study?"

She grinned. "Criminal justice. I want to put bad guys away, not sell them stuff. Or work for them. It'd be cool to bring criminals to justice before I even started…" She trailed off and turned back to her picture. "Bobbert made Marcus put his own name on the underperforming employee certificate of the week. Did you catch that over the transmitter?"

I hadn't. I marinated in the horror of that for a moment. "We have a moral obligation to notify the authorities if something illegal is happening," I acknowledged. "Remember that 'old dude' who works for the unemployment office? Maybe I can ask him how this should be handled."

"You mean cat guy? Look at you with the insider track." She sat back and gave me a huge grin, then eyed her painting. The black dots had blended with the yellow in places, and the effect was striking.

"That's beautiful, Jane," I said, gesturing to her canvas. "I love it."

"Thanks. Dots and haikus are my new specialty," she said. "Do you remember your interview with Directis?"

I nodded. "I met with Bobbert first, then Gary. I didn't meet Xavier until my first day. Things might have been different if he'd interviewed me."

"Me, too!" she said. "For the first half hour, Bobbert went on and on about how they were changing the face of telemarketing and then about how much he loved dinosaurs. Like, why?"

"Yeah. When I interviewed with him, I don't know if he even asked me any questions. It was all him jabbering, with a few tics thrown in."

"And Gary just asked standard HR questions, like about work history, taxes, that sort of stuff."

I thought back to that day. I hadn't had any idea what was coming when I signed on with Directis. "I guess there were red flags, but honestly, it seemed normal. Like typical uncomfortable, unorganized office stuff. Except for the dinosaurs."

She sighed. "If only we'd seen the feet."

"Would that have made the difference? Would you have taken another job if you'd seen the feet?" I asked, genuinely curious.

She tipped her head back, and her messy bun unraveled. She twisted her long hair back up into a ponytail and finally shook her head. "Nah. I needed a job. Besides, all offices are weird. Maybe if I'd known I was going to represent Iraq in a cutthroat wheely chair race, I might have backed up and run." She caught my eye and smiled. "Or not. I've seen some shit now. I'd never go back there, ever, but I don't regret it. I have stories for days. And you and Trisha."

I smiled back. Maybe once all this was wrapped up, I could feel the same way Jane did. Stories for days, but not until I'd aced the interview and could put Xavier Adams behind me, where he belonged.

Chapter 18

There are not more than five musical notes,
yet the combinations of these five give rise
to more melodies than can ever be heard.
—SUN TZU, *THE ART OF WAR*

THE NEXT EVENING, I MADE MYSELF A MUG OF HOT CHOCOLATE AND settled on the couch in leggings, fuzzy socks, and an oversize sweater. Saturday nights weren't the party they'd been in college.

As if I were a magnet, little chonky fluffs waddled over from different spots around the living room, most of them piling on top of each other in my lap, one embedding herself under my arm.

I'd checked in with Jane earlier. She was tending bar at a fancy wine tasting that evening, and Trisha had texted that she was at a Directis Scrabble tournament. Those always sucked—no one wanted to be the one to tell Xavier that whatever he'd played wasn't a word.

I glanced around the living room. Earlier that morning, I'd moved the couch back against the wall where it belonged. Even though the room wasn't completely back to normal, it made me feel better. The Conspiracy Wall was to my back, so I wasn't constantly staring at Bobbert's contorted face. I hated that my mother and her friends had chosen my living room for their arts-and-crafts project, but I had to admit the finished result was a good visual of the Directis rabbit hole. The kittens had taken to climbing the yarn trails that snaked from picture to picture. I planned to call Carter on Monday to ask him a few questions, but in the meantime, I wanted to relax.

I usually listened to the transmitter in the evenings while Jane took the day shift, but with the Scrabble tournament, the office was blessedly quiet, and I felt like I should try to take the night off. My hands still itched to go through those papers Trisha had salvaged, but she said they needed another day to "air out."

I reached for the television remote. Maybe a movie on Netflix would distract me and keep me from worrying about the interview on Monday morning. When the screen loaded, I couldn't help snorting. My mom had shared her Netflix account password with me, and it looked like she'd been binging romantic Christmas movies. Even though she had been driving me crazy lately, video streaming wasn't a necessity for the unemployed, and I was grateful that she'd added me.

While I was scrolling through the trashy movies looking for something with a little more of an edge, my phone buzzed. It took me a minute to find it under all the fluff, but when I saw the message, I had to read it twice.

How's my girl? Carter.

I squinted at it as another message came through. Duo. How's she doing? Also, how're you?

Ah. Less weird. And good timing. Duo is nuts, per usual. And I'm good—I have an interview! I texted. I reached for my hot chocolate and watched the jumping gray dots as he composed his response.

Congrats on the interview, I want to hear all about it.

Thank you. I'm excited about it, I wrote.

What's the job? Is it telemarketing?

No, I texted back. Recruiting. I'd explain more, but too much to text.

More dots, followed by, What're you doing right now?

I put my phone high in the air above me and snapped a photo of my lap, full of kittens on their backs and fast asleep. Pink-padded paws and tiny pink noses everywhere.

Looks like heaven, he said.

I smiled. I knew that picture would crush him. They were so cute when they were sleeping. I reached down to pat one of their little heads and marveled at how soft it was. That kitten started to purr, which started the others purring.

It's not the worst way to spend a Saturday night, I agreed.

Beats mine, he wrote back. I got stood up.

I sat up a little straighter, jostling the fluffs. I didn't care at all if Carter was dating anyone, I reminded myself. But was he texting me as a second choice? Didn't like that.

Sucks, I said.

More dots. My sister got stuck at work. Feel like joining me? We could get dessert to celebrate your interview.

I wavered. I was glad that he hadn't been on a date. I'd also gone through all the desserts my mom's friends had brought to my unemployment wake. If he'd said he wanted to meet for drinks, that would have been a lot easier to turn down. I had told Jane I would ask him how someone should handle a situation like ours, but over dessert, on a Saturday night?

My phone buzzed again. Carter had sent a selfie, and when I touched it with my finger, the photo filled the screen. He was sitting in Brittany's Breakup, an ice cream shop downtown that I'd been to a few times. It was all teal and silver, and the ice cream names played on traditional breakup lines. It was pretty much the antithesis of where I imagined Carter would hang out. He looked completely out of place in his black button-down shirt and dark jeans. I couldn't help but smile at the mildly panicked look in his eyes.

If you were here, I'd look less creepy, he wrote. People are staring at me.

I snorted. Why don't you leave? I texted back.

Another picture filled my screen. It was a luscious strawberry shortcake sundae, with a huge red strawberry dropped into mounds of whipped cream. My mouth watered.

I looked down at the kittens in my lap and then at the trite movie titles on my screen, and I suddenly realized something: I might not be employed, but I also didn't have to attend a Scrabble tournament with an idiot. If I wanted to go out on Saturday night, I could. This was as good a time as any to use Carter as a sounding board for what might be happening at Directis.

With new resolve, I picked up the phone. You convinced me, I texted. See you in 15.

About twenty minutes later, I found myself outside of the ice cream shop on Third Street. I'd taken time to run a comb through my hair and added on some mascara and lip gloss. I'd replaced my fuzzy socks with boots but had left the sweater and leggings. It wasn't a date.

I shivered from the crisp air and pushed open the door. A wave of scent hit me, and I breathed in deeply. It smelled like a birthday cake. The shop was about half-full, mostly a few couples and moms with their daughters. The last time I'd been there, it had been packed; the change in season must have curbed the appetite for more cold.

"Vanessa!" I turned and saw Carter, sitting near the window at a table for two. His blue eyes were full of relief, and I couldn't help smiling. He'd eaten most of his ice cream and clearly could have left at any time.

"Was it good?" I asked as I slipped into the seat opposite him.

"Amazing," he said. "It's called *It's Not You, It's Me*. Would you like to try one?"

I glanced over my shoulder at the menu board and scanned the options before my eyes lit on a picture of a brownie sundae concoction.

"Can we still be friends?" Carter asked.

I turned back to look at him. "I'm sorry, what?"

"*Can We Still Be Friends?* The brownie sundae. Is that the one you're looking at?"

I nodded, and before I could say more, Carter motioned to the woman behind the counter. She was probably in her early sixties with a streak of pink in her hair. He mouthed, "Can We Still Be Friends?" to her, and she grinned, giving him a thumbs-up.

He turned back to me and smiled. "I paid for yours before you got here. So you wouldn't have to wait in line."

"Thank you," I said. "Very thoughtful but not necessary."

"Hey, I pulled you out from under a pile of awesome to come rescue me, so it's the least I could do," he said easily, leaning back in his chair and grinning. "Thanks, by the way. My sister Alayna loves it here. It's not my kind of place normally, but the ice cream is phenomenal. She works the swing shift at Saint Charles Hospital, and her replacement didn't show, so she had to stay. There aren't enough nurses to cover all shifts."

I nodded sympathetically. "That must be hard. Still, that's incredible job security."

"Absolutely, if you've got the stomach for it. Which I'm guessing you don't?" he asked lightly.

"Not at all," I agreed and jumped as the woman from behind the counter placed a gorgeous brownie sundae on the table to my right. "I wish I did, though." I took a bite and felt light-headed. "This is amazing; the brownie is so warm, and the ice cream is so cold!"

"Next time you should try Let's See Other People. It's coffee flavored and mixes well with chocolate."

That *did* sound good. "This place is the epitome of unnecessary for those of us without jobs," I admitted. "Speaking of jobs...do you ever deal with fraud in your line of work?" I bit the inside of my cheek. *Smooth*, I told myself.

He stared at me for a few beats. "There's always fraud when it comes to accessing government funds. I don't deal much with that side of things, but if I see something that looks off, I'm obligated to flag it. I don't usually hear back."

He shifted in his seat, and a thought occurred to me. "Did you flag Directis?" I asked.

"A hundred percent," he answered. "Based on the response we received to the questionnaire alone. But like I said, it seems like those flags go into a black hole and never come out. That's one of the reasons why I'm interested in getting into the investigative side."

"Could that trigger an inquiry into the company as a whole? Like an audit or something?" I kept my voice light and my eyes on the rivulets of chocolate sauce mixing with the ice cream.

"It might," Carter answered carefully. "I think it's unlikely since those are usually handled by the IRS. I have a cousin who works there. They deal with some unusual stuff."

"Tell me more," I said.

"Like people who claim they're not actually people to get out of paying taxes, or that the IRS is really a private organization, or that, you know, it's run by lizard people."

I choked a little on my ice cream as Carter cleared his throat and continued, "People can get extremely creative with fraud, but they usually don't. It's almost always the same stuff."

"Like what?" I asked.

"Falsification of time cards, like getting paid overtime when you're not really working. Another common way is with ghost employees," he said.

I opened my mouth, but he grinned and cut me off. "Not nearly as cool as it sounds. Ghost employees are just people who are on the payroll but don't actually work for the company," he said.

I felt a bead of sweat form on my neck. That sounded about right.

"Sometimes the former employee is in on it, and they split what would be their paycheck with the person working payroll. Other times the employee's bank account number is changed so one person can collect more than one check. There are a few ways to do it." He leaned back.

"But wouldn't they get caught?" I asked, my mouth dry, despite the sundae. "That's like super greedy."

"It can be easy to do if one person handles all the money. That person can pocket the extra paychecks if there isn't anyone else looking through the books," Carter told me. "Which is why it's easier to do with smaller companies. But I think most are caught."

"But how would you ever know about the ones who *aren't* caught?" I asked slowly.

"Fair point," he conceded.

"Surely the more ghost employees you add…" I trailed off.

"If you keep adding them, it's not sustainable," Carter replied. "It usually isn't sustainable anyway. Most cases don't go on long. You're upping your chances of going to jail with each new one. An audit should catch it."

An audit sounded a lot less dangerous than a covert spy mission into secret Directis records.

"There was a case a few years back where a couple of people 'paid' ghost employees by depositing the extra checks into their own bank accounts," Carter went on. "They were only found out when a former employee got a W-2 in the mail, even though he hadn't worked for the company in years. I guess they'd forgotten to change his address in the system."

That little bastard, I thought. Xavier wasn't just an asshole; he was sounding more and more like he was pulling some real Elizabeth Holmes–style shady crap. Minus the blood stuff. But if Carter was right, it really shouldn't be too hard to prove. We were already making a list of ghost employees.

Maybe I could find a way to trigger an audit anonymously. Then I could do my civic duty without calling attention to myself or any of my many helpers. Anger and relief warred for a few seconds.

"Does any of this have to do with Directis?" he asked tentatively. "If there's an actual crime happening there, it should be reported to the police."

Hm. I knew from *Swampy Deaths* that the police always took anonymous tips. "I'm putting that place behind me." If only. "I have an interview day after tomorrow," I said brightly.

He grinned. "Congratulations again. You said it's recruiting?"

I nodded and explained how it was a step beyond what I'd been doing before and that it could have long-term growth potential. "Any advice on how not to blow it?" I asked, swirling my spoon in the chocolate sauce.

"Well, definitely cover your face," he said seriously.

I took a deep breath and felt my cheeks go scarlet.

"It was a joke, I'm sorry, I'm really sorry," he said, reaching for my hand and tripping over himself to apologize. "Too soon?" he asked.

"It'll always be too soon," I answered and pulled my hand away. I suddenly wasn't hungry anymore. I put my elbows on the table and dropped my chin into my hands. "That and my dark soul. Like, why?"

"No one with a dark soul fosters kittens," he said.

I sat up straight. "That's exactly what I told them. I'm glad *you* understand."

"I do, totally. And I have to ask… Do you have a boyfriend or somebody who's been able to help you cope with all this?" His voice went up a little higher on the last couple of words.

I looked down at my hands. "No, I don't," I said. "Work took up most of my free time. And the last guy I dated was kind of a jerk. He broke up with me at the prom."

Carter blinked. "At the what?"

I sighed. "Why does everything sound stupid when I say it out loud? It was a work prom, there was a coronation ceremony and everything, and he walked right out. Which, to be honest, was what we all wanted to do. But trust me, he was still a jerk," I added.

"Were you prom queen?" Carter asked cautiously. "Did he like skip out on the first dance or something?"

Laughter bubbled up in my throat. "God, no. Prom queen? Shoot me now. And it's fine." I shrugged. "I didn't like him that much anyway." I tried to keep my voice light. I *hadn't* liked Quentin that much, but the memory still stung. I looked up at Carter. "What about you?" I asked. "Do you have a girlfriend to help you process stuff?" I was pretty sure the answer was no, but I felt nervous asking the question anyway.

He shook his head. "Single. For a while now. Last girl I dated wasn't the right fit." He caught my eye. "I mean, she didn't dump me at the prom or anything."

I smiled despite myself. "So it couldn't have been *that* bad," I said.

"It was. She didn't like cats."

"She didn't like cats?" I asked sympathetically, remembering the story he had told me about getting a paper route as a child to afford a cat.

He shook his head. "It wasn't just that she didn't want one. It was that she didn't want them to exist in the world."

I gasped. "Like at all?"

He chuckled at the expression on my face. "I'm just kidding, but she didn't like cats."

"Not everybody does. My best friend, Jane, isn't a fan. That in and of itself isn't a deal breaker, as long as it doesn't infringe on my personal cat rights."

"Well…" Carter said, and he leaned back in his chair, averting his eyes. "That wasn't all Haleigh didn't like. She wasn't a fan of my job either. Didn't consider it a career."

I could feel his discomfort as if it were my own. "But you like what you do," I said softly.

"Yes, I do," he answered, his eyes looking directly into mine. "It's hard. I see some of the same people come through over and over, and they can't manage to make progress. I also see new people come in, as shaken by the whole experience as you were. I can't do a lot to help them, but I can ease the transition they're facing. I like it because I make a difference, at least to some people, and I want to do even more."

"Then it's perfect," I said sincerely, not breaking eye contact. "I envy that. *Acta non verba*. Deeds, not words. If it were up to me, I wouldn't go to work and come home every day having done nothing but jump through some dude's, possibly literal, hoops. If you have a sense of purpose, why give it away?"

"It's about priorities, and Haleigh's and mine didn't match up. I think we both tried to change the other, but it didn't work. I moved out about six months ago."

"Oh," I said, feeling an unexpected touch of jealousy. "That's why you're looking to adopt Duo."

"I've got my own place, which, incidentally, is decorated just like this place," he said, gesturing at the teal-and-silver striped walls of Brittany's Breakup.

I snorted. "Duo's going to love it. She's partial to teal. And you're going to give her a great life."

"Hey," he said softly. "You *do* make a difference, you know. To Duo and Uno and all the Kinkies. And all the ones that will come after them. To your friends. And to me."

The shop had gotten quiet, and I looked around to see that they appeared to be closing soon. There were only a few people left. Where had the time gone? "Thank you for saying that." I sighed wistfully. "If I could make a living at it, I'd save all the cats. I've tried to keep up with my volunteer work so I can feel like I'm contributing to the world somehow, even if it isn't the way I want. I haven't been getting it from my job, and I don't want my humanity to…atrophy…I guess. That sounds stupid."

"It doesn't at all. Do you think you'll find that kind of fulfillment at this recruiting place?"

Did I really? I brushed the thought off. "Beggars can't be choosers, but I'm hopeful," I said. "And it'll pay the bills. Maybe I can help people like me find the jobs they want." I stood and grabbed my purse.

"I'm hopeful, too," Carter said and put his hand on the small of my back as he opened the door for me.

My Jeep was parked out front, and when I opened the car door, Carter leaned in and squinted. "The inside of your car has a sheen to it," he said.

"If you mean that fabulous electric blue, then yes, it does," I said then turned to face him.

He leaned against the side of the car, resting his arm on the doorframe. I shifted from one foot to the other. It was chilly outside, and I shivered. "Is everything really okay, Vanessa?" Carter asked quietly. "If you're concerned something illegal might be happening at Directis, maybe you should tell someone. Especially if it could involve past employees. Like you," he said seriously.

"Um, that was totally hypothetical," I reminded him, shivering again.

"You're the worst liar." His eyes dropped to my mouth, and I felt him lean a little closer to me. "The IRS and the police take tips. Theft is a crime. If you think there might be a problem, you can alert them and let them take it from there. If there isn't an issue, no harm done."

"That's not a bad idea," I admitted. My whole body could feel the warmth coming off him. "But you don't need to worry about me. If anything, you should worry about my friends Trisha and Jane," I said softly. I stood completely still, willing myself to breathe.

"You *are* the one I'm worried about," he said, his breath on my lips.

I felt my heart thump a beat too hard. He was too near to me for a casual conversation. This wasn't the time for me to start anything with anyone. Still, my whole body felt tingly with anticipation, with the moment of waiting.

His hand came up to rest on the side of my face, his palm along my jawline, fingers brushing my cheek. My whole body felt tuned to that one spot, and I closed my eyes, letting the sensation wash over me.

"Do you mind…" I heard him breathe against my mouth, his thumb brushing my bottom lip. Not fully trusting my words, I shook my head slightly then felt his lips, featherlight, on mine.

He deepened the kiss, and my adrenaline reached a fever pitch. Then, before I knew it, he was pulling back, his hand falling to rest at his side. I opened my eyes, blinking up at him in the streetlight. He looked as shaken as I was. Then he ran a hand down the length of my hair, letting it curl around his wrist, before he let go. "Have a good evening, Vanessa," he said, his voice slightly unsteady.

I cleared my throat. "You, too, Carter," I said, trying to keep my voice light. He turned and walked in the direction of his car. I gulped in the cold night air, got in the car, started the engine, locked the doors, then rested my head against the back of the seat, trying to slow my heart rate.

When I opened my eyes, Carter's car had left the parking lot. I adjusted the rearview mirror and studied my reflection. I looked flushed and… hopeful? Maybe I could turn Xavier in to the police without it coming back on me or my friends. And maybe if I'd gone to the work prom with Carter instead of Quentin, it would have been a whole different experience.

Chapter 19

Four weeks earlier

I STOOD BACK AND TOOK IN THE ROOM, AN EXPLOSION OF GLOW-IN-the-dark neon for our '80s-themed work prom. Cheryl had improvised on the disco ball, cutting a million tiny squares of tin foil and gluing them to a Styrofoam ball. It wasn't really catching the light, but we'd hung it from the ceiling anyway. The overall effect was glitzy and tacky and kind of fun. Like my outfit. A black velvet and gold lamé off-the-shoulder dress, ending in a puffy balloon skirt. Lots of necklaces and bracelets, along with black lace fingerless gloves and black stockings. Crimped side ponytail and teased bangs. I paused to consider the overall look. I wasn't stoked about being out in public like this, but it could be worse. Early Madonna never fully went out of style, as far as I was concerned. Even if I didn't want to attend a work function channeling "Papa Don't Preach."

Cheryl rushed over to give me a quick hug. "You're adorable. So glad we hit up Goodwill yesterday! Where's your boyfriend?" she asked.

I hesitated for a second. Could I call Quentin my boyfriend? Did I want to? "He should be here any minute," I told her.

"Okay," she air-kissed me then dashed back to the speaker system, which was now blasting Bon Jovi. Geraldine had already told her to turn it down twice.

I scanned the room again before seeing Trisha and Marcus at the punch table, setting out little Dixie cups and several plastic ladles. Marcus had styled his long hair into a mullet and was wearing a white tux with a neon-pink bow tie. Trisha had on large coke-bottle glasses, a high-necked blouse, and knee-length ruffled skirt. She looked like she'd intentionally dressed as a wallflower, the "before" to all '80s movie makeover scenes.

I glanced down at my watch. It was past eight. Quentin was twenty minutes late.

Quentin wasn't my usual type. Most of the time, I crushed on guys in bands who were writing bad poetry to express their existential angst. Quentin wasn't like that. He had a bit of a frat boy feel to him, and I wasn't 100 percent sure how smart he was, which was a little disturbing. We had met after I started working at Directis and had run into each other a couple times getting our morning coffee at Starbucks. Both tall, extra-dry cappuccinos. We'd started talking, and we didn't have a ton in common outside of our need for caffeine, but I liked the idea of him. There weren't fireworks when we kissed or anything, but I was way too practical to believe in love at first sight anyway.

I leaned against the wall and checked my phone for any missed messages when I felt a hand on my shoulder. I jumped and turned. "Quentin!" I said brightly.

He was dressed in khaki pants and a polo shirt, his blond hair cut short. He glanced around the room, then looked me up and down and frowned. He had to lean in so I could hear him over David Bowie. "What're you wearing?" he asked.

I felt a wave of annoyance. "What am I wearing? What are *you* wearing?"

"I'm wearing clothes." He gestured to the room. "You all look like the eighties threw up on you."

My cheeks heated up. "That's kind of the point. This is an eighties-themed work prom. We talked about this."

"I didn't think you were serious," he said.

I looked up at him. "Why would anyone joke about that?"

"Look, babe, we'll get you a change of clothes and go downtown and grab a drink. We can meet up with the others at Ace. I told them we'd be there after we made an appearance at your work thing. I didn't know it was going to be this bad."

I hated that bar, and I didn't really like his friends either. "I have to stay here. It just started."

He rolled his eyes. "It's not part of your job." He snaked his arm around my waist. "C'mon. Let's go get a drink and see where the night takes us."

"I have an unhinged boss," I reminded him, pulling away. "He isn't even here yet. I thought maybe if you and I hung out together, it wouldn't be so bad."

"Nessie," he stated, and I flinched. I hated it when he called me that. He lifted my chin so I was looking him directly in the eye. I hated it when he did that, too. "You blew off our last date for some ridiculous squash tournament—"

"No," I protested. "Also work. Also mandatory. I invited you to go with me—"

He snorted. "Why would I want to do that?"

Irritation bubbled up, and the heat in my cheeks turned angry. "Because you want to spend time with me? Because I went to your company softball game? Because I created your March Madness bracket so you won the office pool? Because—"

"That's different," he said dismissively. "Those things are fun. What you all do at your office is weird."

Wasn't it all weird? I looked down, my eyes coming to rest on the lace booties I'd borrowed from Jane.

I heard a slight commotion to my right and looked over. Geraldine, wearing an honest-to-God authentic '80s prom dress, was wrestling with Trisha over a bottle of Jäger. Geraldine managed to get it away from her and upended the contents into the punch bowl. For once, I agreed with Geraldine. It was going to be that kind of night.

I looked back at Quentin. He had pulled out his phone and was texting. "Get changed, babe. We're leaving."

"No," I said again.

He frowned. "I told the others we'd meet them."

"After the dance," I said firmly.

He stretched his neck to the side until it cracked, and looked up at the ceiling. "I can't believe you're serious right now."

"I can't believe you're serious right now!" I shot back. I was too frustrated for a better comeback.

"Well, maybe if you were better at your job, you wouldn't have to do all this extra stuff to make up for it," he snapped.

That stopped me cold. The music was loud. Surely I hadn't heard him correctly. "You didn't just say what I heard you say," I said, my voice icy.

"What? If your performance were great, then it wouldn't matter if you did this stuff."

I tilted my head at him. "Seriously? What fantasy world are you living in?" Was there any job where security and advancement were decided by performance alone and not other factors, like who was friends with the boss or who was the biggest team player? Or who met at the bar after work for drinks?

"I'm just saying, being a telemarketer can't be that hard," he said.

"I'm excellent at my job," I snapped, "hard or not. And how many lives did you save at the Olive Garden today?"

"Babe," he said and leaned back in. "All I mean is we should spend this evening together."

I stepped back. "Not really feeling it right now."

"If you don't come with me tonight, Nessie, maybe we should take a break from each other."

I sighed loudly, and the stress inside me broke something. "Are you asking me to choose between you and my job? Because both of you eat up my self-esteem and free time, so I'm going to have to go with the one that pays my bills."

He hesitated for a second. "Does that mean you're choosing me? Because I can't really keep up with my own bills, so I don't think—"

"No, I'm not choosing you!" I cried. "I'm staying at this stupid prom, and I'm going to be the 'Owner of a Lonely Heart.'"

"Wait, what?" he asked.

I rolled my eyes. "It's an eighties breakup song. So is 'Dancing with Myself,' which is what I'm going to be doing." I'd listened to Jane's playlist too much recently.

"You don't want to date me anymore?" he asked, astonished.

"Hard pass," I said. "Have a great evening with 'your boys.'"

He walked stiffly toward the door. "Well, 'Every Rose Has Its Thorn,'" he grumbled. "I don't think you're being very smart, babe—"

"That song is about a stripper. Don't disgrace Poison. Goodbye, Quentin."

He opened his mouth to say something, but I turned my back on him and went to find Jane. "'Where Do Lonely Hearts Go?' To the work prom," I said to myself as I made my way over.

I touched her shoulder. "No boyfriend tonight." I had to yell to be heard over Depeche Mode. "'Another One Bites the Dust.'"

She didn't respond. Instead she grabbed my hand and squeezed my fingers tightly. I turned my head to see what she was staring at.

Xavier and his wife, Dawn. The king and queen of the Directis Prom had arrived. She was in a simple white Calvin Klein dress, straight lines and no frills. Her blond hair was pulled back from her face, and her makeup was a masterpiece of contouring. Her classic high heels put her a good five inches over the top of Xavier's head. She was a modern, normal counterpart to her husband, the business in the front to Xavier's party in the back.

Xavier was wearing a dark cashmere suit jacket with a white shirt and knee-length cashmere dress shorts. There was so much calf. He was also wearing shiny oxford loafers and black socks—something I'd never seen on him before. He lifted his feet weirdly with each step.

"He walks like a dog wearing booties for the first time," Jane murmured. "He must save so much money on pants."

"He has to get them tailored that way, don't you think? And when did the eighties theme become optional?" I whispered back.

Xavier smiled and waved at everyone who had stopped to watch them come in. He lurched over to the table next to the speaker and sat, where he methodically began taking off his shoes and socks, flexing each toe individually. Dawn glared at him and put her hand on his shoulder. He shrugged her off and continued to denude his feet. Her face became pinched, but she kept her composure. I was pretty sure his ensemble represented a compromise that was supposed to include that the shoes stayed on.

Suddenly, everything seemed a bit much. I let go of Jane's hand and made a beeline for the punch table. I grabbed a Dixie cup and filled it to the brim then downed it all at once. It tasted like the fires of hell and burned all the way down. It took a second for the aftertaste to fade, and I grabbed the ladle to pour another one.

Geraldine, who was standing by the table, took the ladle from me. "Let me get that for you," she said and filled the cup. She handed it back and poured herself one as well. "Cheers," she said, with a rare smile. I touched the edge of my paper cup to hers, and we both threw back the shot. It burned a little this time but not nearly as much.

"Thanks," I said.

"Do you need another?" she asked.

I hesitated. "Not sure."

"That's a yes." She filled another cup halfway and handed it to me. "Men suck," she said and caught my eye. Then she gestured around the room. "All of them."

I nodded. Had she seen my conversation with Quentin? Did she know I'd just been dumped at the prom like an emo high school girl?

"Sometimes the only thing you can control is how much you drink," she added.

I looked at her with new understanding. "Or what goes in and out of the refrigerator."

She tipped her head. "Or that."

The Paula Abdul song blaring in the background abruptly cut off.

"It's time for the coronation ceremony for prom king and his queen," Marcus said into a microphone. "The ballots have been counted."

The ballots for prom king, which we'd received in an email that afternoon, had Xavier's name with a box to check, and a blank for a write-in candidate. I hoped no one had fallen for that trap.

I handed the Dixie cup back to Geraldine. "Load me up," I sighed.

I took the full cup back from Geraldine as Marcus boomed, "Our winner is…surprise!" His voice cracked a little. "Xavier Adams, and his wife, Dawn Adams!"

Xavier stood and flexed his newly naked feet. He grabbed Dawn's hand and pulled her with him to the microphone, where a spotlight had appeared from God knew where. She resisted and tried to pull away, but he kept hold of her and dragged her behind him. She gave him a murderous look.

Xavier bowed in front of Marcus, and Marcus carefully settled a homemade crown (Cheryl's handiwork, I guessed) onto his thoroughly sprayed hair. Xavier then gestured for Dawn to bow as well. She shook her head hard and managed to get her hand away from his. She pulled out of the spotlight and stepped back into the shadows.

Xavier stood and took the microphone from Marcus. "Thank you, everyone. This is so unexpected. I have a speech prepared…"

I tuned him out and turned back to the punch table. Someone came up beside me. Dawn.

"Hello," she said to Geraldine and me. "Have we met?" she asked. Geraldine filled a cup with punch and passed it to her.

"A couple times," I said.

"Ah. Then nice to see you again." She shook my hand briefly, and up close, I could see how tired her eyes were. She took a sip from the cup, and the harsh licorice taste didn't seem to faze her at all. "Have a good evening," she said and turned to walk away. I saw a few small fluffs detach from her dress and float to the ground. Possibly cat hair? Maybe she wasn't so bad after all.

Had Xavier been wearing shoes when she'd met him? Was she wishing she'd been dumped at the work prom years ago? As bad as it was to work for Xavier, I couldn't imagine the fresh hell it was to be married to him.

Chapter 20

When there is much running about and
the soldiers fall into rank, it means that
the critical moment has come.

—SUN TZU, *THE ART OF WAR*

THAT SUNDAY, I SETTLED ON THE COUCH AND PULLED UP A WEB
browser on my phone while Duo wormed her way under my arm. "I saw
your new dad last night," I told her.

She squeaked back what I imagined translated to, *Did he ask about
me? Did you remind him that I'm a fluffy demon?* I ruffled her ears, and she
bit my finger while I googled how to report fraud to the IRS.

The form that came up made my eyes cross. For one, it couldn't be
submitted online. It had to be mailed to a rando address in California.
Was it 1870 or something? It also asked for a lot of information I didn't
have (like proof? Web photos surely didn't count). And it looked like
their lead time was about a year. Great.

Well, Carter had also suggested calling the police. That made me
nervous, but if it was anonymous, it could absolve me of my moral
responsibility and take the whole thing off my plate for good. "Here
goes," I muttered to Duo and the two others who had crawled in my
lap to join her. I dialed the number and listened to the recorded message with my heart in my throat. The cats wrestled in my lap and
growled at each other. "Shush!" I told them. "If they hear you, they'll
know it's me."

Then the beep sounded. "Um...hi," I said. "I'm calling to report embezzlement. Xavier Adams, Directis. Telemarketing with a personal touch," I stammered. I really should have written something out first. I provided the address then gasped as Duo clawed up my shoulder and bit my ear. "Ghost employees," I managed to choke out like an idiot before I hung up. I turned to her and the others. "Seriously?"

But it felt good. I had an interview, I'd had a nice time with Carter the night before, and Xavier might finally face some consequences for the lives he'd ruined. I'd done my civic duty and finally had a real shot at moving forward. What could possibly go wrong?

"Do you still think about the cat spirits, Haiku?" a voice mused from the laundry room. My body sagged into the couch. I heard Haiku growl a response, which caused all the kittens to perk up. "I do," Xavier continued. "I wonder if they've passed on."

I stifled a groan and imagined him flat on his back on the conference room table, hands behind his head, staring at the ceiling. Had he stuck little glow-in-the-dark stars up there? Haiku was probably cowered near the door, giving Xavier his best bitch face.

"What do you think we're in for?" I asked the kittens. "Platitudes? A dance party? Maybe—" A sudden knock at the door startled me, and I jumped, scattering the cats around the room. My mom was pretty much the only person who showed up without calling, so I gritted my teeth and made my way over to the door. "This isn't the best—" I started but stopped when I saw who it was.

"Carter, hi," I said, my voice going up an octave. Not good. I smoothed down my hair and kept the door cracked. "Um, can I help you?"

"Hey." He smiled at me, and I noticed he had a small box in one hand. "Would you mind if I came in for just a second?"

Panic washed over me. "Uh...." I started, when Duo poked her head through the gap at my feet, meowing loudly.

"Hey there, you." Carter kneeled as she stretched a spotted paw toward him. "Wait, Vanessa, there's something wrong with her mouth. Is she hurt?"

Duo turned and ran back into the apartment, and Carter pushed past me, chasing her down the hall before grabbing her around the middle and holding her up, her legs flailing. He reached into her mouth and unwound a piece of red yarn that was stuck between her teeth. She purred and gnashed on his finger as he sighed in relief. "It's just red yarn. You had me worried," he told her then looked up.

It was like it was all happening in slow motion. A sense of dread and unreality washed over me as I saw him take in the expanse of the wall in front of him. The pictures. The note cards. The yarn. *Fuuuuuuuck.*

His eyes flitted back and forth between Xavier's duck squat, my "innocent victim" photo, resting a beat on a note card that read *Connection to Area 51?* He absently set Duo back on the floor and turned to me. "Vanessa?" he asked softly.

A million explanations flashed through my mind all at once, none of them a good enough excuse for what he was seeing. I grabbed one out of the air and opened my mouth, but Xavier beat me to it.

"I feel like someone's spying on me. Other than you, Haiku," Xavier boomed from the laundry room. "Probably the same person who glitter bombed us." A dramatic sigh. "I hate blue."

Carter's eyes found mine, and I held my breath as a variety of emotions played over his face. "Blue glitter," he mumbled.

"I can explain," I said quickly. "It looks bad because it *is* bad, but—"

Carter held his hand up. "I don't want to hear the explanation," he said. "I don't want to be involved in whatever is going on here. The less I know the better." He put the little box he'd brought down on the table. "I just came by to give you this. Good luck on your interview," he said stiffly. He walked quickly back to the front door, avoiding my eyes.

"Carter, wait—" I started, but he was already out the door, closing it firmly in my face. I took a deep breath to steady myself and picked up the little box. Inside was a small enamel charm of a calico cat, right paw raised beside its head. I turned it over in my palm and picked up the jewelry card inside the box. It read, *Maneki neko: This beckoning cat will bring luck and good fortune to its owner.* I felt like my heart was being crushed.

Chapter 21

The opportunity of defeating the enemy is
provided by the enemy himself.

—SUN TZU, *THE ART OF WAR*

"You got this, you got this," I muttered to myself. It was 11:15 a.m., and I was outside of the Monarch Recruiting office in my car, wiping my sweaty hands on my black dress pants. I'd survived the first two rounds of the gauntlet and had been given a quick break before the third and final round. I checked myself over in the rearview mirror. I had on a soft blue sweater and my hair down and straightened so it lay in sleek lines down my back. I tried to swallow around the dryness in my throat and lint rolled myself a few more times, picking up the last of the cat hair and the glitter still hiding in the seams of the car seats.

Last night had been rough. I'd cried longer than I cared to admit about what had happened with Carter. Afterward, sometime around 10:00 p.m., the transmitter had started emitting a high-pitched whine at ten-minute intervals. The cats and I were completely frazzled by the time it finally stopped, near 2:00 a.m. The only thing that had gotten me through was the hope that it was the swan song of a dying battery. Why couldn't it have died just one day earlier? I'd had several cups of coffee to counteract the sleeplessness, along with quite a few cucumber slices to calm the swelling in my eyes, but so far, thankfully, none of it seemed to have impacted my interview performance.

I was pretty sure the interview had gone well so far, since they'd asked me to stay to meet the boss. There'd been no obviously awkward moments and no curveball questions. I'd met with Stacey and Justin, the marketing directors, both of whom had been polite and mainly talked about Monarch's mission and vision. I tried not to focus on the hope bubbling in my chest or how much of a relief it would be to have a job again.

All my "studying" with Jane had paid off. By the time I'd left her house on Friday, I was the queen of vagueness and had mastered neutral wording for most of the questions she had thrown at me. I just hated interviewing so much. The pretense was physically painful. It was such a weird game of saying, "Why do I want this job? Well, my background is a natural progression toward this role, and I'm excited for the opportunity to apply my past experience…" When all I really wanted to say was, *Because of money. I don't want to be a performing monkey here or anywhere else. I didn't dream about this as a kid, but I need food and cute clothes and fancy coffee. Can we just call it what it is?*

I glanced down at my watch. I had just a few minutes left before I had to go back in and meet with the final interviewer. After one last steadying breath, I got out of the car and walked back into the building, shivering from a combination of the cool air and my nerves. The office was warm, bright, and airy, with an unoccupied receptionist desk near the front door. A full wall of glass bricks extended along the side of the large room, letting in light and creating the illusion of more space. Instead of cubicles, there were about a dozen square tables, with four employees at each. A few of them looked up and smiled at me when I entered.

A blond man I hadn't seen before stood up from one of the tables and came toward me, his hand outstretched. He was pleasant looking, midforties, and wearing khakis and a collared shirt. "Vanessa? I'm Kevin. I just got out of my last meeting, so I'm ready for you. Would you like a cup of coffee?"

I shook his hand and smiled, feeling a little more comfortable. "I'm fine, but thank you."

"Let's head into the conference room so we can sit down and talk."

I followed him into a long room with a large table in the center. This room was different from the one in which I'd spoken to Stacey and Justin. That one had been a lot smaller and tucked away off the main room. This one had a cute single-serve coffee bar tucked into the corner. When he saw me looking, he said, "Our office loves coffee. It has to be fresh every time. We're a bunch of snobs," he confided with a smile.

"I love coffee, too," I told him.

"Then you'll fit right in! I was going through your résumé, and as I said on the phone, it looks like your experience with personalized tele-marketing would transfer well to recruiting. Our office is set up to support different accounts with their recruiting needs. We mainly focus on healthcare, finance, and design, from aides up to directors. The opening we have now would focus on recruiting graphic designers for mid-level positions. Does that sound like it might be of interest to you?"

Did he actually think I might say no?

"Yes! It does! I've wanted to explore recruiting for a long time. I'm interested in full-cycle recruiting and would love to direct my skills toward a new focus." Did that sound convincing enough?

He beamed at me. "We're a smaller company, and we pride ourselves on cultivating room for growth. The right candidate will have an opportunity to take on more responsibility."

"It sounds like a great opportunity, and I like the creative aspect as well."

"Yes, there's definitely a creative edge, especially when looking for designers. We encourage recruiters in that area to find candidates in unorthodox ways: Twitter, social media, online portfolios, pursuing passive candidates."

The job didn't sound terrible—internet research, looking at art, matching people with jobs they'd be perfect for. I might actually be good at that. I might even rescue an artist living under a bridge. If there was cell service there.

He smiled at me. "Your résumé mentions you design the published materials for the Walter Green Animal Shelter. What does that entail?"

I smiled back, feeling more at ease. "I create flyers and brochures for their events and provide content for their social media presence. I also take pictures of the animals and try to present them in the most appealing way to boost adoptions."

"So you know what good design looks like," he said.

"I do. All my work for the shelter is on a volunteer basis, and I would love to incorporate some of that creativity into my work life."

"I figured as much. What contributed to your decision to leave Directis?"

I had known this question was coming, but a knot still formed in my stomach. "Well…career growth is important to me, and I'm looking for an opportunity to improve and expand my skills in recruiting. Directis, as a telemarketing company, didn't offer those possibilities," I said evasively. My answer wasn't a lie, but it also didn't include the word *face*.

"Lack of growth is one of the most common reasons people leave their current jobs," he agreed. "As a recruiter, I interview candidates all the time for a variety of roles. It's a well-established problem in today's workforce." He smiled again and folded his hands on the table. "Can you tell me about a difficult experience you've had in the workplace and how you handled it?"

My mind was suddenly flooded with snapshots of "difficult experiences" I'd had at Directis. Every "extracurricular." Every holiday. Every encounter with Xavier. Pretty much every experience I'd had at Directis had been difficult. I cast my mind around for an ordinary example and launched into an explanation of how I had diffused challenging encounters with clients and customers through my telephone work.

After a series of standard interview questions, which I was pretty sure I nailed, Kevin sat back in his chair and asked me if I had any questions of my own.

There was one question I'd been dreading but had to ask. "What is the office culture like?"

He brightened. "We're all a family. We have holiday parties and pumpkin-patch visits and spend a lot of time together. All of it on the clock, of course," he assured me. "We truly value work-life balance and provide all employees with two weeks of vacation up front."

Oh god. Pumpkin-patch visits? Seriously? But (and I focused furiously on that *but*) he had said it was on the clock. If he wanted to pay me to go on a hayride, I could do that—as long as glitter wasn't involved. I shifted in my seat and tried to glance under the conference room table surreptitiously to make sure he was wearing shoes. All good there.

I took a breath and felt as if a weight had been lifted from my shoulders, and I gave Kevin my first genuine smile. "This sounds like a great opportunity, and I'm excited about the possibility of working here."

He leaned forward a little. "We've interviewed a few people and haven't yet found someone perfect for this role. During the break, I had a few minutes to connect with Justin and Stacey and get their feedback from their interview with you. Both of them think you'd be a stellar candidate and were very impressed with you. And based on our conversation now, I also think you would be a great fit. If you're truly interested in moving forward, we would just need to talk about offer logistics with our HR representative," he said.

"I would like that very much," I answered, tempering my excitement. An offer? A new job? Rent and food and even more space between me and the nightmare of Directis. How much sweeter it would have been if I could have texted Carter afterward to share the good news.

Just then, Kevin's cell phone rang. "One second," he said to me and touched the screen to answer the call. "Oh, hello, Xavier!" Kevin grinned at me while speaking. "Great timing. I'm sitting across the table from Ms. Vanessa Blair, and we've just had a great conversation…" He paused several beats too long, then the smile slowly faded from his face. He swiveled his chair around, turning his back to me.

"I'm not sure I follow you," Kevin said under his breath into the phone. "There aren't any snakes on her head." A pause. "No, I'm sure."

I felt intense dread in the pit of my stomach, and a sense of unreality washed over me. No. This wasn't happening. *Please don't let this be any Xavier I know*, I begged silently. *Please don't let them be talking about me.*

"No," he murmured again. "Nothing's turned to stone yet." He chuckled a little. "Mm-hmm."

I had a suspicion I knew what they were talking about, but I had to be wrong. Kevin glanced at me over his shoulder, and I narrowed my eyes. He shrank back. "Oh," he said into the phone. "I see what you mean." He nervously tapped his pen on the conference room table. "I appreciate the call." He paused again, and I could hear a voice on the other end but couldn't make out the words. "Understood. Bye now." He thumbed off the call.

All the warmth was gone from the room when Kevin turned back around. He cleared his throat. "Thank you for your time here today, Ms. Blair. We'll be in touch."

I felt my cheeks flush, and my neck get splotchy. Had I just been dismissed? "Was that Xavier Adams?" I asked Kevin in a surprisingly steady voice. Had Xavier really called and sabotaged my interview, snatching away a great job before it was even mine? How had he known?

Kevin wouldn't meet my eyes. "Our wives are friends," he answered as though hearing my unspoken question. "Again, Ms. Blair, thank you for your time."

"No more talk of offers?" I asked coldly. "What did he say to you?" Every part of my body felt icy hot, like the last time Xavier Adams had humiliated me. And he'd managed to do it again. The unemployment claim, though horrible in its own way, was one thing. This was another entirely.

"Nothing, Ms. Blair. I'll have Justin walk you to your car. We're finished here."

"Did he compare me to Medusa? Please say I misunderstood." I touched the conference room table, fighting the urge to flip it over.

"He didn't use that word, exactly," Kevin said.

"That's because he doesn't know it!" I spouted. "He said I'm like Medusa, turning people to stone with my face?" I could hear my voice getting louder. "Fine, I'll take the comparison. Medusa was just minding her own goddamn business. She didn't do anything wrong—Poseidon did. And she was the one who was punished, forced to have snake hair and not make eye contact. Poseidon got to keep on being an all-powerful god of the sea. Typical, right? Then Perseus came along to kill her for no reason, except that he was a little bitch. And afterward he carried her head around like a deranged trophy, taking it out at parties to turn random people into rocks." I stopped and took a deep breath. "Perseus thought he was a badass, and history treats him like a hero. Don't make the same mistake with Xavier."

"I don't really understand anything you just said," Kevin replied.

"Well, you would if you'd studied Latin in school, wouldn't you?" I shot back.

He stood and gestured to the door. "Ms. Blair," he said, more pointedly this time.

"I'm pretty sure faces are protected by the Americans with Disabilities Act," I added as I gathered my things. I tried to walk out with as much dignity as I had left. When I got to the door, I turned around one last time and hissed, "You're taking advice from a man who doesn't own a pair of shoes. Maybe you should think about that."

I managed to get to my car on steady feet and sat there, gripping the steering wheel tightly. I was numb with fury and embarrassment and tried to do those stupid breathing exercises I'd learned in yoga class a million years ago. I needed to calm down, not to overreact.

My phone vibrated with a text, and I didn't pick it up. When it vibrated again, I reached for it.

I'm so sorry. Jane.

I stared at the message for a minute and took a few deep breaths. Did you hear Xavier call the interviewer? I texted back.

My nervous system felt like it was on fire as I watched the little gray dots jumping in response. Then her words popped up on the screen.

Yeah, she wrote. Are you okay?

No, I told her. Someone needed to take Xavier down in a spectacular way.

A second text popped up, this one from the group chat. Did someone report something? What's going on? Trisha. It didn't show up with its usual *BFFs* chat name, meaning she'd added another number to the conversation. Marcus.

Not me. Why? Jane answered.

Just curious. Xavier just got a call from somebody and is freaking out. Now Gary's throwing out all sorts of paperwork.

Hell no. They weren't going to get away with it. I had to do something. If only it were possible to turn his stupid ass to stone with my face. This was war.

That would have been me, I wrote. Morituri te salutamus. We who are about to die salute you. I'm all in.

A pause then a message from Marcus. Trisha and I will handle things here. Quid pro quo. That's the only Latin I know.

Chapter 22

Energy may be likened to the bending of
a crossbow; decision, to the
releasing of a trigger.

—SUN TZU, *THE ART OF WAR*

I DROVE HOME SLOWLY AND DELIBERATELY, TRYING TO TAKE DEEP breaths and calm myself. It wouldn't help to turn the car toward the Directis office and storm in on Xavier, no matter how tempting it was to steer the wheel in that direction. I needed to stay rational.

When I got home, I threw my keys and bag in the front hallway and pulled off my heels then dropped them on the floor as I strode into the living room. I opened the windows and turned on the lights. A rush of crisp air ruffled the hair around my face, and I leaned into it, welcoming the chill. Then I grabbed the edge of that sleek, modern couch and jerked it into the middle of the floor, jostling the sleeping kittens piled on one of the cushions. A couple of them meowed loudly in protest. I rammed the couch back under the windows, where my mom and her friends had put it just a few days before. It felt like a lifetime ago.

Then I realized how quiet it was. It was shockingly, blessedly quiet in my apartment. I stood still and listened to the silence. I'd known intellectually that the receiver couldn't broadcast forever, but it had certainly seemed like it would. This should have been the moment when I could officially put Directis behind me for good. A new job, a tip to the police, no more receiver, and a bright future ahead of me. But, once again, Xavier had other plans.

But…when was I going to stop letting other people's plans run my life? Through the anger, a feeling of clarity and a touch of shame settled over me. Monarch wasn't the answer. I knew that; I'd always known it. It was like trading apples for oranges. Kevin might wear shoes, but was going from one dysfunctional work family to another really going to make a difference? Would working at Monarch have made me *happier* than telemarketing had? I already knew the answer.

I felt claws digging into my leg and jumped. A kitten was clawing her way up my dress pants, pulling out threads with each step. I gently disentangled her from my pants and held her up. Her legs thrashed and her potbelly wiggled. No beauty mark. We looked at each other for a moment. Kittens were the worst. They climbed your pants and smelled bad and didn't know how to behave. They lured guys you liked into your apartment and then ruined your chances at a relationship. They were helpless, and they needed me. But I *wasn't* helpless, and it was time to start acting like it.

I thought back through the past few months, or if I was being honest with myself, the past few years. When had I grabbed my opportunities on my own, instead of being shuffled from one place to another by condescending men in suits? You could even throw Quentin into the mix. If I wanted my life to have any sort of meaning, I needed to stop settling. It was time to take control. And the first place to start was showing Xavier he'd messed with the wrong person.

I stepped back and took in the expanse of the wall in front of me. The red yarn spider-webbed out in what appeared to be random directions, with Xavier's duck squat picture directly in the center. I looked at it closely, noticing for the first time that his weird squat was due to one leg resting on a knee scooter. The man's foot (or as Trisha would say, bladder) infection was clearly out of control. Honestly, didn't he have more pressing things to focus on than ruining my life? Like maybe going to the doctor? The face thing was beyond offensive and objectifying (the Medusa comparison still stung), but I'd been at Directis for a long time before my face had come under scrutiny. It was, after all, the face I'd interviewed with.

For the first time, I wasn't angry at my mother for butting in. I had a terrifyingly visual map of the company in front of me, thanks to her. I narrowed my eyes and slowly looked over the pictures, starting at the center and branching out with the yarn. My mother and her friends had not only taken pictures of what I assumed were all the current employees, but it looked like someone printed all the tiny pictures and names of the employees from the Directis website. The same ones Jane, Trisha, Marcus, and I had gone through the other day. I guessed that was Linda's contribution. Each current employee's terribly candid snapshot had a tiny website picture tacked to the wall next to it. It seemed my mother and her friends had indeed noticed the same pattern my friends and I had: there were a lot more website pictures than there were current employees. The extra web images were tacked in vertical lines near the corner where the wall met the windows. An index card above the columns read *ACTORS??* I fought the urge to roll my eyes. Another index card read, *Robbie says FOLLOW THE MONEY.* "Pretty sure Robbie wasn't the one who said that," I muttered to myself. Still another, *NO SHOES— FLAT EARTHER?*

There was a soft knock on the door. I glanced anxiously at the serial killer wall. Not the best time to have people over. Carter's reaction had proven that. I went to the door and opened it a crack. Jane.

I opened the door wider, and she pulled me into a tight hug. "I'm so sorry, Nessa. I hope it's okay that I came over."

She was wearing nice black pants and a tailored white shirt. She must have work later at the wine bar. I allowed myself to relax into the hug and sagged against her for a moment before pulling away.

"They're all bitches," she said. "But don't let it dampen your resolve."

"I won't," I promised.

She grinned at me. "That's my girl."

I closed the door behind her as I gestured for her to make herself comfortable. "I have chocolate chip muffins and coffee," I told her, even though, for the first time in my life, I didn't have an appetite for muffins. I got her a plate and brewed two cups of steaming coffee while she made her way into my living room. I heard a low whistle and knew she must have seen the Wall.

"You don't mess around," she said when I joined her. She'd already taken the remaining yarn and was dangling it in front of a fat sleeping kitten. It didn't wake up, so she reached over and took a muffin. I handed Jane her coffee mug, a ceramic calico cat with a tail for a handle. "This smells amazeballs," she said.

"I didn't make that wall," I said. "It was my mom and her friends. And it made Carter terrified of me." Thinking about it made me feel nauseous.

"What happened?" Jane asked.

"He came over unannounced and saw it. And heard Xavier jabbering like a loon. And now he'll never talk to me again." The weight of it felt suffocating.

Jane's breath hissed between her teeth. "That sucks, for real," she said. "Surely you two can work it out."

I shrugged. "I wouldn't want to talk to me again if I were him," I said.

"Maybe this isn't the best time to mention this, but…your mom and her friends seem like some pretty badass old ladies," she said, taking a sip of coffee. "This wall could be useful. But why is Xavier labeled *Excalibur Lincoln?*"

I shook my head. "There's no reasonable explanation." I sighed.

"You alerted the authorities?" she asked, putting down her cup and settling some sleeping fluff balls into her lap.

I nodded. "Called the police, left a voicemail."

"Did you get Marcus's text? Sounds like the po-po made an appointment to speak to Xavier and Bobbert a couple of weeks from now, giving them an opportunity to destroy all the evidence. I think it's time to put away the glitter and pull out the grenades. Not literally," she clarified.

"I agree," I said. "I'm still figuring out how." I tried to relax into the armchair and watched as a calico kitten gave a big stretch, tail high in the air, and yawned. She made her way over to my chair and climbed up the arm to the headrest. She began licking my hair and emitting a narfy little purr while she groomed me. "There's more," I told her, keeping my eyes closed so I wouldn't have to see her reaction. "You know how Xavier compared me to Medusa? The one who turns people to stone with her face? When they hung up, I yelled at the interview guy about how Medusa was just being herself and not bothering *anybody* when Poseidon and Athena and Perseus teamed up to be bitches. I'm sure I sounded completely unhinged."

Jane looked at me curiously. "Is she, like, the victim in the story? All I know is that she stone part."

"Yeah. She didn't do anything wrong, but Athena cursed her with the stone stuff. Pretty sure she would've scrapped that ability if she'd had a choice. But it gets weirder. A fully grown flying horse jumped out of her neck after Perseus killed her. At least I had the sense to leave that part out," I added.

"So, weird interspecies neck birth aside, it's sort of like he was calling you a strong, badass female?" she asked.

I slumped forward in my chair. "I appreciate you trying to make me feel better, but it's not going to work." I let the kitten bathe me. It was gross but strangely comforting. "Like, Xavier's fired a million people, but is he stopping the rest of them from getting work?"

"Maybe because you're the only one who filed for unemployment?" Jane offered as she took a huge bite of her muffin. "He doesn't want anybody looking into his records. But, to be fair, we don't know that he isn't trying to sabotage other people."

My phone buzzed, and I glanced at it, feeling my heart squeeze in my chest. There was a missed text from Marcus. None from Carter, not that I'd expected it.

Jane was busy staring at the index cards tacked to the wall. "Why does that one say, *Robbie says FOLLOW THE MONEY*?"

"My mom," I replied. "Put your logic away. Why does that one say, *SINGLE BULLET THEORY*?" I said, gesturing to an index card next to Gary's picture. "There are no bullets involved, to the best of my knowledge."

There was a sudden loud knocking at the door. Most of the kittens scattered. I looked at Jane fearfully. "I can't let anyone else see the Wall," I told her anxiously.

"Don't let them in," she whispered back.

I went to the front door nervously, wondering who else could be stopping by. I opened the door a tiny crack and peered out. "Yes?" I said through the thin slot.

"Nessa, it's me," said Trisha.

"Oh, hey," I said, sighing in relief as I opened the door wider. Then I stopped. Trisha wasn't alone. Geraldine stood behind her with an oversize tote bag, tapping her foot impatiently.

"Are you going to let us in, Vanessa, or are you just going to stand there?" Geraldine glared at me.

I looked at Trisha. "Why is she here?"

Trisha glanced back at Geraldine and then lowered her voice. "Is it okay if we come in? We should talk."

"Trisha," I whispered, trying to speak so Geraldine couldn't hear, "my mom and her friends were here the other day. They covered my wall with pictures of Directis employees. It looks like an obsessed conspiracy theorist exploded all over it."

"I get it. You don't want me to see your conspiracy wall," Geraldine barked. "I don't care about your alien theories or your tinfoil hat. Don't be selfish. We're coming in."

Jane came up behind me.

Geraldine stopped immediately. "Oh," she said. "It's you."

"Don't you have a refrigerator to clean out?" Jane snapped.

"Not anymore I don't," she answered and pushed past Jane and me into the apartment.

Jane and I looked at each other as Trisha hurried in after Geraldine, murmuring apologetically.

Geraldine headed straight for the living room and sat on the couch. She barely even glanced at the Wall. She pointed at the lower half of Jane's muffin on the coffee table. "Are you finished with that? I'm gonna throw it out."

Jane snatched it up immediately. "No! Hands off my muffin!"

Geraldine smirked. "Brought a present for you, Vanessa." She reached into the tote bag at her feet and pulled out a wriggling pink mass that vaguely resembled a large rat. It looked like she had it by the scruff.

"Ew!" Jane yelled, causing the creature to thrash around in Geraldine's hands.

"I don't want any gifts!" I blurted before I could stop myself.

"What? Never seen a cat before?" she asked sharply.

The thing squirmed out of her grasp and bolted under the couch. Trisha looked queasy. "So that wasn't your stomach growling in the car," she said to Geraldine. "It was Haiku."

"That can't be Haiku!" Jane yelped. "That's Dobby the house elf!"

"It's a sphynx breed," Geraldine said. "They're very expensive."

"They should be half off if they come without fur," Jane muttered.

"There's a tuft on his rump somewhere," Geraldine said. "I think he's working on his winter coat."

"You stole Xavier's cat? Why would you do that?" I cried as all the kittens squeezed themselves under the couch to greet their new visitor.

Geraldine wavered, and I saw a touch of humanity I wasn't used to seeing. "Animal control was probably going to confiscate him. On account of the diseases," she said matter-of-factly.

I frantically grabbed at the bits of calico fluff still sticking out from under the couch. "Diseases?!" I cried.

Trisha grabbed my arm. "It's okay," she said. "He wasn't exposed to anything, but Geraldine's right. Animal control would've taken him anyway."

I'd gotten a back leg in my hand, but sharp little kitten claws rabbit kicked me, and I let go. "Start from the beginning," I said.

"We got fired today, missy," Geraldine responded. She puffed herself up, even though she was almost as petite as Trisha. "Apparently, I don't care for the refrigerator well enough. And I've invited wildlife into our building." She sniffed indignantly. "As if there weren't already that naked service cat hiding in the Astroturf."

Jane shrugged. "Well…you're the reason for the wild turkeys," she said. "And the raccoons. You fed them our lunches every day. So I kind of get it." She also sat on the couch, squishing herself into the corner, as far away from Geraldine as she could get. Two kittens poked their heads out from under the couch, and Jane scooped them up. She settled them between her and Geraldine as a furry barrier.

Geraldine glowered at her as I turned to Trisha. "What happened?" I asked her.

"It's been a chaotic morning," she replied. "And in the chaos, we got fired."

"Did you have to bring Geraldine?" I whispered.

"I got the impression that if I didn't bring her, she would've followed me. And she had a present for you, so…" I swatted her on the arm. "Besides, she knows things," Trisha said under her breath, her eyes flitting to Geraldine.

"Like what?" I murmured back.

"Like that you're a crazy cat lady but only have rent-a-cats," Geraldine said loudly. She sniffed again. "And you," she said to Jane, "are in love with Man Bun but too wimpy to do anything about it."

Jane's cheeks turned scarlet. "What? Am not."

"Rent-a-cats?" I squeaked.

Geraldine ignored me and turned to Jane. "You always put your leftover pizza next to his vegan, gluten free, not-actually-food nonsense. Like even if you can't be with him, at least your food can." She rolled her eyes.

"Aww, Jane," said Trisha. "Like maybe your hands would touch when you both reached in for lunch."

Jane shot her a death stare.

I looked at Geraldine with new interest. "What else have you noticed?"

"That Brob is getting a divorce—"

"*Brob*?" Jane broke in loudly. "Who the hell is Brob?"

"Bob to the bosses, Robert to the employees. Why? What do you call him?" Geraldine asked.

"Bobbert," we all answered immediately.

She inclined her head. "Not bad. I prefer Brob. Anyway, he used to have a well-packed balanced lunch, like a sandwich, grapes, a cheese stick—like he's a four-year-old child or something—and Go-Gurt. Now he brings in corn chips and throws the bag in the fridge. Who refrigerates corn chips? Only a broken man."

Jane shook her head. "I refuse to feel sorry for Bobbert," she said.

"He'll be so sad to hear that," Geraldine said sarcastically.

"Wait," I said. "Did either of you sign anything? Please tell me you didn't sign the separation agreement."

Trisha and Geraldine looked at each other, then their eyes slid away.

"There wasn't exactly time," Trisha admitted, examining her nails.

Jane and I exchanged glances. "What do you mean, there wasn't time?" I asked.

"Gary was frantically disposing of evidence when Xavier fired us. It got kind of intense when the screeching started."

"Who was screeching?" Jane asked.

"At first, just the turkey," Geraldine replied. "Then pretty much everybody joined in. Except for me," she clarified.

"Was there an actual turkey in the office?" I asked in disbelief.

"Yeah, but I can't understand why people were so scared of it," Geraldine said.

"Probably because it kept charging," Trisha answered.

"It wasn't any scarier than the raccoons," Geraldine said defensively. "They're nasty. That's why I threw Haiku in my purse."

Jane lifted her feet off the ground away from the edge of the couch.

"Everything would have been fine if Xavier hadn't squeaked out on his little scooter to take a look," Geraldine went on. "Not my fault he won't go to the doctor. Maybe if his foot didn't smell so bad, he wouldn't have gotten bitten. He was screaming like a twelve-year-old." Her lips curved in a small smile.

"Eh, still would be your fault," Trisha muttered then looked at me. "Did you know raccoons make a weird chittering noise when they're mad? It's like a chorus of demented parakeets."

"No…I did not know that," I responded.

Jane looked at Geraldine with wide eyes. "I just want to make sure I'm following this. The woodland creatures came in to visit their lunch lady?"

"Not all of them," Trisha clarified. "Just that weird turkey and a couple raccoons. Geraldine let them in. All the cute ones stayed outside."

Geraldine sniffed again. "I did no such thing. I just propped the door open."

"Wow," Jane said softly. "You pulled a Snow White at work. Did you sing to them? Did they help you get dressed?"

"Absolutely not," Geraldine huffed. "And they dress Cinderella, not Snow White. But they did make a huge mess. They're not house-trained."

"Imagine that," I said weakly. Haiku slowly came out from under the couch and hopped up on the coffee table. He sniffed the coffee cups then flopped on his side, exposing a large, pink, hairless belly. If anything, I had imagined Haiku as a fluffy Persian with a squashed face, not a house elf with old-man skin.

"I knew Xavier was going to fire Trisha, and I knew I was next. I did what anyone would do in that situation," Geraldine responded haughtily and patted Haiku on his wrinkled head.

Trisha snorted. "Not anyone, Geraldine."

Geraldine waved her hand dismissively. "Like I said, I just propped open the back door. What happened after was not my fault."

"Wait," I broke in, "how did you know you were next?"

"After they fired Nancy the other day, I started to get behind. So this morning they moved Trisha over to help me on the account and told us we had to sell two hundred units. In one day." Geraldine hmphed. "Have you ever heard anything so stupid?"

We all shook our heads politely.

"Then Miss Trisha here, instead of getting to work, just wanders off." She narrowed her eyes at Trisha. "After about twenty minutes, I went looking for her. And I found her. She was in the restroom painting her toenails!" Geraldine punctuated each word with a smack on the armrest of the couch, her voice louder with each slap. That forced the rest of the kittens out of hiding.

Trisha smiled unapologetically. "I already knew I was on the way out, and I didn't want to learn a whole new account. I just wasn't feeling it." She shrugged. "The bathroom is like the only place you can go in that office where Xavier or Bobbert can't follow."

"Totally," said Jane. "I've cried many times in that stall."

"Me, too," I admitted.

"We get it, you're all crybabies," Geraldine barked. "As I was saying, I dragged her out of there, and then Xavier called her into the conference room to talk with him and Brob. I've seen it happen enough to know that when the door closes with those guys and another employee in the room, someone's not coming out alive."

Jane looked at her in alarm. "Metaphorically," Geraldine snapped. "And I knew I was next."

"We'll never know for sure if you were next," Trisha objected. "You kind of sealed your fate when your forest friends bit everybody."

"I'm not sure who all got bit," Geraldine replied. "It was hard to tell exactly what was going on. Everyone was screaming."

"Pretty sure the whole office will have to get post-exposure prophylaxis," Trisha muttered, pinching the bridge of her nose.

Jane's eyes got huge. "As in the rabies vaccine? Geraldine gave the office rabies?" She turned to look at her. "That's not something Snow White would do."

"I bet she would if she worked for Xavier Adams," Geraldine sniped back. "Even if it *was* my fault, I stand behind it. And you can get the rabies vaccine at Walgreens—it's not a big deal."

"Pretty sure you mean shingles," Jane interjected.

"Same thing," Geraldine dismissed.

"That thing can't stay here," I said, gesturing to the pink lump on the coffee table.

"Would you rather it came home with me?" Geraldine asked. "It can stay in my abandoned storage shed. It's homeless right now."

Trisha looked over at Jane and me. "It was hard to tell what all was going on. Instead of walking me out, Bobbert called animal control and yelled at Geraldine that she was fired. Honestly, I was glad to get out of there at that point."

"Still not sure how he knew it was me, though," Geraldine added.

"I can't imagine," Trisha sighed.

Jane threw her head back against the couch. "I can't believe I missed this," she groaned. "I would have *loved* to have heard it. Too bad I wasn't near the—"

"Ane-jay, ixnay," I muttered at her, making a slashing motion with my hand.

"Wait, you know pig Latin, too?" Jane asked, wide-eyed. "Isn't that, like, a disgrace to your people?"

I looked pointedly in Geraldine's direction. Jane winced and nodded, mouthing, "Sorry." No way was I letting Geraldine know the office had been bugged.

"But enough about that," Geraldine interjected and casually glanced at the Wall. Then she sat up a little straighter and gestured to the pictures in columns near the window. "What's with the pictures over there? They were all fired, right?"

"We think so," I told her. "Maybe some were transferred to the other office."

Geraldine rolled her eyes again. Honestly, how could anyone complain about my face when they also worked with Geraldine? "It's a good thing you have those names printed, even if it makes you look like a serial killer. Gary took the website down this morning. Also, there is no other office."

"Of course, there is," Trisha said. "They're on the We Meeting calls."

Geraldine looked at all three of us in turn. "Are you bitches serious?" she asked.

"Are you sure you aren't mistaken, Geraldine?" Trisha asked. "Why haven't you mentioned this before?"

"It wasn't relevant," she replied.

"But it's also not true," I added. "When Gary got overworked, Bobbert had me process some of the office transfers. Like a couple of the Barbies. Sometimes when people get put on other accounts, they get moved there. I only looked at a couple before Gary found out and made me stop."

"The Barbies?" Geraldine asked. "Oh, you mean the gin-and-tonic, leftover-chicken-parm, and veggie-burger girls? You actually think they're working at the 'other office'?" She let out a loud snort.

We all looked at her.

"Have any of you ever *been* to the other office?" she asked. "Like, for a meeting or something?"

We all shook our heads. I could see Trisha's eyes widening as she thought back through her time at Directis. It couldn't really be true, could it?

"Does anyone else feel like they're in *The Sixth Sense*?" Jane asked with a shudder.

"No one's dead," Trisha reminded her.

Once again, Geraldine rolled her eyes. "Whatever. Put the address into your GPS and see what it says."

I immediately whipped out my phone and keyed in the address for Xavier's other office into my map app and hit GO. "Starting route to—" was drowned out when I saw the final destination. "It's a Dunkin' Donuts?" I managed.

"Yep." Geraldine nodded.

Jane's eyes narrowed. "That's how you figured it out, isn't it? You were googling Dunkin' Donut locations, weren't you?"

For the first time in my memory, Geraldine flushed red. "That part isn't relevant."

"How could you not have told anyone?" I asked.

"Not my business." Geraldine sniffed.

I held up my hands. "Wait. So, even if the police are dragging their feet, Trimaran can still be alerted. They have payroll records, too. The other office is a Dunkin' Donuts. I bet their CEO would act a lot more quickly."

I let the anger from earlier solidify into resolve. We had something that might actually turn Xavier to stone. Maybe I could live up to Medusa's name after all.

Chapter 23

In country where high roads intersect,
join hands with your allies.

—SUN TZU, *THE ART OF WAR*

"Arriving at destination," Siri said blandly as I pulled up in front of a large circular house with a pointed roof and bright red door. It was in an upscale neighborhood, but it was the only house that seemed designed after a pagoda of some kind. I rested my hands on the steering wheel and steadied myself. It was getting dark, but I hadn't wanted to put this off. I was going to be quick. In and out.

A half-hearted hiss issued from the passenger seat. I glanced over at the soft-sided carrier nestled into the seat and made eye contact with a mildly annoyed Haiku. His wrinkled face was scrunched into a soft calico belly, and I shook my head. "I can't believe you made me bring Duo along." The two had quickly developed a weird bond, with Duo riding on Haiku's back like a baby koala. Haiku had growled and snapped and resisted the carrier until I allowed Duo to scoot in after him.

I took a deep breath and got out of the car. Their attachment had ruined my plan of ringing the doorbell, leaving Haiku on the porch, and running back to the car so I could watch from a distance.

I slung the carrier over my shoulder and walked up the sidewalk. Haiku sneezed his displeasure, and I rang the doorbell.

After a few minutes, I heard footsteps on the other side before the door opened a crack and a vaguely familiar face appeared. "What do you want?" she asked hoarsely. Dawn Adams, Xavier's wife.

I caught myself as I took in the dark circles under her eyes, the gray roots in her blond hair, the way she clutched her worn robe tightly around her.

"I just wanted to bring you something," I said awkwardly, stopping myself from blurting, *Brought you a present*, like Geraldine had done.

"I don't think you have anything I want," she said with a tiredness that came across as more beaten down than haughty.

The bag on my hip chose that moment to snort and rumble with a deep, steady vibration. Her eyes went to it immediately, and her whole stance softened. "Haiku?" she asked tentatively.

"Yep," I said and hoisted the carrier up to the porch light so she could see inside. She bent forward and squinted, then smiled joyously. It took years off her face. She quickly unzipped the front of the carrier and pulled the naked, wrinkled lump into her arms, calico koala still attached. She cooed at him and whispered a lullaby as he purred and butted his forehead against hers. Her eyes were damp, and she seemed to be having trouble catching her breath.

Then she frowned slightly and turned to me. "What's that thing stuck to his back?"

"Oh, that's Duo, Haiku's monkey baby. She's one of my foster kittens and apparently the welcoming committee." I scruffed Duo, who thrashed around as I stuffed her back into the carrier.

Dawn rocked Haiku back and forth and closed her eyes tightly. "How did you find him?"

"Umm, I guess there was a kerfuffle in the office where he'd been staying, and there was fear for his safety. I foster animals, so he was brought to me," I said evasively. "I didn't realize he had such a loud purr." The cat was thundering away like an express train.

"His purr is the best part of him," she answered softly. "That and his smooth baby skin."

"Gross," I muttered to myself then cleared my throat and backed a few steps away from Dawn. "I'm going to head out now," I said.

She touched my arm, keeping me in the circle of the porch light. "Have we met?" she asked.

At least a dozen times. "I'm Vanessa. We had a drink together at the work prom. I used to work for your—" I caught myself just in time. *Bony-eared assfish* had been on the tip of my tongue. Where had that come from?

She squeezed my arm. "Thank you," she said earnestly. "Sometimes I think this cat is the only good thing in my life." Haiku's naked belly spilled out over her arm, and his spindly legs dangled back and forth as she rocked him.

Well, *that* was sad. I felt my heart soften. "Then I'm glad I got him back to you," I said as I walked down the porch steps.

"Thank you again, Vanessa. It was nice meeting you."

I'd almost gotten to my car when I heard her voice again across the distance. "It wasn't always like this, you know. When I met him, he was wearing shoes."

She went back inside and closed the door. I walked the rest of the way to my car, holding the zipper closed to keep Duo from wriggling her tiny head through the gap. It'd been a hard day, but I took a moment to be grateful for what I had.

I woke the next morning to sharp, repeated knocking on my front door. I sighed deeply into my pillow and stretched into the tangle of blankets, not ready to leave the dream I'd been having. Finally, I looked over at the clock. 8:00 a.m. Why in the world would someone be here this early? I'd stayed up late the night before, cataloging and updating the grants spreadsheet I had been keeping for the shelter. I sat up and stretched again; then I looked down at myself. Tank top and plush, furry pajama pants. I knew from a lifetime of experience that my hair would be sticking up in all directions. Not the way I usually liked to greet guests.

I trudged from my bed into the living room and past the laundry room to the front door. I knew it wasn't the Bridge Brigade since I hadn't gotten around to changing the locks. They would have made themselves at home and likely taught the cats circus tricks by now.

Why were people showing up uninvited at indecent hours these days? The one perk of being unemployed was sleeping in every morning.

When I opened the door a crack, Trisha's smiling face greeted me. I opened the door wider and gestured for her to come in. "Why is your tail so bushy?" I griped.

She shuffled past me into the apartment, carrying a laptop bag and a large box of coffee, which looked like it held enough for at least a dozen cups. "What is that?" I asked, pointing at it. My eyes took in her full appearance. Slate-blue sweater that looked great with her dark hair, straight-leg trousers, and wedged ankle boots. Her eyeliner and brows were on point. I looked down at myself again. "I haven't run a comb through my hair yet," I mumbled.

Trisha smiled sympathetically and hurried into my kitchen to grab a coffee mug from the cabinet over my stove. She poured a steaming cup from the spout at the bottom of the coffee box and handed it to me. "You look great," she said unconvincingly.

I glanced up at the wall clock. "It's eight oh two, Trisha. What fresh hell is this?"

She blinked. "We were going to have a meeting today."

"We agreed on nine a.m.," I said.

Trisha sat on the sofa and stared at her hands. "I didn't know what else to do," she admitted quietly. "This is my first real day without a job."

Guilt washed over me. "I'm sorry, Trisha. I shouldn't be snappy. I'm glad you came here in your work clothes, ready to kick ass."

She grinned at me, looking relieved. "I did. I put on my ass-kicking shoes."

I glanced down again at her little booties and tried not to snort. Then I inhaled the smell of Panera coffee and took a little sip. "But it's just going to be us and Jane and Marcus. I texted him last night. Why bring so much coffee?" I asked. "I know I can drink my weight, but still...."

Trisha averted her eyes again and shifted uncomfortably. "Well, actually...."

Just then, there was a loud banging on the door, as if someone were kicking it instead of knocking on it.

I narrowed my eyes at Trisha, then went to answer the door. As soon as I opened it, Geraldine barreled past me carrying several large garbage bags full of what looked like paper. "Make way for your guest," she barked. Then she paused to look at me over one of the bags. "Kittens sleep in your hair last night?" she asked then smirked.

"Maybe," I said under my breath and touched my hair self-consciously. For someone whose own hair channeled 1994 for the bangs and hair spray alone, Geraldine was quick to throw out the insults. She was also dressed for a day at the office, which, in her case, meant a flowery, shapeless dress with an attached lace collar. "Are those things fumigated?" I asked.

"They were, at least before Geraldine touched them," Trisha called from the living room. "We separated out just the paper to bring over."

Marcus ducked his head through the open door. "Hey," he said as he followed Geraldine into the apartment, carrying a big box of what looked like folders and at least two tablets. "Nice place, Vanessa. Oh, look, you have kittens!"

I took a breath and downed my cup in two big swallows, then went to put my mug in the kitchen. Now the coffee box made sense. We'd need it all to get through the morning. From the kitchen, I heard Marcus exclaim, "Oh, and look, you have a murder wall!"

"Did you invite anyone else?" I muttered to Trisha. I needed to put on some real clothes, stat.

"Why, because no one wanted Geraldine to come?" Geraldine said loudly as she dropped the garbage bags in the middle of my living room floor.

"That wasn't what I meant," I said quickly, though it clearly was. "And either way, it doesn't warrant talking about yourself in the third person."

"Geraldine does what she wants," Geraldine shot back. "And Geraldine is a part of this, whether you like it or not."

I sighed and tried not to give in to the headache that was forming. "Fine. Let me brush my teeth and throw on some clothes, and we can get started."

"Don't forget to do something about your hair," Geraldine called after me as I headed toward the bedroom. "And where's that wrinkly old man cat?"

A quick hot shower and some jeans and a sweater later, I had rejoined them in the living room. By this time, Jane had also dragged herself over, in an old off-the-shoulder sweatshirt and leggings. Her eyes were barely open, and she was nestled on the loveseat with a cup of coffee and a fat kitten chewing on her sleeve.

"Everybody ready?" Geraldine asked loudly.

"Do you have a volume control?" Jane asked meekly and touched her temples. "I work evenings now. This is the crack of dawn."

"How about you go in the bathroom and cry about it?" Geraldine snapped back.

I stood and ignored the rude gesture Jane made in response to

Geraldine. "Jane, Trisha, and I are going to make phone calls. Marcus and Geraldine are going to go through all this stuff."

"What is it?" Jane asked.

"The box is what I was able to save during Gary's big purge. I started hiding things as soon as I saw him tossing documents. It's not much, but I think there's some good stuff in here," Marcus said. He grinned at Jane, and she smiled back shyly.

"The bags are what Xavier made me clean out of the dumpsters. I also took the liberty of going through the recycling," Trisha piped up. "I saved all of it. Sun Tzu says that victory comes from finding opportunities in problems. You know, in war."

"When he says that, what do you say back?" Jane asked.

Trisha ignored her. "They didn't tell me to clean those, but I was feeling extra helpful."

"You did great," I told them. "I bet all the evidence we need is here. I also might have access to some information myself."

Trisha looked pretty pleased with herself. "I hope so. But going through it isn't going to be quick. There's a ton of unnecessary crap in there."

"Who are we supposed to call anyway?" Jane asked.

"We're calling all the fired employees that were still on the Directis website," I went on, gesturing at the Wall. "If our current theory is correct, some of these people may still be listed as employees. It would be great to have their support."

"But why would they talk to us?" Jane asked. "Maybe I should go through the papers instead."

Geraldine looked at the ceiling. "You have to help make the calls because, inexplicably, people seem to like you more than me. You'll probably be more successful," she added, as if it physically hurt her to say it.

"That's a good point." Jane nodded sagely.

"It's not like we're asking them to do anything that would break that contract," Trisha interjected.

"We're way past that," I said. "These people have also been the victim of fraud and maybe identity theft. And some of them are still dealing with the effects of it. They need this as much as we do. But," I conceded, "we still need to use some finesse when we call them. We're salespeople. We've got this."

I thought for a moment. "And we should start with the Barbies. Anyone who's been 'transferred' to a nonexistent doughnut shop would definitely be on the list. And keep an eye out for any mention of transfers in the documents." A memory resurfaced of an incident at Directis a few weeks back. Maybe there had been more to me being fired than my face after all.

Chapter 24

Three weeks earlier

I PUT DOWN THE PHONE AND GLANCED AT THE CLOCK. 3:12 P.M. How could it only be four minutes since I'd last looked at it? At this rate it would be nighttime before it was 3:30. Two days in a row with almost no responses from the millions of calls I'd made. Some days were like that, and I dreaded them. I looked at the clock again. Still 3:12. I fought the urge to stand and announce loudly that in the twenty-first century, people didn't answer phones anymore, and we were all better for it. Times had changed, and cold-calling was severely outdated. It had been brought up before, but Xavier and Bobbert the Luddites were having none of it.

I picked up my pink cat mug and brought it to my lips before I realized it was completely empty. Already? With a sigh, I rolled my neck on my shoulders and slipped my feet back into my pumps under the desk. Cup in hand, I stood and walked toward the break room for a refill. The coffee was terrible and wasn't free, but when you're desperate, you do what you have to do. I got halfway across the office when I heard what sounded like snaps.

"You! Over here!" I looked down a row of cubicles and saw Bobbert snapping his fingers at me from his office. I grimaced and made my way down an aisle of cubicles to his doorway. Bobbert's office was claustrophobic, and I hated having to sit in it. Narrow, no windows, with a closet feel. And some pretty unsettling decor. I scanned the professional-looking pictures of him with his family on the desk, and my gaze was drawn, as always, to the dozen or so inexplicable models of dinosaurs. I tried to look away, but I couldn't. A two-foot-tall realistic-looking velociraptor glared from his desk, snout frozen in what I assumed was a terrifying dinosaur war cry. The brachiosaur on the floor beside his wastebasket was a little less intimidating but every bit as ugly. A stegosaurus gawked on the bookshelf in the corner.

"Did you need something?" I asked. A support group?

"Yeah, I do," Bobbert said distractedly, touching the velociraptor's foot. Gross. "Gary got held up, and we need to process some transfers. Take care of that, will you?" Then he turned his back to me and bent over his laptop.

"Do you have names? Locations? Dates? Any additional information would be useful," I said, trying to hold back the snark. It seemed like the brachiosaur was looking at me.

He glanced at me over his shoulder. "Hm? Oh. I don't remember. Let me just add you to the Google Doc, and you can work with that." He smacked the keys for a few seconds. "It won't add you," he said. "Do you have a Google account?"

I hesitated, not wanting to give out a personal email for whatever this was, but sighed and told him anyway.

"Great, you're set," he said. He had started to sweat, once again focused on his screen. I backed out of his office and headed toward the break room for that cup of coffee.

"Hey!" Bobbert yelled, with further wet-fingered snapping.

I leaned back into his office doorframe and narrowed my eyes. "Yes?"

He shrank back in his chair but said, "Now," and gestured in the direction of my desk.

My ears burned, but I walked back to my desk with my empty mug. Now I wasn't caffeinated, and I'd been snapped at like a small dog. And I still had to meet the call-time quota, or my name would be on the board. Again.

I sat back down at my desk with a hmph and pulled my phone out of my bag to shoot off a quick text to Jane. Bobbert is holding the coffee hostage until I complete an inexplicable task.

She wrote back almost immediately. Was that YOU he was snapping at? I thought maybe he was listening to poetry on his headphones or something. More jumping gray dots. I can grab you a cup if you want.

Bless you, I texted back then opened my personal email on my computer, something I never did. Sure enough, there was an invitation to a Google Doc from Robert Ruddy. I clicked on it, trying not to roll my eyes at the ecstatic smile Bobbert was wearing in his little profile picture, and immediately saved a copy of the file to my own Google Drive. I'd been in enough shared documents to know to make a backup. I knew Google Docs saved automatically but also knew it could be a bitch getting back to where I'd been if I messed up, which I was likely to do, given I had zero direction.

The document had about a half dozen names in it with salaries listed and a column for the transfer date and a column for the new location. It looked like these employees were all going to Xavier's more recent office location, but how was I supposed to "process" the transfer?

Another buzz from my phone. So…I got up for coffee and was also summoned by the dino enthusiast. Looks like no caffeine for either of us. Jane again.

Sorry, I texted and turned back to the document, trying not to be too grumpy. I looked for other tabs, embedded formulas, and the document change history for some clue as to what to do when suddenly a hand came out of nowhere and snatched my laptop computer off my desk and snapped it shut.

I turned around in anger to find myself looking up at a flushed Gary. "That's enough, Ms. Blair," he said through gritted teeth.

"What? Bobbert snapped a request—" I began before Gary cut me off.

"I'll talk with Bob," he said shortly. "I'm going to have to take this," he said, gesturing to my computer.

"You can't take my computer," I said, but he had already turned and was marching back to his office with my laptop gripped under his arm.

What the hell was that about?

Chapter 25

On contentious ground,
I would hurry up my rear.

—SUN TZU, *THE ART OF WAR*

MY IMAGINED DIRECTIS COLONY WAS REAL. AND IT WAS HERE, crowded inside the large glass-walled lobby of Trimaran Corp, to the clear dismay of the receptionist at the main desk.

Mary-Anne Dubler was front and center—high-waisted jeans, round glasses, and beaded glasses chain. She blinked owlishly at me. "This isn't going to interfere with the three days' pay they gave me, is it? I don't have that money anymore." Trisha reassured her quickly, while I took in the Barbies to my left, who were pretending this was a happy reunion, chatting and hugging and gossiping. Burned-Out Barbie had a flask in her hand. Behind them was Nancy, along with Geraldine and several other faces, some of whom I recognized and some I didn't. Jane was manning the door to the lobby. She looked great. Simple black-and-white work clothes, but with a flashy Betsey Johnson necklace for flair.

Beside me, Trisha smiled encouragingly and squeezed my hand. "There're at least thirty people here," she murmured.

I squeezed her hand back. "I know. Maybe after this, we'll all be able to move on with our lives," I said.

"Yeah." She gestured around the lobby. "This actually looks like a pretty nice place to work."

I stared at her as if she had two heads. "Are you serious?"

She nodded. "Totally. But Jane had the same reaction you did. Said she'd rather pull off her own fingernails. So dramatic."

She and I were both dressed professionally. I was in pin-striped, straight-leg pants with a button-down shirt under a soft V-neck sweater. Trisha had on a black blouse and scarf, and I grinned as I snuck a look at her feet. Little wedge-heeled booties. Ass-kicking shoes. It didn't matter, I told myself, if Mary-Anne looked homeless or Nancy hadn't bothered to brush her hair. They'd been through a lot. Trisha, Jane, and I looked put together, and we were here to speak for them.

Out of the corner of my eye, I saw the receptionist waving her hand in the air from her seat at her computer. I made my way over to her.

"Is Mr. Dyer ready to see us now?" I asked.

"He's been called into a meeting. We're going to have to reschedule. All of you," she said. "Who exactly *are* all of you?" she asked, glancing at the ragtag group of people crammed into the lobby.

I looked her over. She was likely midforties, slightly round, and had shoulder-length brown hair. Her eyes had a scared look, as if not usually confronted with the chaos I'd brought. The name on her desk plate read *Doris Jenson*. "Directis 'employees' that Brenn really should meet. I appreciate your help, Doris," I said. "It's important."

Brenn Dyer, the CFO of Trimaran, was busy. I was willing to concede to that. But too busy to spare a couple of minutes? A few minutes now would save him untold minutes later.

There was a commotion behind us, and Doris and I both turned. Cheryl, who used to make cookies for the office and had been knocked on her ass during the wheely chair race, had pushed her way into the lobby. She marched straight over to Geraldine. I didn't hear what they were saying, but they were nose to nose, and it looked pretty contentious (maybe the altercation during the Office Olympics? The need for a rabies vaccine? It honestly could have been anything), and Doris gasped. She grabbed the phone receiver and punched a key for one of the interoffice lines. "We need a security presence in the main lobby, stat."

I shrugged. She probably wasn't wrong. I had thought the visual impact of a room full of "ghosts" would stress to Brenn the importance of taking this information seriously, but perhaps it hadn't been one of my best ideas.

Doris grabbed the phone and made another call. "Hello? With whom am I speaking?" A pause. "Yes, it's nice to speak with you as well, Mr. Ruddy."

Wait, she was calling Bobbert?

"Just wanted to inform the Directis branch that it appears some of your employees have gone rogue—"

"What? No—" I started, but Doris turned her back.

"Please come and remove them from the lobby of Trimaran. Thank you and bye," she said and glanced at me nervously.

I spun on my heel, almost running into Geraldine and Trisha.

"What's the holdup?" Geraldine barked at me.

I gestured to Doris. "Apparently Dyer needs to reschedule, and she just called security *and* Bobbert—"

"Oh, for God's sake," Geraldine snapped. She leaned over the counter and snatched Doris's employee badge off the desk before Doris could react. Then she marched straight past the reception desk and toward the glass doors that led into the main office. She scanned the badge then yanked one of the doors open. "Brenn Dyer!" she bellowed. "Get your ass out here!"

Behind her, Doris gasped again, and Trisha offered helpfully, "Sun Tzu says if the enemy leaves a door open, you must rush in."

I turned to her. "I swear, you talk to Sun Tzu way more than you talk to any of us."

"Not as much as you talk to old Latin dudes."

I nodded. "Touché."

On the other side of the glass wall, employees were looking over the tops of their gray cubicles and into the lobby to see what was going on. Who made walls totally of glass and then stuck people in cubicles? Geraldine had time to yell another particularly loud "Brenn!" before Doris had gotten over her shock, shot out from behind her desk, and grabbed Geraldine's arm to drag her back into the lobby.

The lobby had gotten quiet. I glanced behind me and saw two men in blue security uniforms ambling down the glass hallway on the right. They didn't appear to be in a hurry. Jogging down the left hall, however, was a clean-shaven man with short dark hair in a button-down shirt, dress pants, and dark blue tie with no jacket. My heart fluttered with hope. Was that the mysterious Brenn? As he got closer, the hope faded. Surely not. This guy looked like he was in middle school and was already winded. Another reason the glass walls weren't the best idea; it gave us plenty of time to watch him run out of steam, and by the time he reached the door, I knew everyone in the lobby was thinking the same thing I was: this guy wouldn't last a day in the Office Olympics. He and the two security officers reached the door at the same time. One of the officers opened it for him, and the man stuck his head in the lobby. "What can I do for you?" he asked.

"Go get Brenn Dyer," Geraldine snapped at him. "Chop, chop," she said, clapping her hands.

He smiled at her but didn't look amused. "I'm Brenn Dyer," he said.

"Then go get Brenn Dyer Senior," she shot back.

"Geraldine, hush," I growled.

She looked over her shoulder and glared at me. "But he's twelve," she said loudly.

The security guards looked at each other. This wasn't good. I opened my mouth to respond, but Brenn Dyer waved me off. "My father is retired and currently in Boca Raton," he told Geraldine. "His name is Roger. Again, is there something *I* can do for you?"

Geraldine sniffed, but I stepped forward and inserted myself slightly in front of her. "Mr. Dyer, we appreciate you coming out here. Would you have a few minutes to speak with us? We won't keep you long."

The smile he gave me was real. But damn, Geraldine was right. No one would promote a twelve-year-old, even a tall one, to head a company. Right? Was this some sort of weird form of nepotism?

He came into the lobby, brushing off Doris's fluttering protests and taking my hand in a warm, firm grip. "And you are?" he asked.

"Vanessa Blair," I said. "I recently worked for Directis. And I've brought with me some of your current employees." I gestured around the room.

"I suppose I have a few minutes," he said, glancing at his watch.

"Great," I said. "There is a serious situation at Directis. Embezzlement, fraud, identity—"

"*Stop!*" A loud voice rang out. I spun toward the entrance just as Mary-Anne let out a little gasp. Standing just inside the lobby doors was Xavier. Marcus had gotten him here just in time.

He looked like he'd aged a decade since I'd last seen him. His clothes were disheveled, there were circles under his eyes, and his gray hair looked to be newly thinning. To my relief, it seemed his mangy foot had received some sort of medical treatment and had been wrapped in gauze and taped. He still had his little knee scooter. His untraumatized foot was bare.

"Oh good, his turkey bite healed," Trisha whispered. "I hope they fixed the bladder disease, too."

Xavier's eyes scanned the lobby, and I watched his horror grow until his gaze came to rest on me. That horror turned to anger then to purple-faced hatred. "You," he sputtered.

I did the only thing I could think of; I gave a little wave. "Yep, the one with the face," I said.

Xavier hobbled slowly up to us, his knee scooter squeaking, and he looked straight at Brenn. "Don't listen to a word she says. She was fired. She's out for revenge. And don't look directly at that face," he stage-whispered.

I couldn't help it. "Seriously? Still?" I asked. "Have you tried therapy?"

Brenn looked back and forth between the two of us, his gaze coming to rest on Xavier's bare toes.

From across the room, Geraldine boomed, "Hey, Xavier, did you get that rabies taken care of? You allowed to be out of quarantine?"

Brenn drew back.

"Mr. Dyer, Xavier Adams has been defrauding Trimaran out of hundreds of thousands of dollars. Everyone in this lobby, except me"—I rolled my eyes—"is still on your payroll as a current employee at a non-existent satellite office, but we were all fired, some as long as a year ago. Xavier's been collecting the paychecks and making it appear that Directis is growing. He's stealing from you."

Xavier's head whipped around, and he shouted a mostly incoherent diatribe, the gist of which was that I was out to sabotage him, there were phantom cats in the conference room, his service animal had been stolen, a meeting had been bombed, and someone had trained a wild turkey to attack.

"He's lost his mind," I said to Brenn.

Geraldine smacked a folder down on the reception counter. "Proof of the embezzlement with the transactions and account numbers, going all the way back."

Trisha narrowed her eyes at Xavier. "You really should shred your documents before you ask an employee on probation to clean out the bins. And I take back what I said in my thousand-word essay. I've given thought to the kind of person I want to be, and it's someone with a dark soul, all the way."

I loved her so much in that moment.

The ugly purple flush came back to Xavier's cheeks. "Are you serious? You guys think you're a group of loveable underdogs who'll win against me because you've got pluck?"

"This isn't *The Mighty Ducks*," Jane said, speaking for the first time.

Brenn grabbed Geraldine's folder and frantically flipped through the pages. His hands shook, and he loosened his tie. He grabbed his phone from his back pocket and tapped in a number. "We need a forensic accountant, stat."

From out of nowhere, Mary-Anne bumped up against Brenn. "Excuse me. I'm Mary-Anne Dubler, and they're about to foreclose on my house, so if I can get the money you've been paying him for me not working, that'd be great."

Brenn looked at her with distaste, and I felt a fierce wave of protectiveness for this woman I barely knew. "This is Mary-Anne. She was told she was fired almost a year ago by Xavier Adams. She can't find work and has lost her family and self-esteem, while Xavier has been collecting her checks. Real lives have been destroyed over this."

Mary-Anne's eyes filled with tears as she blinked at me, but before Brenn could respond, the door to the outside swung open again, and Bobbert trotted in. Xavier's eyes lit on him, and he pointed. "It was him! It was all him," he said viciously.

"What was me?" Bobbert asked politely.

"He's the one who did this to you," Xavier yelled at Brenn. "He has no respect for Trimaran or Directis. I just figured out he was embezzling and came here to tell you."

"What is he talking about?" Bobbert asked.

"He's saying you're responsible for the ghost employees," I told him.

He gasped. "I don't even know what that means!" His eyes focused on me. "You look familiar. Do I know you?"

"I worked for you for almost two years!" I exclaimed. "Of course, you know me."

Xavier looked up at Bobbert and scowled. "Don't pretend you're not responsible for the ghosts."

"I'm Catholic!" he protested.

"Quiet!" Brenn Dyer suddenly yelled. He gestured to Xavier, Bobbert, and me. "You three," he said, his voice low and hard. "Come with me."

I nodded and immediately followed Brenn to the glass doors leading into the office area. He gestured for the younger of the two security guards to come with us. Xavier and Bobbert hadn't moved. "Come on!" Brenn demanded again, and they trudged after us, Xavier's scooter squeaking all the way.

At the end of the hall, we entered an office with a four-foot sand-pattern pendulum on the floor, lots of bamboo, and a couple of large, potted ferns. It was like magazine-quality Zen. I would have loved an office like this when I was in middle school.

Brenn sat behind a teak desk and gestured to one of the two leather armchairs facing him. "It's okay; I'll stand," I told him. "I think they need to sit more than I do." The security guard stood behind Brenn's desk and crossed his arms over his chest. He looked bored.

Xavier and Bobbert each sank into an armchair. Xavier positioned his little knee wheelie in front of him. He stared daggers at me but looked away quickly when I stared back. Bobbert seemed close to tears.

Xavier leaned forward and held out his hand. "Brenn, my man, there's been a terrible misunderstanding—"

Brenn immediately pulled his hands into his chest. "No need to shake hands, thank you," he said. "A forensic accountant is on the way, so this will be your only opportunity to explain yourselves before I turn this all over to the authorities." He steepled his fingers.

"She did it," Xavier said immediately, pointing at me.

I snorted. "When would I have been able to do it? When I was dressed as a pilgrim for Thanksgiving week? In between meeting my ridiculous phone goals and mandatory after-hours ladder golf? I spent every day in that office living the 'dweam,' Xavier. I couldn't have pulled this off if I'd wanted to."

"I thought you said Bob was responsible," Brenn said in a cold tone.

"They're in it together," Xavier corrected himself.

Bobbert looked back and forth between Xavier and me. "Come again?"

Brenn focused on me. "What is your involvement in this?"

"None, directly. I was recently let go from Directis because Xavier didn't like my face."

Brenn blinked slowly. "Excuse me?"

"Well, just look at it," Xavier hissed.

I sighed loudly. "And I noticed a pattern. So many people were being fired from the Directis branch, but their photos were never taken down from the website. New ones were being added, however. And Xavier was raising the goals of the remaining employees past what was possible. So I looked into it further. The fired employees haven't been removed from the payroll. They'd been 'transferred' to a nonexistent satellite office with a separate accounting system. The documents in front of you show their paychecks are being deposited into a single bank account. And some of your 'current' employees are in your lobby, happy to explain that they haven't worked for Directis in some time. As Mary-Anne will tell you, they haven't received any of the money allegedly paid to them."

"How did you get this paperwork?" Brenn demanded.

"I didn't get the paperwork. It was given to me," I said evasively. "And the rest of it is in the process of being destroyed, so I suggest you look into it quickly." I was 90 percent sure going through someone's garbage was legal, but it was better not to risk it.

"She's a thief," Xavier blurted. "She needs to be arrested."

Bobbert looked alarmed. "Wow, Xavier, I know you've been going through a rough time, but you didn't do that, did you?"

Brenn spoke softly. "A scam like this couldn't be done by one person unless it was someone in payroll. Who handles your payroll?"

Xavier's eyes lit up. "Gary Gallard!" he exclaimed. "This is all *his* fault! He handles all the money, and I don't have any idea how he does it. I guess this is what you get for trusting peons." He put his hand on his cheek dramatically. "How could Gary and Bob have done this to us?"

I rolled my eyes again. "One more thing," I said to Brenn. "Don't go to the address of Directis's other office unless you're in the mood for doughnuts."

Xavier let out a little strangled sound. He shot me a look of fury and mouthed, "I hate you," before suddenly shifting forward in his chair and lunging for me.

"Are you kidding me?" I yelped as I sidestepped his "attack."

"Ross, get the real police in here," Brenn ordered. The security guard pushed Xavier back into his chair. Then he turned his back to us and put the phone to his ear.

There was a sudden commotion outside the door. I turned to see a half dozen people I knew only too well pushing their way into the office.

I squeezed my eyes shut tight. "Mom?" I asked. "Why are you here?"

She smiled brightly at me, dressed in her typical uniform of jeans and a button-down shirt. No spy gear today, thank goodness. "Trisha filled me in on the plan over coffee. Where have you been keeping your friend Geraldine? She's delightful," my mom said.

"This isn't happening," I whispered to myself.

Behind her, Geraldine barked, "I joined the Bridge Brigade, Vanessa. Your mom's a lot cooler than you are."

I'd imagined how this meeting would go many times, but none of my scenarios had been like this. "How did you get in?"

Linda's cheeks turned pink, and Tammy piped up, "Our girl Linda used to, you know, have a little side action with Arnold, the security guard in the lobby. He let us walk right in."

"It's not side action if we're both single," Linda protested, her purple lipstick contrasting with her cheeks. "More of a friends-with-benefits situation."

"Please wait in the lobby, Mom. I've got this," I said in a low voice, the tone she knew meant I was serious.

She pushed her way farther into the room, Linda, Tammy, and Sharon on her heels. "I'm sorry, Vanessa," my mom said. "I know you don't like us meddling. But technically we still haven't broken the twenty-foot rule." She paused to take a breath.

"Those were the people I saw in the bushes outside of Directis," Xavier said, pointing. "They're spies." Brenn looked like he'd swallowed something bad.

"I tried to find Excalibur's mother to let her know what her son had been up to," my mom told Brenn. "Unfortunately, I couldn't track her down. We're pretty sure he's operating under an assumed name." She looked at her friends conspiratorially then smiled brightly at me. "But I *did* find this delightful woman who agreed to come with us." She stepped to the side and gestured toward the back of the group.

A svelte blond in a Kate Spade dress pushed forward. My eyes widened at the same time as Xavier gasped.

"Dawn!" he said in a high-pitched voice. "What're *you* doing here?"

She looked better rested than she had on the porch. Her eyes met mine, and she nodded, a brief acknowledgment that we'd shared a moment. Then she leaned toward Xavier and looked him dead in the eye. "You shouldn't have taken Haiku," she said, her voice low and threatening.

"He's been stolen! I don't know what happened," Xavier pleaded. "I don't even want—"

Geraldine coughed from her position behind my mother.

Dawn's eyes narrowed. "All bets are off, Xavier," she hissed. She looked at Brenn. "I'm not sure what information you need, but I'm happy to answer any questions about Xavier's activities over the past decade. There are also a dozen filing cabinets in my home that might be useful to you. I'm granting you full access. You won't need a warrant." She threw Xavier a fierce look.

I couldn't help it. I had to ask before Xavier got arrested and I lost my chance forever. "Out of all these women that hate you, how did *I* become Medusa?"

"Who?" he asked distractedly.

"I still don't know what's happening here," Bobbert muttered. He turned to Brenn, who hadn't moved during the whole exchange. "I've been going through a divorce, a separation, really—" he started to confide, but Xavier interrupted.

"That's me, Bob, you got us confused."

"No," Bobbert protested, "my wife moved out—"

Xavier cut him off again. "No, I moved out, and my wife stayed in the house—"

"Oh my god," I broke in. "You can both go through divorces at the same time." I turned to Brenn. "I think my contribution is over. Are we good? If you have any other questions, I'm sure Dawn will have more information than I do."

"Happy to assist," Dawn said, still glaring at Xavier.

I pushed my way through the crowd of people in the room and

down the hall to a full view of the chaos in the lobby. Former Directis employees, security officers, police, and of course, Doris, who was clapping her hands and trying to bring order. I felt a kinship to her in that moment, trying to bring order to chaos, but it quickly faded as I glanced behind me. Nope, I still had it worse. I was the mother duck to the saddest-looking ducklings. Following behind me single file were Brenn, my mother, Linda, Tammy, Sharon, Geraldine, Dawn, and finally, Xavier scooting along and Bobbert walking closely with the security guard.

I exhaled slowly and held open the glass door to the lobby as they all trudged through. "Hey, Arnold." Linda giggled at the older-looking guard at the door. He winked at her.

"Xavier Adams and Bob Ruddy, over here," Brenn called to the four police officers in the crowd in the lobby. The officers immediately handcuffed them and read them their Miranda rights.

Xavier sputtered through the whole thing. "You've got the wrong guy. It's just Bob. And Gary. And her, over there." He tried to point at me, but his hands were cuffed.

"Just shut up," Dawn hissed at him.

"This affects you, too," he snarled back. "How do you think we're able to afford that house and all your trips?"

"You think I want money you stole from Mom Jeans over there? I'd rather ask my father," she cried.

She leaned in and growled something I couldn't hear in his ear. I tried to just take in the scene. This guy, who had humiliated me and my friends and tried to trash my future, was being publicly arrested. In front of former employees, his boss, his soon-to-be ex-wife, and at least one coworker. Mary-Anne and a couple of the Barbies were snapping pictures on their phones. This would be all over social media in under an hour, if it wasn't already.

Weirdly, seeing someone else humiliated, even if they deserved it, didn't feel awesome. Especially when they were handcuffed and on a knee scooter with a clearly untreated narcissistic personality disorder. But it *was* satisfying. I felt my lips curve into a small smile. But something was missing. Sharing the achievement with Trisha and Jane.

I scanned the crowd for them and found them with the Bridge Brigade and Geraldine, avidly watching the chaos from the side of the room. I pulled my phone out of my pocket as I made my way over. I'd set it to Do Not Disturb when I'd arrived earlier. There were a few missed texts from my mom and Marcus. Perhaps I should have checked it earlier.

"Jane!" someone yelled. I turned and saw Marcus rush in, carrying a blast of cold air with him. His hair had come down, brushing against his chin, and he'd clearly been running. "Nobody touch Jane!" he bellowed.

Jane cleared her throat and ran a hand nervously down her sleeve. "Over here, Marcus. Nobody's touching me," she said, her voice higher than usual. It always surprised me to see her transform from her normally confident self to someone so self-conscious when Marcus was around.

"Thank goodness," Marcus panted as he made his way over. "After I got Xavier to come over, Bob/Rob took off, and I couldn't get ahold of Vanessa. Then these images started showing up on Instagram." He pulled out his phone and turned the screen so we could see it. Xavier with his knee scooter. Dawn growling at Xavier. Mary-Anne taking selfies with the Barbies. Jane in the background appearing to yell at someone.

"But I'm fine," Jane said.

"While you were meeting here, Gary took off through the back door. I have no idea where he went. He and Xavier are dangerous," Marcus said seriously. "I heard him on the phone, mentioning something about identity theft and possible past warrants. I didn't catch it all."

My mom glanced over at her bridge friends. "We knew about the assumed names. *Excalibur* and *Xavier* are both ridiculous things to call a child. His name is probably Ronald or something."

"But why would anyone hurt me?" Jane asked. "Nessa and Trisha have done more dirty work than I have."

"I just—" Marcus blew out a breath. "I like you, okay? I was worried. I have anxiety." He paused again and squared his shoulders. "I would like the opportunity to focus that anxiety on you," he said, staring at her earnestly.

A tremulous smile lit up Jane's face. "That's the most romantic thing anyone's ever said to me, Marcus. I would be honored to be the object of your anxiety."

His face broke into a huge grin. He looked over at me with relief, and I gave him a thumbs-up. *Go Marcus.* "Anyone mind if I steal Jane for a date?" he asked.

"Don't bring her back," Geraldine barked.

My mom tittered. "Your friend is hilarious," she told me.

Marcus tentatively took Jane's hand in his own. "See you later!" she said brightly, and they walked out hand in hand.

Behind me someone sniffled. Tammy and Linda, who had both been quiet through the whole exchange, looked very moved.

"That was beautiful," Trisha sighed.

"Nothing more romantic than mental illness," Geraldine said sarcastically.

Doris cleared her throat from her place behind the desk. "We all need to get back to work, if you don't mind," she said loudly.

"She's right, we need to go," I said to the group and led them out into the parking lot. "I'll catch up with each of you later," I said as I headed over to my Jeep, wondering about how many potential lawsuits could arise from all of this. For anyone who hadn't gotten a job after checking that "FIRED" box on their applications.

Trisha was parked near me, so we walked together as my mom and her friends went back to Sharon's minivan. "Is it just me, or do you feel exhausted and relieved?"

"Not just you," I told her. "It's all someone else's sleepless night now."

"Totally," she answered. "But overall, it went okay. Definitely could've been worse."

I let out a laugh. "And better. Definitely could have been better."

Chapter 26

A kingdom that has once been destroyed can
never come again into being.

—SUN TZU, *THE ART OF WAR*

THE ENTIRE DAY, AND ALL THE PEOPLE, REALLY WORE ME OUT. WHEN
I got home, I kept the lights low in the apartment and went straight
for the shower. I turned the water on steaming hot and stood under it
for a long time, letting it relax me and drain away the tension and the
embarrassment. A couple of kittens sat at the bathroom door, meowing
loudly, as if warning me away from the water. I scrubbed my hair and
tried to tune them out and enjoy the moment. I'd been vindicated. Sort
of. The guy who had fired me for something that was inherent about me
had been fired himself. Sort of. At the very least, I'd accomplished what
I set out to do. Xavier would never again keep me, or anyone else, from
getting a job. And I didn't have to check that "FIRED" box now, right? I
paused. Right?

When I got out of the shower, I made sure the kittens were fed and
scooped; then I slipped on a robe and took my laptop into the living
room. Now that I'd made it this far in my plan to take control of my
life, it was time to tackle the next step. I spent the rest of the evening
meticulously creating a PowerPoint presentation that would, hopefully,
be impossible to resist. I'd been applying for shelter grants for months,
and the bulk of them had started to come in, which was going to be key.
I'd asked Danielle to add me to the board meeting agenda for tomorrow,

and I wanted to be ready. When it was time to knock off, I flopped down on my queen-size bed.

"It's your last meal before you get spayed tomorrow," I told the kittens. My phone dinged, and I grabbed it from the bedside table. The banner alert flashed *Email from Job and Family Services* across the screen. I sat up and opened the message. There were a lot of words, but my eyes focused halfway down the screen, where, in all capital letters, were the words BENEFITS ALLOWED. I let out a deep breath as I scanned the rest. I'd been approved for half of my original salary, and it was enough to cover rent while I looked for another job. I could collect it until I received a job offer or the allowed amount ran out. I leaned my head back on the pillow and gazed at the ceiling. All in all, Trisha was right. It could have been a worse day. Only one thing would have made it better. I reached over to the nightstand and picked up the cat charm Carter had given me. Was there truly a way to explain everything to him? I put the little figure back and grabbed my phone again. If I didn't do it now, I might never get the courage.

I dialed his number and held my breath until a familiar deep voice said, "Hello?"

"Hi, it's Vanessa," I said quickly. "Please don't say anything. I just wanted to let you know something. I'm lucky to have a lot of people in my life who care about me." It was the most diplomatic way I could put it. "My mom and her friends felt bad that I'd been fired and wanted to 'help.' They made that conspiracy wall display you saw. And when Trisha bugged the office, Duo hid the transmitter in my laundry room, so I couldn't turn it off. You shouldn't hold it against her, though," I rushed on. "Once she's older, she'll probably just become lethargic and obese like most cats, so it should be fine."

"Vanessa," he said, but I cut him off.

"Anyway, that's all I wanted to say. I like you, and I couldn't leave things with you thinking I'm someone I'm not. Thanks for coming to my TED Talk—bye," I said and hung up before I could embarrass myself further.

I flopped back on the pillow and tried to put it all out of my mind. I'd done what I could. I stretched my arms over my head as the kittens came from their hiding places to snuggle against my legs. I didn't bother to change out of my robe or dry my hair. I fell asleep on top of the covers and slept deeply, straight through the night, for the first time in ages.

———

The next morning I took down the photos on the crime wall, and the index cards, and unwound the red spiderweb of yarn that stretched from the center outward. It took a while, since the kittens grappled for the string and hung from it whenever I tried to roll it back up into a ball. They were getting so big. I piled them all into my lap and looked down at their sweet little furry faces. "Your vet visit is this afternoon. Our time together is coming to an end. And you've been very difficult," I told them seriously. All five of them looked up at me and, one by one, began to purr. I sighed and relented. "But I love you guys. And I'm going to miss you." I leaned my head on the back of the couch and told myself not to get sad. Things were okay. It was the end of an era all the way around, and I was going to get some control back in my life. And one of my little fosters would be getting the best home possible, and I could take credit for that. I gathered them all together and placed them in their carrier for our last trip to the shelter.

The weather outside was getting colder, so I threw a blanket over their carrier to keep them warm. When I got to the shelter, there were about a half dozen cars in the parking lot. They didn't open for adoptions until noon, but it looked like the board of directors had arrived, as well as Danielle and the shelter veterinarian.

"Vanessa! How are you?" Danielle asked when I entered the tiny lobby. "Our girls ready for surgery?"

I nodded. "Nothing to eat or drink today, so they should be good." I felt like a giant next to her in the tiny lobby. She had such a big personality that sometimes I forgot she was only about five feet tall.

"Great!" She took the carrier from me. "Are you sad to see them go?"

I opened my mouth to speak then stopped. Was I actually going to get emotional over this? I swallowed hard. "I mean…yeah. I am. They're absolute hellions. But they're *my* hellions."

She nodded sympathetically. "Fostering is the hardest. I'm going to take them into the back to get prepped, but you can go on ahead into the cat room. The board members are already in there having coffee."

She went down the hallway to the vet room, and I watched the carrier until it disappeared through the door. Then I shook my head. I was being ridiculous. It was time to pitch my case. I turned the other way and entered the cat room. A few women and two men were already seated, discussing a recent adoption event. I waved hello and set up my laptop. We made small talk until Danielle entered a few minutes later.

"What happened to the white cat that always greets me?" I asked her.

She grinned. "He was adopted a couple of days ago. He charmed the pants off an older couple who stopped in to donate some food. They took him home the same day."

"That's awesome," I said. "He was like the little welcoming committee here."

"Yeah," she agreed. "Everything about shelter work is bittersweet, isn't it?"

I nodded. "But it's worth it."

She sat next to another board member. "I'm glad you feel that way.

As you know, we've been grateful you've been able to help us even though your job was so demanding." The others nodded in agreement.

"Thank you," I said. "I've always tried to make time for the shelter. What we do here is important, and so much of what I've been doing, well, isn't." I stood straighter and addressed the group. "I'd like to change that." I turned on the screen and began the PowerPoint. "As you know, in my capacity as a fundraising volunteer, I've done my best to increase financial resources. I'm happy to announce that several of the grants I've applied for have come through."

I flipped the next slide, featuring a spreadsheet and graph. "We've received funds for these areas of shelter operations," I said, pointing. "This frees up our resources for other areas. There are a few different ways to allocate the funds, but I wanted to put forth a proposal. The grant money allows the possibility of creating a permanent position for a fundraising and marketing director. This position has the potential to increase the current revenue stream significantly." I flipped through the next few slides and detailed how the plan could change the cash issues we were experiencing. "I believe that, given the opportunity, I would be able to double our revenue if hired into this position."

Danielle squirmed in her seat and bounced a little as I finished up my presentation. "Vanessa, this is so exciting!" she exclaimed. "The board has been talking about needing a director of fundraising and marketing for a while now. We need someone focused on fundraising and events, who can address the media—who can increase our presence in the community. And you've found us additional money to do it."

I smiled at her enthusiasm. "Thank you for taking the time to listen. I left copies of the grant paperwork in the shelter office, and I look forwarding to hearing from you."

They were already murmuring among themselves when I let myself out and trudged back to the car. Putting myself out there was hard, and so was leaving behind a bunch of furry monsters.

I'd opened the driver's side door when Danielle came bounding out of the shelter toward me.

"Vanessa!" she cried. Her excitement was contagious. "You did great! I told the board that if we didn't jump on this, you were going to get some sort of boring corporate job and we'd have to rely on your midnight contributions until you got sick of us and quit."

"Thanks." I grinned.

"They don't know how we got so lucky with you in the first place. The vote was unanimous. We would like you to be the face of the shelter."

"The...face...of the shelter?" I asked softly. "You want my face?"

"Of course we do!" she exclaimed. "I'm going to go through the paperwork you left and realign the finances. Afterward, I'll email you an official offer, with the responsibilities and benefits package, and we can meet next week to go over all the details and make sure you're comfortable with it."

"The funding doesn't come in for another three weeks," I said, feeling dizzy at the possibility.

"We can aim for a start date at the first of the month, then," she said.

"Are you kidding?" I asked. "This is my dream job. Thank you, Danielle. Thank you for doing this for me."

She laughed brightly. "This is all your doing. Because of you, I think we can finally afford you."

I felt a lump form in my throat and blinked rapidly. *Be cool*, I told myself. *This is potentially your new boss.*

She turned back toward the shelter door. "I have to go check on your Latin litter. Does Monday work for you to discuss a formal offer?"

"Absolutely," I said. "And please let me know how they're doing."

She gave me a quick happy wave and hurried back into the building. I sat a second longer, savoring the moment. I smiled when I thought of all the effort to get unemployment payments, only to have a prospect so quickly. A spring of happiness welled in my chest.

Chapter 27

Anger may in time change to gladness;
vexation may be succeeded by content.

—SUN ZHU, *THE ART OF WAR*

DANIELLE TEXTED THE NEXT MORNING TO LET ME KNOW THE LATIN litter had all done well with their surgeries and were recuperating.

I texted Trisha and Jane. Uno through Quinque are at the shelter for adoption, I said.

How're you holding up? Trisha.

Eh, I said.

Let's stop by to see them for a minute, Trisha suggested. Maybe that would help, Nessa. We couldn't have done this without them.

Says who? Jane.

I'm so proud of us, Trisha texted, ignoring her. We made the world a better place. We're like the Powerpuff Girls.

I ignored their jabber as I got dressed. But I appreciated the sentiment. It would be nice to stop by the shelter and see the kittens one last time. Besides, I was excited about the offer Danielle and I had talked about.

When I got to the shelter, Trisha was walking the length of the room, pausing every so often to coo at the cats and tell them how pretty they were. She was very careful to allow hand sniffing before stroking any ears. Jane sat awkwardly on the patio chair, looking as though she wasn't sure she wanted to touch anything. Cats were coming down from their ledges and beds to sniff at her pants and shoes, all jumping back in unison whenever she shifted in her seat. Finally, one jumped into her lap and rolled onto its back. Jane eyed it nervously. "That's a trap," she said, pointing at the belly. "If I touch it, he's going to kick me."

The cat twitched and purred, looking up at her. Jane slowly reached her hand down to the soft fur on the cat's stomach. It immediately wrapped its front paws around her arm and rabbit kicked her enthusiastically. She jerked her hand back. "This is why I don't do cats," she told me. "They're weird, and I don't understand them."

"Sounds to me like you understand them perfectly," I said.

"They just need love, Jane," Trisha said, reaching under a cabinet to pet a small black cat with white feet. "I love you," she told him.

"When I want someone to love me, I don't kick them," Jane answered.

I went over to the large cage my kittens were recovering in. "Hello, you little weirdos," I told them. One of them bit the bars while another tried to squeeze her little head through an opening to get to me. I opened the cage, and Duo immediately climbed out and onto my shoulder.

I nodded to Trisha, where she was crouched on the floor trying to coax a little tuxedo cat out from under the cabinet. Once he emerged, she gently folded him in her arms. "Found one you like?" I asked her.

"I don't want to put him back," she said.

"Is he your child now?" Jane asked her.

"I like you," Trisha told him softly. Then she looked up at me. "I'm still unemployed, so it's not time to add a new family member."

"Mommy just wants to give you a better life," Jane told the cat.

Just then, the door to the cat room opened, and I looked up. Carter. He must have stopped by to pick up Duo. My heart rate kicked up, and the awkwardness threatened to swallow me. "Hi," I said, going for a neutral tone. "Here for Duo?"

He carefully closed the door behind him to keep any cats from escaping and nodded. "*Danielle said to stop by so she could finalize everything.*"

"She's getting a little chunky. She's gained three ounces since her last visit," I said, my voice light. I didn't make eye contact as I disentangled her from my shoulder and thrust the thrashing little potbellied kitten at him.

His face immediately melted. "Hi, itty floof," he cooed at her. She immediately streaked up past his elbow, her claws digging into his leather jacket and leaving scratch marks as she climbed her way up to his shoulder. I cringed.

Jane cleared her throat from the patio chair. She was looking back and forth between Carter and me with extreme interest. "Hi there, I'm Jane," she said loudly.

Carter smiled and immediately reached out his hand to shake hers. "I'm Carter," he said. "Vanessa has mentioned you a few times." Duo dug her claws farther into his jacket to steady herself as he bent forward.

Jane looked at me sideways as Trisha piped up, "I'm Trisha."

"It's nice to meet you, Trisha," he said, smiling at her. "Vanessa told me you haven't been having the easiest time lately. I'm sorry to hear that."

"Things are getting better," Jane said happily. "You're the unemployment dude, right?"

"That kitten is ruining your jacket," I interrupted, wishing fervently that they would stop talking. And that Duo could keep her manners until the adoption papers were finalized. I'd told Trisha and Jane the basics about what had happened with Carter, but that was it.

"It's okay," he said, scritching her chin. "She just missed me." She stretched her tiny pink nose up to his face then headbutted his cheek. "It's okay if I can't have nice things," he told her.

As if the awkwardness couldn't get worse, Trisha's phone rang. She pulled it out, grinned, and set the phone on speaker. "Hi, Kathy!" she said. "I'm with Vanessa right now."

"Wait, what?" I asked. "Mom?"

"Oh, hi, honey!" she yelled through the crackled static. "Am I on speaker? I love your friend Trisha. We have so much in common. We have plans later!"

Trisha's cheeks colored a little, but she didn't look nearly embarrassed enough.

"Jane's here and Vanessa's friend Carter is, too. We're at the animal shelter," Trisha said.

"Of course you are," my mother sighed. "Did you say *Carter*? Is he the one that got scared by my strategy board in Vanessa's living room? Carter, sweetie, it's Vanessa's mother, Kathy. Sorry about the murder wall, that was my bad," she yelled. "Vanessa doesn't have any friends, so I got keys to her place for my girls, and we started meeting there. She freaked out about the wall, too. And the stalking. I personally don't get what the big deal is. We got the idea from that show *Just Around the Coroner* on cable."

Inadvertently, my eyes drifted up to Carter's. He was looking directly at me. "The stalking?" he asked.

"Yes! Stalking Excalibur." My mother sounded delighted. "I didn't bug the office, but—"

"That was me," Trisha inserted proudly.

"We tried to get Vanessa involved in the espionage, and she always threw a fit and got mad," my mom shouted. "She doesn't take risks! I raised her better than that."

"That's not true," I interjected. "Xavier's been arrested, and all the evidence we gave Trimaran was legal. And I created, funded, and pitched the idea of my dream job to the shelter board, and convinced them to hire me. So you're wrong, Mom," I said, leaning closer to Trisha's phone. "I do stand up for myself. And I take control of my life." No matter how embarrassing.

"Congratulations about the job, Vanessa. *Acta non verba*. This is what you wanted," Carter said.

"Thank you," I said. "They asked me to be the face of the shelter."

"I always said you had a great face," he told me, his eyes soft.

"Are they being cute?" my mother shouted through the line. "I wish I could see."

"Yeah, it's cute," Trisha agreed as I tried to melt into the floor. I glanced up at Carter, in time to see a grin on his face before I looked back down quickly, suddenly needing to examine my shoes. Yep, still on my feet.

"Oh good!" my mom exclaimed. "Are you going to be her new boyfriend? She's the best. I know there are things that can take some getting used to, like her obsession with furry animals. I certainly hope you're not allergic. Vanessa's dad can't even be in the same room with—"

"Mom!" I cried.

Carter leaned toward the receiver but kept his eyes on me. "Not currently her boyfriend, but I'm auditioning for the part. And I'm partial to 'furry animals' as well."

She tittered over the line. "Oh no, if you two ever get married, you're going to have a house full of cats."

"My mom likes true crime shows, too," Carter said to me. "Her favorite is *Bridal Showers of Blood*."

"Oh, I haven't tried that one!" My mom said. "Would it be possible to get her phone number so I could—"

I grabbed for Trisha's phone and yelped, "Gotta go, bye!" and thumbed off the call. I busied myself examining the calicos. "This might be the most embarrassed I've ever been in my whole life," I mumbled into their fur.

"See?" Jane exclaimed. "I told you that being fired wouldn't be the most embarrassing moment of your life forever. I was right."

Awesome. Another one of the kittens climbed out of the cage and up Carter's arm.

"How do you tell them apart?" Jane asked him.

"If you look closely, their markings are all different," he said as the other kitten straddled his arm. "My girl here has a little spot on her cheek and longer ears. But the others *do* blend a bit."

"If they didn't lick off the Sharpie, it'd be so much easier," I muttered.

"Septem, Octem, and Novem are particularly hard to distinguish," Carter said.

"That's because they don't exist!" I looked up to find Carter smiling at me. "There're only five."

"Seems like more," Carter said.

"That's only because we're in the cat room and this place is full of calicos. Only five of them are"—the words lodged in my throat—"my rent-a-cats. And you left out the number six."

"That's because *six* in Latin translates to *sex*. I figured you wouldn't do that to a kitten," he said.

I inclined my head. He was right, I would've skipped Sex the kitten. Too easy. "You get extra points for knowing the next numbers in Latin," I said. "I'm impressed."

He looked sideways at me and gave me a slow grin. "I looked it up."

"It seems like more than five when you're drunk, too," Jane broke in.

While Carter bent over to say hi to the kitten on his arm, Jane snuck a glance at me. She gave me a thumbs-up and pointed obviously at Carter. I fought the urge to hide my face. Meeting my friends this early was not a good idea. Yet here I was. Story of my life.

"I don't know exactly what's going on at your former company, but I wanted to let you know that I think it's probably best you never sign anything without consulting a lawyer," Carter said to Trisha and Jane, looking fully at ease with a plumed tail wrapped around his neck and two tiny kittens clinging to him.

"Trisha didn't. Because of the turkey," Jane answered. "I did, though." She shrugged. "I needed the money, and I didn't know I had an option."

"Turkey?" he asked. "Metaphorical?"

"No," I answered.

"Sounds like there's a lot of this story that I haven't heard," Carter said.

"Oh, it's not a big thing. It's just that earlier, there was a turkey and a rabies scare, and some wild raccoons, and—" Jane began.

I sucked in a breath. "I can fill Carter in on what happened if he's interested," I told Jane.

Carter smiled at me and nodded. "I am."

My shoulders felt ten pounds lighter. "Great. *Ad meliora,*" I said. "Toward better things."

"Does she do that a lot?" Carter asked Trisha and Jane.

"All the time. It's like a tic," Jane answered, rolling her eyes.

"*Meliorare* is a verb," I said. "And—"

"We get it," Jane groaned. "Old Latin people knew everything; they were a bunch of smarty-pants."

"Oh, they were," Trisha added helpfully. "I googled them. Maybe their pants weren't quite as smart as Sun Tzu's, but—"

Danielle came in, saving Trisha from being strangled. "I gotta head out, got plans," Trisha said, noticing my look.

"Oh, me, too!" Jane added. "We'll text you later!" They both scooted out the door, leaving me with Carter and Danielle and my embarrassment, which stood like a fourth person in the room.

"Have you thought any more about maybe taking two of them, Carter?" Danielle asked him, oblivious to the tension.

He turned to me speculatively. "Based on your knowledge as Duo's foster mom, would she do better with a friend?"

I paused. "It's usually a good idea to adopt in pairs if that's an option for you. Especially when they're rambunctious. But it's not necessary. I should probably head out, too," I said, as I edged toward the door.

"I'll walk you," he said. "Be right back, Danielle." She smiled and waved at both of us.

I couldn't quite look him in the eye as we walked to my car. "About everything…" I began softly.

"Your mom seems great," he said.

I couldn't hold back the snort. "She can be pretty embarrassing," I admitted.

He chuckled. "Yeah, that part came through. I might have overreacted the other night. I should have listened to what you were going to say. I'm sorry. I'd like to try all of this again if that's okay with you."

My cheeks flushed. "That's fine," I said, my voice barely above a whisper. I felt like I was in middle school again, a bundle of nerves and no finesse. Like asking a friend to ask a guy if he *like* likes you or just likes you.

"About my audition to be your boyfriend. How's it working out?"

I grinned shyly. "You survived the first few interviews, so pretty good."

Chapter 28

Such is the art of warfare.

—SUN TZU, *THE ART OF WAR*

THE APARTMENT FELT STRANGELY EMPTY WHEN I GOT HOME. No fluffs crowded around me when I sat on the couch, and no one frantically scattered when I dropped the television remote onto the floor. It was too quiet. I got up and headed to the tiny kitchen to make a cup of coffee. I reached into the cabinet for a calico mug but stopped. I was starting a new chapter in my life. Xavier was in jail. I had an amazing job opportunity. My kittens were all grown up. Even my face felt redeemed. I closed the cabinet and walked back to my living room. I had about a half hour before I was supposed to meet Carter for coffee at the Steam Room.

My phone dinged. I'm already on my way, he wrote back. See you in ten?

Not enough time to straighten my hair and add a little highlighter, but I took a few minutes to change into a fitted T-shirt free of cat hair. See you then.

When I pulled up outside the coffee shop, Carter's car was already there. I quickly walked to the front door. It was cold, and I sent a quick mental hug to Marcus for returning my jacket.

Inside was warmer. The green-haired barista smiled at me, and I saw Carter wave from a corner booth. There were two cups of coffee on the table in front of him. One appeared black, extra strong, and one was a dry cappuccino. I couldn't help smiling.

"You remembered," I said.

"Of course." He leaned back and stretched his arms out along the top of the booth. "How're you holding up? It's been an interesting few days."

I closed my eyes and inhaled the coffee. It smelled so good. "It definitely has. Duo should be ready to go home tomorrow. Are you excited?"

He sat up straighter and grinned. "I'm all ready for her: I got her food, a bed, a litter box. A tiny collar."

His enthusiasm was contagious. "Do you have a name picked out for her yet?"

He blinked at me. "Her name is Duo."

I took a sip of my coffee, but it was too hot, so I had to set it back down. "That name just means *two*. And there's only going to be one."

"But that's what *you* named her," he said, and reached for my hand across the table. His fingers were warm, and I felt a little light-headed.

The barista with the green-tipped hair made her way over. "You doing okay?" she asked.

"We're good," I smiled at her.

"You still looking for a job?" she asked me. "Right now, we're getting along fine with the reduced staff, since business has been pretty slow, but I can keep your name on a list for Tom if you'd like to be considered."

"Actually"—I smiled up at her—"I'm not. I have a position at the animal shelter lined up."

"Awesome, I'm so happy for you!" the barista said. "Probably for the best anyway. I'm not sure how long the Steam Room is going to last these days, with Starbucks and Tim Hortons and everything else. I'll probably be headed into your office soon, Carter," she said with a sigh. "We don't have a good enough gimmick."

"That's disappointing to hear," Carter murmured quietly. "I love coming here. I was even going to bring my new kitten by to say hi."

A thought suddenly struck me. "I'm just tossing out an idea, but let me know if Tom might be interested in trying out a cat café vibe. We don't have one nearby, and they've been very successful in other cities. If there were a few adoptable shelter cats here, maybe we could get some articles in the newspaper and some exposure, both for the shelter and for the Steam Room."

She practically squealed. "Oh my god, I'm texting Tom right now. Can I get your contact info?"

I wrote my name and email on a napkin and handed it back to her. "Just an idea."

She took it and practically ran back to the counter, where I could see her on her phone.

"Your talents were wasted at Directis," Carter said.

"So was my time," I replied. "But thanks. Oh!" I said, suddenly remembering. "I got approved for benefits."

He looked at me slyly.

"You already knew!"

"I work for the unemployment office, remember? But awesome!" he said. "You got them. Just in time not to need them."

"Totally. But look where it got us," I said, feeling shy again as I looked down at our entwined hands.

He squeezed my hand tighter. "Look where it got us," he repeated softly.

When I got home, I was so buoyant from my afternoon with Carter that I barely noticed how empty the apartment felt. After coffee, we'd wandered around downtown and I'd filled him in on everything that had happened with Xavier, my mom, and everything else. We had eventually gotten dinner together before we called it a night. The whole day had felt like springtime, even though it was only about thirty degrees outside.

I wanted to hold on to the lightness I was feeling. I slept well, only to wake up cold, with no fluffy, purring blanket on my legs. I wasn't ready yet for another batch of fosters. I'd gotten more attached to my hellions than I'd realized.

I spent the morning going through the offer Danielle had sent me. It was exactly what I wanted to be doing. Even though it still stung a little to think about Directis, I'd gone from there to a place I had desperately wanted to be, and I couldn't help feeling grateful.

My phone buzzed with a number I didn't recognize. That usually didn't bode well. "Hello?" I asked.

A voice I knew but couldn't place answered, "Looking for Vanessa Blair, please."

"Speaking," I replied, racking my brain. Where did I know him from?

"Ah, Vanessa. Hello, how are you?" the voice asked.

"Who is this?" I replied.

"Brenn Dyer," he answered quickly. "We met at my office. I head Trimaran."

Like I could have forgotten who Brenn Dyer was.

"Hi, Mr. Dyer. I remember," I said.

"Please call me *Brenn*. I wanted to give you a call and thank you for what you did as a whistleblower. You brought the problem straight to me, and I appreciate your fortitude."

I hadn't been expecting this. "Thank you?" I said, struggling to keep the question mark to myself.

"Employee loyalty is hard to find, and your ability to see a pattern of behavior that no one else saw is impressive."

Well, the whole thing had been a little more complicated than that, but okay. Where was he going with this?

As if answering my unspoken question, he paused dramatically. "I've called to offer you a job, Vanessa. Would you consider working for Trimaran?"

When it rains, it pours. "That's a very kind offer," I started but didn't say the rest: *But I would rather jam hot pokers in my eyes than go back to anything connected to Directis.* I cleared my throat to get rid of the words and continued, "But I think you've misread what happened, Brenn. Trisha Lam was the one who collected the evidence of embezzling at Directis. She and Geraldine Foster put the pieces together and approached me with their theories." I knew Jane felt like I did and would never want to be connected with Directis or Trimaran ever again, so I didn't mention her name. "I'd recommend touching base with them instead."

"Trisha Lam," Brenn said. "Was she one of the ones with you? Blond or brunette?"

"Brunette," I answered.

"I appreciate your honesty. I'll reach out to Trisha. And Geraldine... is she the one who said I was twelve?"

I winced. I'd forgotten about that. "She can be a bit abrasive," I allowed.

"I'll think on that one," he said. "Are you sure you're not interested in an opportunity with Trimaran?"

Even without the shelter offer open on my computer, a thousand times yes. "I'm sure. Thank you for the offer. You might have already thought of this, Brenn, but this story is going to be on the news. It would benefit Trimaran if there was a positive spin for you, such as providing job assistance and good work records for those who have been the victim of fraud under your watch. Makes you look less complicit and shows a moral compass that will help your image."

"Are you sure I can't convince you to join my staff? I'd like to make you head of my public relations team. I think you'd be a natural."

"I appreciate it, and that's what I plan to do. But not for Trimaran."

"Well, I appreciate the advice, Vanessa. Good luck in the future. If you ever need a job recommendation, I'd be happy to supply one."

I thanked him again and hung up, crossing my fingers that he really would give Trisha a call so she, Jane, and I could all move on from Directis to new, and better, employment.

Epilogue

Three months later

I GRIPPED CARTER'S HAND TIGHTER THAN I SHOULD HAVE. HE leaned over and kissed the top of my head. "You okay? Having flashbacks?" he asked.

"No, and yes," I replied.

We'd reached the pine tree farm on the edge of town that held the Trimaran employee picnic. Despite the crispness in the air, it was a beautiful day to be outside. Someone had stretched a banner across the archway at the entrance. *Trimaran Winter Extravaganza* was printed in Comic Sans across it. I could smell a cozy fire and hot chocolate even from the entrance, but it didn't cover the distinctive smell of farm animals. I didn't want to step foot under that archway. "We don't even work here. I don't know why we have to come—" I started as a familiar face caught sight of me from the edge of the corral offering pony rides and began waving frantically.

"Nessa!" Trisha called, and I waved back weakly as she bounded over to me, full of excitement. "So glad you could come!"

"You didn't leave me much choice," I grouched. "You begged and begged. And someone invited my mom."

Trisha grinned. "Kathy's having a great time. She's so good at making friends. Last I saw her, she was teaching Brenn how to cheat at poker.

Actually, the whole Bridge Brigade is here. But if we're being honest, I don't think they play bridge," she confided.

I tried to brush the thought away as I looked at her more closely. "Is that a…prom queen sash?"

She raised her arms and twirled. "Sort of! Read it."

"Employee of the Month," I murmured as I took in her sash, a shiny white polyester with gold embroidery. I looked up at Carter, at a loss for words. Apparently, nothing had truly changed in the circus of the corporately employed.

"You look lovely," he told her, but Trisha saw my mouth opening and closing, unable to form words.

"Don't worry," she said. "It's an honor, not like those certificates we used to get. It means they think I'm the coolest!"

"And you are," I answered her, ignoring the bile in my throat. Trisha had been working in the Trimaran office for the past couple months, and she was clearly enjoying herself. Her salary was higher, and her job duties involved a little espionage, which gave her a rush.

"Where's everyone else?"

"Geraldine is over in the petting zoo. She's been hanging out with the goats for a while now. C'mon, Jane's over by the fire having some hot chocolate," she said, gesturing for us to follow her.

As we walked over toward the warmth, I craned my neck to get a glimpse of Geraldine. She sat just inside the barn entrance, tossing whole hot dogs to the goats and sheep and whatever else was in there. At least half a dozen practically crawled up onto the bench to get closer.

When we got to the picnic table, Jane jumped and gave me a quick hug, and Marcus, who sat beside her, waved hello.

"I didn't expect to see you here," I muttered in her ear before she sat back down.

"Marcus asked me to come, and we're not far enough along in

our relationship for me to openly mock him," she whispered back. Jane and Marcus's relationship was new, but she'd already moved out of her parents' house and into his condo. It was closer to her classes at the university anyway. Marcus was still the receptionist at Directis, but everything else there had changed. No one had managed to find Gary, and Xavier and Bobbert were still being held without bail awaiting trial.

"How's it going with the brood at home?" Jane asked Carter as he poured two mugs of hot chocolate and sat on the bench beside me.

He passed one to me as I shook my head. "I still can't believe he adopted all five kittens."

"Well, I panicked," he defended himself. "They say to adopt in pairs, and Danielle and I talked about how Duo needed a friend, and we got out the checklist, but it was still hard to tell who was who. And they were all curled up in a pile, like a family. So I got them all." Carter shrugged and stretched his arm around me, shifting on the bench.

"We have a lot of dependents now," I said.

"We," he repeated and caught my eye again with his bright blue ones. "I like that you said *we*."

"Barf," a voice said loudly behind me, and I turned to find Geraldine stomping over, trailed by a handful of goats and several ponies.

"Geraldine, I don't think you're supposed to let the animals out of the barn," Trisha said.

"I didn't," she snapped back. "I just left the gate open." She slipped a mug of hot chocolate to one of the goats. Trisha wrestled it out of her hand.

Carter leaned close so only I could hear. "How about we stay for just a few more minutes then go to the Steam Room?" Carter said. "Afterward, we can go back to my place and hang out, just you and me. And, you know, all the cats." I'd spent more time there than at my own apartment over the past few months, and it really felt like home.

"Okay," I said and leaned against him, closing my eyes. My whole body relaxed. Despite the cold, and the barnyard smell, and the snark, and the work event, things were good.

There was a tap on my shoulder, and my eyes snapped open. Tammy, one of my mom's friends, was staring down at me through her false lashes and shifting from foot to foot. "Vanessa, sweetie, your mother brought her binoculars, and she thinks that fugitive escapee from Directis is hiding in the Christmas trees."

I sat bolt upright. "No, no, and no. Carter, we gotta go. The cats need to be fed."

He got the hint. "Sorry we have to take off," he said to the table. "We left the animals to starve."

I grabbed his arm and pulled him up from the bench and toward the parking lot. I was done with Directis. And murder boards. And tapping offices. And catching fugitives. And tweams. And anything corporate in general. Even when it wasn't bad, it was still pretty bad.

I heard my mother yell, "Vanessa Leigh, get back here—" just as I slammed the car door closed.

"Drive!" I ordered Carter, and we sped away.

I breathed a sigh of relief as the picnic disappeared from the rear-view mirror. "Before we hit the Steam Room, do you mind if we swing past the shelter? I have to pick up some marketing materials for the next fundraiser."

"Sure," he replied, and soon enough we were pulling into the parking lot outside of the Walter Green Animal Shelter.

"I'll just be a minute," I promised. The shelter was closed for the afternoon, but I let myself in with a key and flipped on the lights.

And there I was. Everywhere. My face smiled back at me from the posters on the walls and the brochures lining the entrance. Me, with Duo perched on my shoulder. Me again, holding a pit bull puppy with a cast on its leg, a recent surrender who had already been adopted. The name of the shelter was above me, along with *Adopt. Volunteer. Donate.* underneath. Danielle had told me I would be the face of the shelter, but seeing it for the first time staggered me.

My face. My dark soul. I sucked in a breath and let the feelings wash over me. *Ad astra per aspera.* Through adversity to the stars. Then I stopped. Should I be quoting Sun Tzu when I talked to myself now? Maybe this weekend would be a good time to reread *The Art of War.* As someone who had survived an '80s-era work prom, I knew love was a battlefield. But so was the workplace. Maybe I could swing by the bookstore later and grab a copy. Or two. You never knew when you might have to go to war.

Acknowledgments

Thank you to my mom, dad, Miellyn, Jeff, Chance, and Sam for your help. This book wouldn't have been possible without the plotting sessions, revision advice, and general support you gave me. You all rock.

And thank you to Jennifer Wills and Deb Werksman for believing in me. I'm forever grateful.

About the Author

Anastasia Ryan writes about what she loves best: humor, coffee, and cats. She has several useless degrees and fills her time listening to true crime podcasts. *You Should Smile More* is her first novel, focusing on what happens when your resting bitch face is wide awake…at work.

WITH NEIGHBORS LIKE THIS

Uplifting, feel-good fiction from *USA Today*
bestselling author Tracy Goodwin

When divorced mom of two Amelia Marsh relocates to a northern suburb of Houston, all she wants is a bit of normalcy for her children. The last thing she needs is to be the center of community gossip. But that's what happens when Amelia clashes with the HOA representative over her children's garden gnome. HOA president Kyle Sanders could be a good friend—and something more—if Amelia wasn't gearing up for battle with the HOA in her determination to make her house a home and her neighborhood a community...

"Tracy Goodwin delivers every time!"

—Sophie Jordan, *New York Times* bestselling author

For more info about Sourcebooks's books and authors, visit:
sourcebooks.com

THE SUMMER OF CHRISTMAS

Experience the behind-the-scenes magic of your favorite
holiday movie in this fun movie set rom-com

Up-and-coming LA screenwriter Ivy Green is about to have her life turned
upside down. Her movie, based on her and her high school sweetheart,
Nick Shepherd, is being filmed in her hometown. In the middle of summer,
during the month of July, the production crew creates a winter wonderland
Christmas. But when drama on set and adoring fans make it harder for the
movie to get made, Nick is the one Ivy turns to. With old feelings bubbling
up and her dream on the line, Ivy will need to re-write her life script to finally
get everything she ever wanted.

**"Fans of small-town romances, second-chance romances,
and Christmas love stories...will feel like Christmas
has, indeed, arrived early with this romp."**

—*Booklist*

THE STAND-IN

A hilarious and heartwarming story of fame, family, and love

Gracie Reed is doing just fine. Sure, she was fired by her overly "friendly" boss, and no, she still hasn't gotten her mother into the nursing home of their dreams, but she's healthy, she's (somewhat) happy, and she's (mostly) holding it all together.

But when a mysterious SUV pulls up beside her, revealing Chinese cinema's golden couple Wei Fangli and Sam Yao, Gracie's world is turned on its head. The famous actress has a proposition: due to their uncanny resemblance, Fangli wants Gracie to be her stand-in. The catch? Gracie will have to be escorted by Sam, the most attractive—and infuriating—man Gracie's ever met...

"A sparkly, cinematic adventure that combines emotional drama with hilarious and relatable moments."

—Talia Hibbert, *USA Today* bestselling author

For more info about Sourcebooks's books and authors, visit:

sourcebooks.com

THE UNPLANNED LIFE
OF JOSIE HALE

Hilarious, heartwarming fiction from Stephanie Eding that
reminds us it's always a good idea to expect the unexpected...

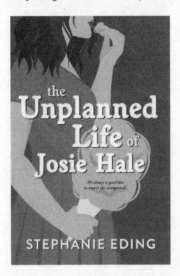

When Josie discovers that she's unexpectedly pregnant with her ex-
husband's baby (darn that last attempt to save their marriage), she seeks
comfort in deep-fried food at the county fair. There she runs into her two
old friends, Ben and Kevin. While sharing their own disappointments
with adult life, they devise a plan to move in together and turn their lives
around. Soon Ben and Kevin make it their mission to prepare for Josie's
baby. Maybe together they can discover the true meaning of family and
second chances in life...

For more info about Sourcebooks's books and authors, visit:

sourcebooks.com